TRADE DEADLINE

CHICAGO THUNDER HOCKEY

JODI OLIVER

Dedication

To those who don't believe they are worthy of love,
you are worthy, I promise.

One

Blaine

The irritating sound of my phone vibrating on my nightstand sounds like a siren in my otherwise silent room, causing me to bolt up in a delirious haze. Who the fuck would be calling me at this hour? The sun isn't even up yet.

I lean over, stifling a groan, and aimlessly slap my hand against my phone, hoping that if I hit it hard enough, it'll make the noise stop.

Seconds later, my wish is granted, and the room drops into a peaceful silence.

"Mm, thank fuck," I mumble as I lay back down.

Pulling the covers up over my head, I let out a happy sigh and nuzzle my face into the pillow. It's too early. I have at least another hour until I need to get up for morning skate, so it's time to get cozy again. Whoever it is can wait.

Maybe I can get back to that dream I was having where this gorgeous guy was about to go to town on my dick.

Wishful thinking, though, because the annoying sound starts up again.

"For fuck's sake!"

I grab my phone and quickly sit up, staring at the screen, when I see Hayden's name displayed on the caller ID.

My agent is calling at six thirty in the fucking morning.

Nothing good comes with your agent calling at six thirty in the morning.

My heart beats like a crazy drummer in my chest as I swipe on the screen to accept his call and raise my phone to my ear.

"Hello?" My voice comes out croaky. I clear my throat and try again. "Hayden?"

"At least one of us has had some sleep," Hayden grumbles.

"Well, good morning to you too," I scoff, stretching my arm above my head.

He wakes me up at this time and doesn't even have the decency to say hello? Christ.

"Fucking hell, Blaine! Do you realize what kinda shit you're in? Do you seriously not give a single fucking fuck?"

"Whoa, that was a lot of fucks for this time of the day." I rub my eyes with the heel of my palm. "What have I done?" comes out in a garbled yawn.

Scooting up the bed, I lean back against the headboard, bringing the comforter with me.

"Do you recall the night you spent with three puck bunnies?"

I grin at the memory. "Mm, yeah, I do. Quite the wild night, that was."

It's not often I get involved in a tryst of multiples, but I couldn't turn down those three beauties the other night. It was like a trio of decadent desserts.

One light, one dark, one cherry.

The way their bodies moved on the dance floor, their sexy clothes teasing me about what was beneath under the flashing lights of the club. All luscious curves and dangerous smiles.

"Blaine!" he shouts, pulling me out of my wayward thoughts. I pull the phone away from my ear with a wince. "Quit joking around, okay? It's four thirty here in LA, and I'm not in the mood. I've been up all fucking night trying to put out this wildfire, so the least you can do is listen to me."

Suddenly, the tiredness I was feeling evaporates. My spine goes as stiff as a rod, and my eyes are no longer heavy with sleep.

"What?" I whisper.

"They posted some bullshit on that bunny blog, *The Warren Post*, going into detail…" He trails off, not needing to elaborate any more because I know from experience what gets posted on there. A heavy sigh echoes through the phone. "Blaine, there's photos."

Dread pools in the pit of my stomach. Twisting and churning as my hands start to shake. It's easy when it's just some text claiming I did this or that, it can be brushed off as fabricated, but when there's photos? That's when it gets harder. That's the proof I can't deny.

"Photos?"

"Yeah. We've managed to get them taken down, but the Thunder PR team has been working throughout the night as they keep reappearing."

"What kind of photos are we talking about here? Is my dick on Twitter?"

It wouldn't be the first time there's been something incriminating posted about me. Luckily, my dick hasn't graced the world wide web.

Yet.

"No, thank God. They are all from behind, so all you can see is your back and ass, but everyone can tell it's you because of your tattoo. They must have set up a camera, or one of them took it while you were entertaining another, I don't know, but there's also a photo of the three of them posing by your Frozen Four jersey with a rather … inelegant caption."

I squeeze my eyes closed, raking my hand through my hair.

I've always been super careful with everyone I brought back here. Taking them to my spare room like I always do because it's so fucking minimalist that there's no way they can take anything as a trophy or go snooping where I don't want them. I was naive not to think about the jerseys on the wall in my hallway.

Because if they wanted a *hey, I was here!* brag post, it would be the perfect one.

My heart thumps wildly in my chest. Anxiety crawls across my skin like an army of fire ants.

As I said, nothing good comes from your agent calling at six thirty in the morning.

"Has Coach…?" I trail off.

"Yeah, he's pissed. The only reason why you're not packing your bags right now is because I've given him my word that we're going to work on cleaning up your image."

"This fucking sucks," I grumble.

I'm a fucking amazing hockey player, with the stats to prove it. I'm currently sitting second in points in the league. It's not my fault that everyone wants to hook up with me for bragging rights. It's hard not to give into the temptation of a good time when I have attractive people throwing themselves at me in every city. It's part and parcel of being a professional hockey player in the NHL.

Plus, I always make it crystal clear that this is a no-strings-attached, fun time in fucktown. No false hopes and empty promises of something more.

Sex.

Just sex.

An aid to help blow off steam and tension.

"I suggest you keep your head down for a while, at least until the trade deadline has passed. The GM isn't happy with you either, so we need to work on ensuring that you keep your spot on this team because you deserve it. You're an incredible hockey player, Blaine, and I would hate to see you lose everything you've worked so hard for because of people who only care about your status."

I drop my head into my hand and pinch the bridge of my nose.

I want to stay on this team. It means more to me than just a paycheck. These guys have become my family, and I don't want to lose them. I know it comes with the territory, but I *love* it here.

"I'm putting my reputation on the line for you, Blaine. Don't let me down. Your contract is up at the end of this season, and while I'm still working on negotiations, the last thing we need is this kind of attention. I'm about to board my flight to Chicago, so I'll see you in a few hours before my meeting to discuss a plan for what's next."

He doesn't give me a chance to respond before he hangs up.

The room plummets into silence apart from the blood thumping in my ears as I stare out of my bedroom window overlooking Lake Michigan. I don't usually close the drapes when I sleep, except when I have my pre-game nap. The bustling streets of Chicago and the expanse of water is usually soothing. Only now, the lake is rippling with waves from the wind, crashing aggressively against the shoreline.

It's chaotic.

Turbulent.

Which is strangely apt for this moment, especially as the sky is gray and cloudy. Like a storm is brewing, threatening a torrential downpour.

Just like my career.

You could say I've always had a bit of a reckless streak. When I was a kid, I would always be the one pushing the boundaries, seeing how close to breaking the rules I could get without being reprimanded. Then, before I left college, I fully embraced the perks of being a hockey player and the attention that came with it. The thrill of being wanted became a drug I craved, constantly feeding my ego—essentially feeding a monster. And now it could be what potentially causes my career to crash if I'm not careful.

All I've ever wanted since I was a kid was to play hockey in the NHL.

To play the best sport in the world on the biggest stage.

I can't let someone take that away from me, even if that person is *me*.

With a sigh, I kick the sheets off and get in the shower. I don't need to be at the rink for practice until eight thirty, but there's no way I'll be able to go back to sleep now.

My jaw ticks as frustration creeps in as I stand under the warm spray. It's bullshit. I'm just a guy living his dream and making the most of the opportunities that are presented to me.

Once I've showered and shaved, I slip on my matching team sweatpants and hoodie and head out with a thermos of coffee in hand, descending two flights of stairs to knock on the door to my brother's apartment.

Elliot is my twin brother and the newest goaltender for the Chicago Thunder. He came here in the summer when his contract was up with Vancouver, and we're finally getting to play on the same team together.

The door swings open to reveal a fresh-faced Elliot, his hair slicked back from his shower. We're not identical twins, as Elliot was blessed with my mom's genes. Strawberry-blond hair, green eyes, and light freckles sprinkled across his nose. We often joke that he has a face for magazine covers rather than guarding the net.

He looks at his watch, then back at me, confusion lining his forehead.

"I'm early, I know," I drawl.

"Just checking I hadn't overslept, and this was some weird dream," he chuckles, stepping aside so I can enter.

I rub my face with my hand as I lean against the back of the couch. His apartment has the same layout as mine. Floor-to-ceiling windows overlooking the lake. Open floor-plan kitchen and living room, although his is still a little chaotic. Boxes are piled up waiting to be unpacked from his move nearly four months ago, claiming he'll do it another day.

"Hayden is on his way," I announce, figuring I should let him know as we share the same agent.

Elliot's brows furrow. "Why? What did you do?"

I roll my eyes. "How do you know it's something I did?"

"Isn't it?"

"Hayden called me this morning. You know those girls I hooked up with the other night?"

"The awesome foursome you had?"

I nod. "Well, turns out they've framed me big time. They've shared some photos online, and they've written some post on the bunny blog, a play-by-play about that night."

His jaw drops and his eyes widen as the word "no" comes out in a shocked gasp.

"I wish I was joking," I grunt. "Hayden said I've gotta keep my head down, at least until the trade deadline passes. I'm guessing he's worried that Coach might cut me because of it."

"You're gonna do what he says, right?" Elliot chews on the side of his thumb, his eyes filled with worry. "Like, you can't be traded. I just got here! We have our whole dream to live out, like we've planned since we were kids."

Knowing he can feel the inner turmoil that's running wild through my mind right now, I place my hands on his shoulders in reassurance.

"I promise you, I'll do whatever he tells me. I'm just pissed that this happened, you know?" I shrug, shoving my hands into the pockets of my sweats. "I was just having fun. I didn't want to cause any trouble."

Ever since I was drafted, I've been sucked into the vortex of people wanting a piece of me. Guys, girls, the media. I relished it. I felt in control for once, that everything was happening on my terms, and I craved the attention they gave me.

But maybe I became too greedy, and this is my reckoning.

When I enter the locker room twenty minutes later, everything seems normal. The rookies are shooting the shit on the far side of the room, throwing wads of tape at one another, while the rest of the guys are either listening to music or deep in conversation as they get ready.

Everything *is* normal.

Blissfully unaware that this morning I woke up to a shitshow.

We're on fire this season. Currently top of our division, and if we keep up this momentum, the playoffs are well within our sights.

Another reason why I can't get traded.

"Blaine, you got a sec?" Ethan, the team captain, asks.

"Of course." I nod and follow him to the player lounge.

He grabs two bottles of water from the fridge and passes one to me, where I'm propped against the counter. His brown eyes remain fixed on me as he takes a few gulps.

My skin prickles, knowing this is going to be an uncomfortable conversation.

"I spoke to Coach this morning about what happened," he begins.

I'm not surprised Ethan's already been made aware. Ethan Parkes is the best captain I have ever known. He's grumpy and broody, but he will have your back no matter what.

Guilt weighs me down.

"Yeah, shit. I wish I could turn back time and erase it."

"I'm sure you do, but you can't. I think I've gotten to know you well enough over the years you've been here to believe you wouldn't have followed through with that night had you known what they were going to do."

I shake my head.

"What's done is done. You can't change what's happened, but I can help you move on from this, help keep you focused on what's important, but you also need to help yourself now, Blaine."

I'm expecting a similar conversation with Hayden when he lands in a few hours from Los Angeles, but I know Ethan has mine—and the teams'—best interests at the forefront of his mind.

"No more hookups. No distractions. Channel every ounce of energy into hockey," Ethan says, counting them off on his fingers, leaving no room for argument.

I nod firmly, promising I will be better, when Coach Harris appears in the doorway. His thick arms are crossed over his equally thick chest. He was a big guy when he played defense for Dallas seven years ago, and even though he's retired from playing, he's worked hard not to lose too much muscle mass. The frown lines on his forehead are so deep, though, that they add decades to his forty-two years.

"Blaine, my office. Now," he orders.

I swallow the lump that's lodged in my throat.

Fuck.

I quickly follow him with my tail between my legs. I wince when he slams the door hard, surprised that it's still on the hinges. The framed photographs on his wall shake from the impact.

Sitting down in the leather chairs opposite his desk, I risk a glance up at him. His jaw clenches as he grinds his molars, his glare burning a hole straight through me. His anger is so palpable, I'm just waiting for steam to come out of his ears.

He turns his laptop around, and there on the screen is a photo of the three puck bunnies I hooked up with, posing in front of the jersey I wore when I won the Frozen Four my junior year. They're grinning from ear to ear, but it's the caption that causes me to drop my head into my hands in shame.

Pucks in the net and his dick's getting wet—hat trick for Blaine Olsen!

It's followed by a photo of my very naked ass mid-thrust. You can't see my face, but as Hayden said, there's a clear image of the Spartan warrior tattoo on my upper back.

"Do you realize how bad this looks? Not just on you, but the team?"

This isn't the first time we've been in this exact same situation. Something bad about me plastered across the puck bunny blogs, shaming me for whatever I had done the night before. Shining a negative light on me like I'm some kind of sexual deviant.

My hands begin to sweat. I wipe them down the front of my sweatpants, but no matter how many times my palms brush against the fabric, nothing seems to dry them. My throat clams up, and my skin suddenly feels too tight for my body.

"I worked so fucking hard to get Elliot on the team, knowing how much it meant to you, and this is how you repay me?"

I stare down at my feet. Struggling to find my breath as guilt weighs heavy in my chest, pressing against my lungs.

Do I regret every reckless thing I've ever done? No.

But apparently this is the wakeup call I needed.

Being one of the few twins in NHL history has given Elliot and I an automatic entry in the hockey record books, and we're the second set of twins to play on the same team in the NHL. Which means more to me than I could ever explain.

Coach waves toward the screen of his laptop, motioning to the photo again. "This behavior needs to end. Now. Stay away from the bunnies. I don't want to see your name on this shit again. The only thing I want to see on the internet about you is how good of a fucking hockey player you are, how many goals and assists you have after each game, and how you deserve to be an Art Ross finalist." He slams the laptop closed and crosses his arms over his chest. "Do you hear me?"

"Yes, Coach," I nod, clearing my throat. "I'm sorry."

He lets out a tired sigh and runs a hand down his face. "Your sorry means jack shit to me right now. *Show me* that you're sorry, Blaine. Show me you want your fucking spot on this team. Show me that you respect me, your team, and your-fucking-self. Now get ready for practice, you're on the ice in five," he stands to step behind his desk. "And don't think for a fucking second that I'm not having you run bag skates for this bullshit."

I grimace. I suppose it's better than getting benched.

Two

Alex

"You've got us rink-side seats?" I shriek when I reach the bottom of the stairs, spinning on my heels to face Nate, my best friend and clearly a very sneaky fucker.

His face lights up with a sheepish grin, his head bobbing in an excitable nod. "Hell yeah, I did! I haven't seen you in, like, a month, and I wanted to spoil you."

I press my hand against the boards and gaze over the pristine white ice. It looks like a mirror with the colored lights flashing from above.

There's something so majestic about ice hockey arenas.

The vibrating energy of a packed stadium. The anticipation of puck drop. The accolade banners spanning decades of accomplishments; retired numbers of legendary players, Conference Champions, Division Champions, Stanley Cup Champions. These walls have seen so much history that it feels surreal to be standing here.

Ice hockey has been a love of mine since I was a child, when I used to sit with my grandpa to watch the Chicago Thunder on TV. The speed, the determination, the passion, the aggression. It sucks you into its orbit and keeps you hooked. It's an incredible sport, and I haven't been able to indulge in it in a while due to a few issues.

The biggest one of them being money.

"These must have cost you a fortune," I say quietly.

Guilt churns in my stomach; there's no way I can repay him for even half of my ticket. I nearly cried when I spent twenty bucks on a hot dog and beer ten minutes ago, and these seats often sell for hundreds of dollars.

Money isn't a luxury I have at the moment, and I always feel bad whenever people spend their hard-earned cash on me, even though I know they wouldn't do it if they didn't want to.

Nate comes up beside me, wrapping his arm around my shoulders, and gives me a small squeeze. "You deserve it after everything you've been dealing with over the last couple of years. Losing your grandparents, graduating college while grieving. Now you're working yourself into the ground trying to make ends meet."

He turns me to face him, his smile tinged with a hint of sadness. "I fucking love you, Alex, and it's been killing me to see you lose that sparkle in your eyes. Plus, I can tell it's currently eating at you that you want to pay me back but don't know how, but look at it this way…" He brings me into a hug, kissing the side of my head. "This is your combined Christmas and birthday gift. Let me treat you, please; you deserve it."

Wrapping my arms around his waist, I swallow the lump

in my throat at his words, blinking away the tears in my eyes.

Nate has been my rock throughout these last two years.

My grandparents raised my brother and me, they were the pillars of strength in our lives after we lost our parents at a young age. Losing them both within a week of each other was heartbreaking in ways I could never explain.

"Thank you. I love you too," I croak in his ear, giving him a squeeze, then shaking off my emotions.

We walk down the aisle to our seats, and once again I'm nearly knocked off my feet with shock. "We're next to the penalty box, too?"

Nate beams, rocking back on his heels as he rubs his hands together like a happy otter. "Oh yeah, I have a feeling tonight's going to be *pretty* exciting on the penalty front, so we have front-row seats to the good stuff, literally." He wiggles his brows.

I laugh, wiping away tears from my eyes with my thumb. I'm so overwhelmed with emotion right now. I can't believe this is happening.

The handful of times I've been to the Thunder arena was with my grandpa when I was in high school. We were so high up we could almost touch the rafters, so being down here, so close to the action that we'll be able to see the facial expressions of every player as they fight for the puck...

It feels out of this world.

With the clock on the jumbotron counting down to warm up, we both unwrap our insanely expensive hot dogs and settle into our seats.

"I think we should hit up Gino's after the game," Nate

suggests, screwing his foil into a ball and balancing it on the ledge of the boards in front of us.

"Do you think they'll be there?" I point to the empty ice, referring to the players.

"If they win, yeah," he props his feet up on the ledge. "They usually go there after a win; people don't always see them after a loss, but it has happened."

I chew on the inside of my lip.

The first thought running through my head is *can I afford this?*, and the simple answer is no, but I've been lacking on the social life front, especially since I graduated college and started working full time.

Surely one night with my best friend won't do too much harm if I'm sensible.

"Okay, we'll go, but I have to be up at four for work, so I don't want to be out too late."

Plus, my brother Jacob won't let me hear the end of it if I'm late, seeing as we both get to the shop at five to start baking the day's selection of desserts.

As the arena begins to fill ahead of warm-up, people of all ages stand by the boards with homemade signs. Nate and I take endless photos and selfies with the ice behind us and beside the penalty box. Some people might think it's pathetic to be so elated over some seats, but when you've been a fan for as long as I have, it's exhilarating to be this close.

The chances of reliving this experience are slim, so I'm making the most of every second.

And let's face it, there's something undeniably sexy about hockey players.

These big men fighting over a tiny, rubberized disc is

what dirty fantasies are made of. And to be this close? I'm in heaven.

My crushes on hockey players began in college when Nate took me to a game during our freshman year, and since then, they've been my kryptonite.

And the reason why my heart constantly gets broken.

I have vowed not to give in to temptation anymore because hockey players definitely don't equal Prince Charming.

Goose bumps erupt across my skin as the lights go up and the iconic notes of their warm-up intro song, Thunderstruck, blast from the sound system.

"Welcome to the ice, your Chicago Thunderrrr!" The announcer's voice booms throughout the arena.

My heart rate goes to a thousand as the players step out onto the ice one by one, knocking over the neatly stacked pucks as they go. I slap my hands against the boards as player after player skates by, my cheeks beginning to ache from the uncontainable grin on my face.

The first one to drop down onto the ice in front of us is Zach Reid. The defenseman looks even bigger in person, and a quick Google search tells me he's six foot six without skates and one of the heaviest players in the league.

My tongue suddenly feels too big in my mouth. My pulse increasing at a dangerous pace as I watch the players in various positions, absolutely mesmerized by how flexible they are. Even with all the goalie padding on, Elliot Olsen is nearly doing splits.

I fumble with my phone, making sure to capture this on video so I have something to look back on.

Next to skate toward us is the team captain and left

winger, Ethan Parkes. His signature broody scowl does nothing to hinder how handsome he is. He's all dark hair and darker eyes. He leans back against the boards between Nate and me, and we both glance at each other with large grins on our faces.

"So fucking hot!" He mouths, pressing his hand against the bottom of the glass, pretending to squeeze his ass, and rolls his eyes to the back of his head with a moan.

I laugh hard. "You're ridiculous."

Nate winks, then presses a kiss to the boards behind Ethan's head.

We watch the warm-up in contented silence. Our gazes jump from watching them stretch to skating so seamlessly and effortlessly on the ice. Some players are standing off to the side, working on solo puck handling, while others are running different passing drills and shooting pucks at the goalie in the net.

After I take a sip from my beer, hoping it can cool my blazing insides, I set it on the small ledge as Blaine Olsen skates toward us, wearing what could only be described as a mischievous smirk.

I realize my mistake seconds too late, when I realize exactly what that smirk means. The noise from the arena becomes distant, and the panic bursting in my chest keeps me rooted in place. Time seems to slow down as Blaine turns on his skates, jumping up and slamming his shoulder into the plexi. It bows under his weight, causing my beer to fall and spill across the front of my jeans. Nate erupts into laughter beside me, tears beginning to stream down his face.

Glancing down at my now-beer-soaked jeans, I can't help but laugh. "Oh shit."

I'd heard about people being soaked when their own drink gets knocked over by a player, but I never would have imagined it happening to me.

Regardless of the fact I've never been so embarrassed as I am right now, I kinda like it.

But that may be more to do with the guy than anything else.

Looking back up at Blaine, the stare in his light gray eyes is intense, his wicked grin doing nothing but adding kerosene to the fire that is currently burning inside me. He flicks a puck up over the boards, but I'm so enthralled that it drops to the ground at my feet.

Our eyes remain locked in a heated stare. His gaze is a heady mix of determination and desire, and with all his focus on me, it's like the thousands of people in the arena have disappeared and it's just the two of us.

I'm pretty sure my poor little heart stops beating.

If I die right now, surrounded by hot hockey men, I'll die a very, very happy guy.

He winks, a playful grin on his full lips, and I can't help but wonder what he'd look like wearing only that grin, but I quickly shake those thoughts away as my face heats.

"Whoa, talk about an eye fuck," Nate says under his breath as Blaine turns and skates away, hitting puck after puck into the net where his twin brother, Elliot, tends the goal. Nate hands over the puck that landed at my feet. "I've heard he's a bit of a playboy, so maybe he can help you destress." He winks.

As I stare at the solid rubber disc in my hand, my thoughts running wild at the possibility. It would no doubt be the hottest night of my life, but Blaine and I are worlds apart. I take my eyes off the godlike human to face my best friend.

Smoothing both my hands around his head, I check for any possible injuries. "Are you okay? Did the puck hit you on the head and make you delirious?" I pat his chest in equal measure before shaking my head. "Don't be ridiculous. Men like that are unattainable, and how do you know he's into guys?"

I glance over my shoulder at some super pretty, petite girls a few rows behind and let out a defeated sigh. "They have a type, you know that. I don't fall under that bracket."

The buzzer sounds, indicating the end of warm-up, and we watch the players continue to hit pucks into the net, ignoring the shouts telling them to leave the ice so the Zamboni can resurface.

The last one to leave the ice is Blaine, and when he reaches the small door to the home bench, he looks over his shoulder in my direction. Our eyes lock once again, the corner of his lips tilting in a teasing smirk before he winks and jumps over the small ledge, disappearing down the tunnel.

"You could've fooled me if it wasn't for the way he was pretty much undressing you with his eyes," Nate says with a smirk.

This game is intense.

St. Louis is out for blood, determination written across every player's face as they give hit after heavy hit to try and weaken Thunder's offense. The atmosphere in the arena is wild when the puck drops in the third period, the score currently tied two-two.

The Thunder must have received a grilling from their head coach during the intermission, as they win the face off and are instantly on the attack. Before St. Louis can even react, Ethan Parkes slips one between the goalies' legs nine seconds into the period. The crowd erupts and the goal horn blasts. My eyes find Blaine, watching him skate past the bench, tapping gloves with his teammates before going to center ice to line up for the next face off.

But even with the lead in hand, the pressure doesn't ease up.

As play continues, the Thunder are all over them like a bad rash, causing St. Louis to miss several scoring chances. Elliot is on fire in front of the net, his arms and legs are shooting in every direction, blocking every shot. He covers the puck with his glove and the official blows the whistle. Elliot scoops up the puck with his glove and flicks the puck over to the official. As the official catches it, one of the St. Louis players aggressively shoves Elliot, causing him to lose his balance and fall back awkwardly into the pipes.

Within an instant, Blaine drops his gloves and stick. He grabs a fistful of the offender's jersey and slams his other fist into the guy's face. The air is filled with electricity as the crowd goes wild. Blaine gets hit a few times, one catching his lip and drawing blood. After breaking up the fight the ref gives them both a penalty. It's only when he's heading this way that I let out the breath I've been holding.

Rivulets of sweat drip down Blaine's face as he pulls off his helmet and takes a seat in the penalty box.

"You think you're cool, bud? Cheap shot going after my

brother, ya fuckin' nerd," he shouts to the St. Louis d-man, then shakes his head, blood spilling from his busted lip onto his jersey before he wipes his face on a towel. I'm in a trance, watching it happen almost in slow-motion as Blaine grabs a bottle to squirt water into his mouth, and then squirts it over his face and hair.

"Chicago, number eighty, five minutes for fighting," the referee announces.

The crowd boos in response, then cheers when the ref announces two plus five minutes for St. Louis for instigating and fighting—essentially, for being a douchebag. Blaine grins at their reaction, then shakes his head again, causing water to spray everywhere like a wet dog, and wipes his face once more with the towel.

"He's so fucking hot," I mumble under my breath.

His thick, solid neck glistens with sweat, droplets trailing down and disappearing under the collar of his jersey. He runs his fingers through his hair, slicking it back, showcasing his billboard-worthy face.

He's rocking a few days' worth of stubble, slightly lighter than his hair, a crooked nose from being broken more than once, no doubt. It takes me a few moments to realize he's caught me staring. That smug grin is back, causing my face to heat again.

Fuck.

I'm ridiculous. Blushing like a teenager. But I can't tear my eyes away as he runs the tip of his tongue across his bottom lip, catching a stray drop of water.

"What are you waiting for?" Nate's voice breaks the moment.

I turn to my friend, who is waving my phone. "Get a photo! The five minutes will be up before you know it."

I take my phone from him and swipe my finger across the screen to my camera, changing it to selfie mode then hold it up high enough to get both myself and Blaine in the shot. He must see me in his peripheral vision because he scoots closer on the bench until his shoulder is pressed up against the plexi, and this time gives me a jaw-dropping smile. I know I'm blushing even harder, but I take a few photos before dropping my phone into my lap. When I glance up, he's still looking at me. His gray eyes have turned dark, but it only lasts a few moments until his attention is torn away as Ethan attempts another shot on goal.

"Why are the hot ones so unattainable?" I sigh.

Blaine Olsen is no stranger when it comes to being featured on the bunny blogs. There seems to be an endless supply of girls sharing bedtime stories of their nights with the center.

"He would be the perfect candidate to get you back in the saddle though." Nate nudges me with his elbow. "You gotta start living again. Find a hottie to help you destress and distract you from everything. I bet he would be down to do just that."

I shake my head.

Only in my wildest dreams.

Three

Blaine

"Great game, boys! Fuckin' A!" Ethan claps his hands.

The locker room fills with back pats and ass slaps as we strip out of our gear. Someone connects their phone to the built-in sound system, and within seconds, our standard post-W playlist is blaring through the speakers. Gloves are thrown in the air, along with sweaty jerseys and the odd sock, in celebration. Some teams might not celebrate a win like we do, but it's become a tradition.

It helps keep morale up throughout the season, plus a hard-fought win against St. Louis is fucking fantastic. It was a close call to overtime, but I managed to pocket one in the top left corner with twelve seconds left in the third.

Earlier today, after morning skate, I showered before returning to Coach Harris's office, like a kid being sent to the principal's office. When I got there, I found Hayden waiting outside, dark shadows under his eyes, which only caused my guilt to grow. They ordered me not to engage with any puck bunnies, hookup apps, or any form of distraction that would take my focus away from hockey.

"I want you to succeed, Blaine. I know what it's like to have temptation dangled under your nose like a carrot. I've lived it, remember? Breathed it. But you're better than this. Take this as your final warning, and don't let yourself be caught in their trap," Hayden told me once Coach dismissed us.

Hayden had played for Boston for twelve years before he retired six years ago from an ACL injury. Even though he was the one all the girls wanted to fuck, and the one guys wanted to be, including me, he managed to stay on the right side of the press.

Like I need to now.

Once our post-W dance and singalong is over, we stand in front of our cubbies, each of us in various stages of undress, when Ethan steps up to award our "player of the game".

"That win was very well deserved, boys. We played hard, we fought hard, but I'm sure you will agree that the player of the game tonight was the one who stepped in when his brother was in need and still managed to sink two in the net... Blaine, congrats, man." Ethan heads toward me and hands over the "award", which is a costume helmet based on Odin's.

I give an *aw-shucks* grin as I put it on my head. The boys cheer and clap, and I bend at the hips with my arms out wide, bowing like I'm center stage.

"Thanks, Cap. You know I'll have every one of your backs. Nobody touches my guys. Each one of you gave it your all out there, so let's keep that up. But tonight, let's hit up Gino's, celebrate in style, and get ready to kick some Detroit ass!"

After a final cheer, I place the headpiece on top of my cubby. Some of the guys head off to do press while the rest of us use the bikes to cool down before taking a shower and getting ready to celebrate at our favorite bar.

The moment we step through the doors to Gino's, we're surrounded by fans congratulating us on our win. A sea of black and red jerseys fills the space from wall to wall.

"That uppercut on DeLuca was incredible!" One fan slaps me on the shoulder, a wide grin across his face.

"Thanks," I answer back, blowing on my knuckles and rubbing them against my shirt. They're bruised as fuck, but it was worth it. I meant what I said in the locker room—nobody touches my teammates, let alone my brother. "I hope he feels it tomorrow."

I leave the fan laughing and make my way through the crowd toward the bar.

I like Gino's.

A family-run bar that's filled with sports memorabilia—hockey, football, baseball—you name a sport, and it will have some form of history displayed on the walls here.

It's a large open space, a sectioned-off area of a converted warehouse; exposed brick, high ceilings with lighting hanging down from the metal beams casting a warm glow. There's also this silent agreement that fans can drink here on game nights on the basis that we can hang out here without being swamped.

I love our fans. We have the best fans in the league, but sometimes I just wanted to shoot some pool and drink a beer with my bros, and Gino's is the place that lets us do that.

They also make the most amazing bourbon chicken wings I've ever tasted.

As I reach the bar, I nod and wave at Dylan as he serves some people further down. We hooked up once a few months ago after one too many tequilas, and he's the only person I've ever hooked up with where there's no lingering animosity.

It was a mutual sharing of orgasms, just as it should be.

On my right, Zach leans against the bar, typing away on his phone, while on my left, Ethan scans the space with his signature stern expression. If you didn't know him, you would think he's wishing everyone would disappear, but it turns out it's just his face.

I turn and rest my elbows on the wooden bar top, silently cursing as I stretch my aching body. I took a few hits tonight, aside from the fight, and even with the hotter than normal shower, I still ache.

In hindsight, I probably should have gone to see Joe for a massage instead of just doing a cooldown and some stretches.

Oh well, there's always tomorrow.

I look over my shoulder and groan as a flash of skin catches my eye.

"You need to keep them away from me," I say under my breath.

The bunnies are already swarming like a pack of hungry hyenas. Although this morning's drama wasn't created by them as individuals, I still have this bitter taste in my mouth.

Coach's words play through my mind on repeat, and I refuse to make the same mistake.

I'm not going to let anyone threaten my spot on this team, or risk me losing this family I've found.

Ethan glances over his shoulder to where the bunnies are circling their prey and rolls his eyes. I can't recall a time when he's ever gotten involved with them, in any city.

In fact, he's never talked about hookups at all.

Huh.

"Ignore them. You need to keep your head down for the next few months. I don't want to piss on your fun parade, but you need to take Coach's threat seriously. He won't think twice about putting your name on the trade table if you carry on."

My shoulders sag at his words.

The only time I was able to shut out Coach's words was when I was on the ice. The second my ass was back on the bench, they were swirling through my mind like a verbal hurricane.

"Excellent game tonight. First round is on the house," Dylan announces, planting his hands on the bar, leaning in so he can be heard over the loud, pumping music. "What can I get ya?"

We order a round of beers before Elliot pops his head over my shoulder and adds, "Tequila us, amigo!"

Dylan's eyes cut to me, obviously remembering the last time we had tequila. He shakes his head, hiding his smile, before he starts lining the beers up on the wooden bar top.

"Why? Why are we always ordering tequila?" Mitch Henry whines, his bottom lip pouting out like a child. "You know I can't handle it."

"Then you need to learn, my young padawan." Elliot wraps his arm around the young rookie's shoulders, who is already looking a little green around the gills at the mention of the drink. "Tequila is scientifically proven to make you lose your clothes and heighten your sexy time mojo with its aphrodisiac properties."

Mitch's eyes go wide in awe. "Really?"

I chuckle behind my bottle. "Gullible fuck."

Elliot nods at Mitch. "Yeah! It's also scientifically proven to enhance bedroom activities."

"Scientifically proven?" I scoff.

Elliot's attention flicks to me, giving me a grin which has been dubbed by the media as the 'cheeky Olsen grin', because we both do it. "Yeah, twinny, didn't ya know?"

I shake my head, swallowing my laughter, as Mitch asks about how many tequilas he needs to have to be in "top form for the bedroom Olympics".

Poor kid hasn't got a chance.

After our shots, we squeeze through the throng to our usual section, which has been roped off. I take a seat beside Zach, his focus still on his phone, no doubt texting his buddy Carter in Denver, and look out at the faces in the crowd as Ethan slides in next to me.

"Who's on the menu tonight, then, Blaine?" Mitch sits down opposite me, his cheeks already flushed from the one drink he's had.

Lightweight.

Shaking my head, I reply, "No one. I'm on a bunny-free diet for a while."

Mitch's eyes bug out as he shrieks, "What? Are you insane?"

"Maybe you need to find yourself someone more permanent," Elliot suggests with a shrug. "You know Mom would love someone else to fuss over at Christmas."

I snap my head up at that comment. "And why would I subject myself to that particular torture?"

"Because it would be good for you to have some stability," he replies. "And it'll keep your ass off the blogs."

"Literally." Mitch cackles, snorting at his own joke.

They high-five across the table. Morons.

I flip them both the bird. "Fuck no. The day I get into another relationship is the day hell freezes over."

Because I'm not going down that road of hurt again.

The whole reason I'm in this position now is because I took advantage of how bunnies threw themselves at me everywhere after every failed relationship attempt.

Maybe love just isn't for me.

"Your brother has a point," Ethan pipes up. "I know we said zero distractions, but it could do you some good to have someone steady. You just gotta find the right person, the one who can handle what being with you entails. But you won't find them while you're fucking your way through North America".

"Please." I roll my eyes. "I don't want to be tied down. I'm happy as I am, I just need to stay away from hookups for a little while. Why would I want to deprive everyone of a night in the sack with me for eternity?"

I would never admit it out loud since I'd never hear the end of it, but they have a valid point. The only thing stopping me is the crippling fear that if I give in, and give relationships another chance, I'll fall in love with someone, and they'll never love me back.

I've been there before, got the heartbreak t-shirt, and swore I would never wear it again.

I pull my attention away from my teammates, who are busy making jokes at my expense, and glance out at the bustling bar. There's so many people around, and the atmosphere feels awesome, everyone buzzing from our win.

And then it's like the sea of bodies parts, and the universe decides to hit me with the biggest temptation. Stealing my breath away like a slap shot to the sternum.

"Fuck," I groan, my head hitting the back of the booth.

When I need to be on my best behavior, life decides to throw weakness into my path.

Because the blond guy from the penalty box has just walked into Gino's.

The guy I soaked with his own beer during warm-ups.

The guy with the bluest eyes I have ever seen.

He's temptation personified.

He's walking toward the bar, his head tipped back in laughter at something his friend said.

I hope he's only a friend.

They slip into a gap just in front of Dylan, and it's like my body is drawn to his. I'm standing before I know it, ignoring Ethan's questioning eyes as I slide past him.

"Blaine? What are you doing?" His voice is low and commanding behind me.

I come to a halt a few feet away, allowing myself to take in the blond hottie before he sees me. He must only be a few inches shorter than me. Hair shaved short on the sides, left longer on top, so much so that it's beginning to curl. When I saw him during warm-up, it was the color of his eyes that captivated me. Bright blue, like the ocean in the Maldives.

And those sinful, plump lips?

Fuck. I can just imagine them stretched around my cock while those big blue eyes look up at me.

The jersey he's wearing does nothing to hide his rounded shoulders. Black skinny jeans highlight long, lean legs that would look so fucking good wrapped around my waist.

"Blaine…" Ethan warns. "Don't even think about it."

But there's something in my gut saying this guy might be different. It's like my Spidey senses are telling me he won't cause me media nightmares, despite the fact I can hear Hayden and Coach Harris' voices in my head warning me about distractions.

Still…

"What if he's different? What if he's the right person you just mentioned?" I voice my thoughts out loud.

But as I take another step closer, I hit another wall of doubt.

Would someone want to get to know me for me? Not because I'm Blaine Olsen, NHL player with millions in the bank, ass all over the Internet, sitting second in the points, but for *me*? The guy off the ice, the guy who doesn't like to be front and center of the scandals?

The guy who uses meaningless hookups as a chance to feel? Even if the feelings are only short-lived?

The guy who has never really known what it's like to be loved by someone other than the person I shared a womb with and my family?

I have no fucking idea, and I still have no idea what I'm doing when I find myself closing the distance to this guy, sliding into a gap beside him and his friend at the bar. The warning bells are still buzzing in my ears.

"Hey." I plaster on my most charming smile. "I think I owe you a drink."

I can't help but glance at where his beer spilled down on him earlier to see that his jeans are now dry.

He startles, those hot-as-sin lips parting on a gasp, almost like he's shocked I remembered him, let alone come over. It takes all my restraint not to lean in and press my lips against that spot above his collar just to see if his pulse is fluttering as wildly as I think it is.

"I'm Blaine. I'm sorry for knocking your drink over earlier." I hold my hand out.

He slips his hand against mine, and goose bumps erupt over my skin. I lean in closer, inhaling his delicious scent. He smells like citrus and pine, mixed with the lingering smell of the rink.

He says nothing, so I go on.

"Only a little bit, though." I step in close, angling my head so my lips brush against the shell of his ear. "I would have fucking loved to have helped peel you out of those soaked jeans."

His fair brows hit his hairline, and his eyes go wide. He stares at me, his mouth gaping like a fish. It seems to take him a few beats to come back to his senses.

"I'm Alex." His voice is smoky, the kind that could get you hard just from listening to them recite the alphabet. "And I would have loved to have you help me out of my pants."

Well, fuck me sideways.

And Alex?

Now that's a name I haven't moaned before.

I create some distance between us. One, I know I'm playing with fire, and I can sense Ethan's eagle-eyed stare in the back of my head; and second, I'm already half hard from the way his tongue keeps darting out to wet his bottom lip.

He tugs at the front of his jersey nervously, bringing my attention to the "*C*" stitched to the front. What is it with Ethan trying to fucking cockblock me tonight?

"Alex, you wound me." I place my hand over my heart, feigning hurt. "Here's me hitting on you, and you're wearing another man's jersey."

He looks down at his chest, letting out a nervous laugh. "Sorry, I've had this for years. It's the only one I have."

When he raises his head, the expression on his face surprises me. He looks genuinely… apologetic?

"I'm only messin' with you." I cup his elbow, bringing him to stand next to me. "What can I get you?"

Alex looks over his shoulder to where his friend went. As if sensing his eyes on him, his friend turns his head and winks before returning his attention to the guy he's talking to. I send a telepathic thank you for allowing me some uninterrupted time with Alex.

"I'll have a beer, please."

I wave to get Dylan's attention before looking back at Alex. I take in his features, a cute button nose, full, pillowy lips. A cupid's bow that's just begging to be kissed. His face has a youthful glow but a jawline so sharp it could cut glass. He looks younger than me, possibly a senior in college based on this air of innocence about him.

And not just because of his fucking adorable blushing, but a sense of purity.

Purity ready for me to corrupt.

He's fucking breathtaking.

When Dylan slides the beers across, I raise mine for a toast, clinking our bottles together, and I watch intently as he takes a swig, at how his throat bobs when he swallows. I take a sip of mine, running my tongue over my lips slowly, keeping my eyes locked on his.

He follows the movement, teasing the tip of his tongue over his lower lip.

I'm burning with the inferno that I'm playing with, but nothing could stop me.

Not Coach.

Not Ethan.

Not Hayden.

Most certainly not myself.

"I haven't seen you here before."

Cringe, is that really the line you're coming out with, Olsen?

"That's because I haven't been here before." He tilts his head curiously. "Do you make a habit of knocking people's drinks over and then hitting on them later?"

Well, shit.

I chuckle nervously. "What can I say? I thought you were hot and needed to cool down a bit. You were distracting me."

He raises an eyebrow, his full lips twitching in amusement, and takes a sip of his beer. When he leans his head back, I take a chance and step into his space. Our chests press together, the hitch in his breath making all the blood in my body rush straight to my cock.

Blaine Olsen, two minutes for popping a boner in public.

"You're fucking gorgeous."

His face lights up with a shy smile at my compliment. I press my finger under his chin when his head drops, lifting it to make him look at me. His blue eyes have turned dark with desire. The rise and fall of his chest tells me he feels this.

This electric current between us. It's palpable, like lightning hitting the ocean in the middle of a storm. It was there during warm-ups and again when I was sent to the box.

"Did you enjoy the game?"

He nods. "It was amazing; that slap shot of yours was something else." I'm hypnotized by his smile. "And that fight?"

I'm taken by surprise as he cups my jaw with his hand, brushing his thumb gently over the cut on my lip. A low purr rumbles deep in my chest under his touch. It's so gentle, but at the same time, it's like my body has been charged with a thousand volts. I'm vibrating with need.

A need to taste him.

A need to hear him moan.

A need to know just how low that fucking blush goes.

"It was so fucking hot," he whispers, teasing me.

Fuck, he's killing me.

"Yeah?"

He nods, sucking on his bottom lip as his hooded gaze moves from my mouth to my eyes. "Does it hurt?"

I nip the tip of his thumb with my teeth. My dick jerks against the fly of my pants as he lets out a shaky breath.

"No, but if I said yes, would you kiss it better?"

That gorgeous blush spreads across his cheeks, tipping down his neck and under his collar.

I place my bottle on the bar top behind me before sliding my hands around his trim waist, pulling him close. A low groan escapes me when our erections brush together, and then I run my nose up the slender column of his neck, breathing in his heady scent. Once I reach his ear, his entire body shudders as I flick my tongue over the lobe.

He's so fucking responsive.

I want to strip him naked, explore his body with my tongue, and elicit the filthiest noises from him.

"Come home with me."

My heart is going wild. I'm high on him. I want him under me. Riding me. I want to hear his gasps as I fill him up with my cock. I want to hear him moaning my name, begging me for more. I want to watch his face as his body is overcome with pleasure only I can give him.

I want it all.

I want…

"No."

Wait…

What?

I take a step back to look him in the eye. There's no way I heard that right.

Did he just say… "No?"

He shakes his head. His neck flushes a deep pink, and his eyes close and his jaw clenches, like it's taking every ounce of willpower in his body. He bites his bottom lip, and when he opens his eyes again, those radiant blues are completely blown out with desire.

I take a quick glance down. The bulge of his erection is visible in his jeans. He's just as turned on as I am, but he said no?

I don't understand. This is a first for me. I can't recall a situation where both parties have wanted one another so blatantly, yet nothing is going to happen.

"I'm sorry, Blaine." He raises a hand to cup my jaw again. "You have no idea how sorry I am, but boys like you are my kryptonite, and I'm so tired of being hurt." He leans in, pressing those delicious lips to the corner of my mouth in a tender kiss. "You might be used to getting anyone you want with a snap of your fingers, but if you want me, you're gonna have to work a little harder than just laying on the charm. It may work on everyone else, but I'm not everyone else, and I don't want to be another notch in your bedpost."

I watch as he walks away, losing sight of him as the crowd swallows him.

Never in my twenty-seven years has anyone ever turned me down.

Everyone wants me.

Everyone wants a piece of me.

Instead, I'm left speechless and insanely hard.

Did he just... turn me down?

Four

Blaine

"I'm not angry, I'm just disappointed." Joe, the team's physician, gives me a pointed look.

Why is it that whenever someone says that, you immediately regret everything?

I drop my head between my shoulders. "I know, I know! I'm paying for it now."

"Why didn't you come and see me after the game? I could have helped you."

"It didn't feel as bad, probably because I was just hopped up on the adrenaline, but Joe," I whine playfully, although I know he's going to take zero pity on me. "It really hurts."

With a roll of his eyes, he pats the table. I climb up, screwing my face up when my hip twinges. I took a big hit in the third period last night, and my left hip has been sore since. I spent some time on the bike and did some stretches after the game, followed by a quick ice bath before jumping into a long, extra-hot shower. Although I was starting to ache last night, I didn't think it was this bad, but this morning I woke up feeling like an eighty-six-year-old.

"You know better than that, Blaine. Have I taught you nothing since we've been working together?"

I sigh.

He's right. I skipped protocol last night—despite the fact that I thought I was okay—and reconditioning and recovery is essential.

"Or was it you were too eager to go and see a certain blond that was by the boards?" I open my eyes at his teasing tone and throw a glare over to Ethan on the next table over. His shoulders are shaking as he silently laughs to himself.

"Fuck you, Ethan," I grumble.

He flips his middle finger over his shoulder at me before groaning when the other therapist works on the back of his thigh.

"I'm guessing everyone knows?"

Joe nods, a small smile playing on his lips. "You can thank the rookie for that. He's been blowing up everyone's phones, sharing the news that Mister Bachelor-for-life himself got turned down for the first time in history."

Fucking Mitch.

After Alex disappeared into the crowd last night, I headed back to the table, uncertain for the first time in a while.

"What happened?" Ethan asked, his annoyance evident, as was his surprise at my re-appearance.

Alone.

I shrugged, slumping into the seat next to him. "He turned me down."

Ethan's jaw dropped open, and the rest of the boys leaned forward.

"Shut the front door!" Elliot gasped. "You got rejected?"

I flipped him off. "Fuck off."

He slapped his palm against the table, his head tipped back in laughter. "This is amazing. Broski got rejected!"

I scowled at my twin brother, hoping our telepathic senses were working so he could feel the wrath that would be coming his way if he didn't quit it.

"What did he say, exactly?" Kendrick asked in amusement.

"Just that he's been hurt by guys like me in the past and that if I want him, I'll have to work for him."

"Ouch!" Zach grimaced. "You've never had to work for anyone's attention in your life."

"I know!" I sighed, running an aggravated hand through my hair. "I'm feeling kinda… stunned."

Ethan smirked. "Hell, I wanna meet this guy."

I'm still kinda baffled now.

There's never been a time where there was an obvious mutual attraction and they haven't wanted something from me. It's left me off-kilter.

All thoughts of Alex are pushed to the back of my mind as Joe begins to work on my hip, and we start discussing tactics ahead of our game against Detroit tomorrow.

A few hours later, I'm about to drift off on the couch to the sound of SportsCenter on the TV and the image of Alex running through my mind when the door to my apartment swings open, quickly followed by the sound of Elliot's voice.

"Yeah, yeah, it was so funny, Mom." He's practically howling with laughter, and by the time he appears in front of me in basketball shorts and a Thunder training tee, his eyes are creased with laughter lines.

I cast a glare at him, mouthing, "What?"

"I was just telling Mom about how you got turned down last night," he says between laughter and gasping for breath.

"Blaine?" My mom's voice echoes through the speaker on Elliot's phone. "Elliot, leave your brother alone and give him the phone." He hands it over to me before disappearing to look in the fridge. I can't help but smile at the sight of my mom filling the small screen.

With bright red hair, freckles dotted across her nose, and porcelain skin, she's glowing under the Californian sunshine where she sits on the porch of our childhood home. A far cry from the cloudy skies of Chicago currently outside my window.

"Hey, Mom."

"Hey, how are you? Great game last night!" Her delicate brows turn downward in a frown. "And I know you were protecting your brother, but that doesn't mean I condone the fighting."

I smother my laughter with my hand. "Sorry, Mom."

Her face softens. "You've always had that protective streak when it comes to Elliot."

Isn't that the truth.

Ever since we were kids, my mom says I've always acted like Elliot's protector. I didn't realize the complications my parents had with Elliot's birth until I was older, and how they thought they were going to lose him. Twins are often high-risk, and apparently I was a greedy baby, which meant Elliot was a lot smaller than he was supposed to be. It was like my subconscious mind knew that, so I was always there for him, even before we could walk and talk.

Elliot returns from the kitchen with a bowl filled with grapes and mango and slumps on the couch next to me. I haven't moved from my spot since getting back from the conditioning session at the training facility. I usually try to make the most of our off days. Sometimes I end up using them to nap and do some stretching, and when the weather's nice, Elliot, Zach, and I will go on a walk or something. The rain has put a damper on that plan today, though.

"I also saw that article that was posted about you." She frowns. "That photo wasn't something I ever wanted to see of my son, but I'm angry at those girls for doing that to you."

"Yeah, me too."

"I'm also angry at you for putting yourself in that position. I don't know why you can't find yourself someone nice to settle down with."

I roll my eyes. "Don't you start, too. I had Elliot and Ethan give me that talk last night."

She purses her lips, clearly wanting to argue but deciding against it. "What does Hayden have to say about it?"

"He wants me to keep my head down, at least until the trade deadline has passed."

"Is he worried?"

I nod, sinking further into the cushions. "Yeah, Coach

pretty much said the same because it sheds a bad light on the team too."

She hums, nodding in agreement, then takes a sip of her coffee. "They're both right. You and Elliot have worked so hard to be where you are; don't allow people to ruin that for you, to ruin your dream."

I look over at my brother. He's got this sad puppy-dog face going on that makes my heart hurt. I hold my fist out to him, giving him a smile when he returns the bump.

"And what's this your brother told me about you getting turned down last night? How is that keeping your head down if you're running after people?"

Elliot grins around a mouthful of fruit, enjoying the fact that Mom is grilling me far too much.

I flip him off.

"I saw this guy during warm-up. Super hot, blond hair, and the bluest fucking eyes I've ever seen."

"Language!" Mom scolds.

"Sorry." I grimace, rubbing the back of my neck. "He was beautiful, Mom, which I know sounds stupid. Anyway, I purposely knocked into the boards to get his attention, but I didn't realize he had put his drink on the ledge, so I ended up completely soaking him with his beer."

Mom gasps. "Blaine William Olsen! Why would you do such a cruel thing? No wonder he said no if you humiliated him like that."

Elliot laughs, throwing grapes up in the air and catching them in his mouth.

I shrug. "I dunno… I dunno what compelled me to do it, but I did, and we just…" I trail off, rubbing my face with my palm and mumble, "Had this moment."

"What was that, sweetie?"

"We had a moment… In the penalty box…"

Elliot erupts into laughter again. I scowl, flipping him off for the second time in a couple of minutes. My middle finger might as well be permanently up with the number of times I've flipped the bird in the last twenty-four hours.

"Then," he leans over, pushing my head out of the way. "He saw him again at Gino's after the game. He was at the bar, and Blaine was over there like a rocket, trying to be all swoony and seductive, and when he suggested going back to his place, the guy said no!"

Mom rolls her lips; they're twitching with laughter. She tries to put on a typical sympathetic-mom face as she says, "Oh honey!" but then a giggle escapes. Next thing I know, both my mom and Elliot are belly laughing.

"I don't find this very funny," I grumble.

If I could stomp my foot on the floor like a child, I would, because I don't like being the center of this "let's make a joke out of Blaine" parade.

"Aw, honey. Maybe he isn't like the rest of the people you… you know, *date*." My mom doesn't like the whole hookup culture. "Why don't you ask this nice guy on a date?"

I sigh, shaking my head.

"Not everyone is going to be like the others, sweetie. You can't keep up this persona forever. Isn't it lonely?"

Yeah, it is really fucking lonely, but it's better than feeling vulnerable and getting your heart broken.

It's easier to jump from bed to bed. Having a different partner every night.

Because it means I'm in control of the narrative.

I get to decide whether I take them up on their offer or not, and I get to set the ground rules that are strictly no feelings, one night only, and no strings attached.

Because every person I thought could be the one turned out to have an ulterior motive. Like my college girlfriend, Kelly, when I overheard her talking to her friends in junior year.

I'd just gotten back from an away game at UMass where we lost spectacularly, and there was nothing I wanted more than to just chill with my girl, but as soon as I stepped through the door of her house, I heard her saying that she was only with me for the clout. Once I went pro, she would be able to live the life she'd always wanted; she wouldn't need to work because I'd have enough money in the bank to support her, and she could buy anything she wanted. She went on to say that she didn't really love me. I later found out she was sleeping with a guy from the basketball team.

We had been together since freshman year, and the whole time had been a lie.

Nearly three years built on deception.

But I kept trying and kept ending up disheartened.

My mom must notice I've disappeared into my own head because she says, "Your dad and I were thinking we might try and come to Chicago for Christmas."

"Yeah, that would be nice. You can stay here or at El's. I'm happy to host it here."

She beams. "Invite all the boys too."

I chuckle. All the guys love our mom. "I'm sure they'll snap that invitation up in a heartbeat."

She asks us how we're feeling ahead of our eight-day road trip to the West Coast, then fills us in on my cousin, who started college this year. Once we say our goodbyes, I'm beat, emotionally drained after my throwback thoughts.

"Wanna go see what Zach's up to?" Elliot says, clearly noticing I need the distraction.

"Yeah, sounds good."

I grab my things, and we head down the hall to Zach's apartment.

When I moved to Chicago, we clicked instantly. He is one of the best defensemen I've ever played with, and became my closest friend on the team, so when this apartment came up for sale opposite his, buying it was a no-brainer.

We've become the Luke, Chewbacca, and Han Solo of Chicago, and I'm Han, of course, because I'm awesome.

Footsteps and a muffled voice sound from his apartment when we knock on the door. Zach answers with his phone to his ear

"Hey," he says with an upturn of his chin and mouths, "Sorry, just on the phone to Carter." He steps aside to let us in, closing the door behind us. His apartment has the same layout as mine and Elliot's, and we've been here so often that we pretty much know it like our own.

Retrieving two bottles of water from the fridge, I toss one to Elliot, and take a seat on the couch. SportsCenter plays on the large flat-screen TV mounted on the wall above a fireplace, showing clips from last night's New Jersey and Toronto game.

"Yeah, that's cool; I'll speak to you later," Zach says into the phone, and I'm certain he whispers, "I miss you," but I can't quite be sure.

"What's up?" he asks, sitting down on the other end of

the sectional. "It's only been two hours. Did you miss me or something?"

"Yes!" Elliot says dramatically, throwing his thumb over his shoulder toward me. "I'm so bored of this one moping."

"I am not moping!"

My brother rolls his eyes. "Puh-lease. Even mom could see you were moping."

"Well, it's not like I'm ever gonna see him again."

I can't pinpoint why that pains me the way it does.

I don't miss people, except my parents, but that's normal.

It's not normal to miss someone you just met and know nothing about except for their name, their scent, the color of their eyes, or the sound of their voice.

"Got any plans this afternoon?" Zach asks.

I shrug. "I was just gonna play some video games and take a nap."

"Wanna come with me to my favorite place?" His eyes sparkle with mischief.

"I do not wanna see Carter naked, thank you very much." Elliot holds his hands up.

A quick flash of panic flashes in Zach's eyes before he blinks it away. "I didn't mean that."

Elliot lets out an exaggerated sigh of relief. "Well, thank Gretzky for that. You had me worried for a moment."

Zach looks at him, his forehead furrowed in a frown. "I meant this dessert place in Lincoln Park. They do the most amazing donuts and cupcakes there." He practically drools before patting his solid stomach. "I like to treat myself after a win."

"Sure, sounds good!" I nod.

"I'll meet you downstairs in ten, I gotta put some pants on." Elliot sprints out of the door, allowing it to slam shut behind him. When the coast is clear, Zach turns to me, frowning.

"Why does he think my favorite place is Carter naked?"

I shake my head, a rumble of laughter escaping my throat. "Ignore him; you know what he's like. He's just messin'."

Zach hums, making me a little suspicious that maybe Elliot was closer to the mark than we might think.

Five

Alex

The door flies open, causing the bell to chime wildly like an alarm, followed by a bellowing voice that startles me. I briefly lose my footing and nearly drop an entire tray of freshly baked Biscoff donuts onto the floor.

"You need to tell me everything!"

Tightening my grip on the tray, I close my eyes for a moment to compose myself, taking a few deep, steadying breaths when I see it's only Nate.

"Jesus, Nate! Why can't you enter a building like a normal person?" I slide the tray into the glass display before placing my palm over my rapidly beating heart. "If I had dropped those donuts, you would've been a dead man."

He shrugs, resting his elbows on the counter and placing his chin in his palms. "And what fun would that be? You know I like to make an entrance." He flutters his long eyelashes, a move that has always gotten him out of trouble.

I roll my eyes. My traitorous lips can't help but smile. Some things never change.

We became best friends on our first day of college, when we found out we were going to be sharing a dorm room. I was midway through unpacking my clothes when my grandma began to give me a lecture on how it would be rude to "service the little general" when sharing a room with someone. She continued on to suggest the sock on the door handle method when we realized Nate had been standing at the doorway, holding a box of "welcome roomie" cookies. I was mortified because he'd witnessed the entire thing, but he started laughing so hard that he ended up curling up on the floor because his stomach ached.

We have been stuck together like glue ever since.

He's been there through the highest and the lowest moments of my life, and I couldn't wish for a better friend.

"Anyway, so a little birdie told me you rejected Blaine Olsen last night. Wanna tell me what that's all about? Are you sick?"

Nate paid for me to take an Uber home as he ended up staying later with a guy he met. I text him when I got home letting him know I had fun, and I bumped into Blaine, but that was all I shared.

I glance around the shop but thankfully, we've just finished the lunchtime rush, so the shop is empty.

"I guess I didn't want to be just another number."

Nate frowns. "But he was the perfect candidate for some meaningless fun."

"I know that, but what if I had a bad experience? Then the team that I have known and loved for as long as I can remember would be tainted by it." I shake my head.

"Players are just that, players. I've learned my lesson over the years, and I don't think I could put myself through that again."

Anyone else in my shoes would be jumping at the chance to get in bed with a professional hockey player, but my heart has been through a lot. I've dated a few athletes, and while they are fun, their egos are bigger than the moon, and they thrive on attention. Every one of them cheated on me, and I let them manipulate their way back into my life because I thought I was in love.

I'm not sure I'm one of those who can separate actions from emotions anymore. I may be at the point where I don't think I can do hookups.

I want to date, do the whole getting to know someone, and build something meaningful. It was fun while it lasted in college, but now I want something real.

I want that connection.

Plus, the team genuinely means a lot to me. It's a lasting link to my grandpa.

Nate leans over the counter with a sigh, giving my bicep a comforting squeeze. "It's just sex… It doesn't have to mean anything."

"And I can get *just sex* from someone else when I want it, but the Thunder means too much to me to get involved with a player and for it all to go wrong."

Which it will, no doubt about it.

Nate nods, disappointed, but I know he understands where I'm coming from.

Am I shocked that I had the willpower to say no to a night of what would have been wild-hot sex with a hockey player?

Yes. I'm very shocked.

More so because Blaine is my type with a capital T.

Nate fills me in on the guy he went home with after I left him at Gino's last night and all about his class at the gym where he works when the bell rings above the door again— less frantic this time. Our conversation halts, and I switch into professional mode, but when three figures enter the shop, my mouth goes dry.

Blaine, Elliot, and Zach's huge bodies suddenly make the shop feel small. They're wearing hats low over their faces to try and hide their identity, but the disguise doesn't work on me. I've watched too many games not to know who they are at a glance.

"Oh, this is going to be so good," Nate whispers gleefully.

When they look up, my eyes lock with familiar, stormy gray eyes that seem to light up at the sight of me.

"Well, hello, Alex," Blaine says, a smug grin on his lips. "Fancy seeing you here."

My face heats. Fuck.

I hate how my body instantly becomes alert around him. Electricity prickles at the base of my spine, and my heart kicks against my chest.

He makes me nervous, but like a good nervous. I need to play it cool so he doesn't see the kind of effect he has on me. Leaning my hip against the counter, I fold my arms across my chest and cool my features.

Raising a brow, I ask, "Are you following me?"

I know he isn't. It's simply a coincidence—I hope—but I can't help the laugh that escapes me when his face morphs into a mixture of shock, nerves, and embarrassment.

"Uh, no," he splutters, the tips of his ears turning the deepest shade of pink. "W—we were in the area as Zach wanted these donuts, and I—"

"I'm kidding," I chuckle, interrupting his cute ramble.

He pulls off his ball cap with a sigh, running his hand nervously through his hair and gripping the back of his neck. "You got me good, then." He looks down at his feet, hiding a sheepish smile.

I flash him a toothy grin. "What can I get for you guys?"

Blaine looks at Zach, who's crouching down in front of the glass cabinet, his hand resting against the glass as he scans the selection on offer like a child, and Elliot is grinning gleefully at the two of us.

Nate's looking at Elliot, eyes roaming his long, lean form like a predator would his prey.

I clear my throat when his tongue darts out to lick his lips, and shake my head when Nate turns to look at me.

Don't even think about pouncing on him, I mentally say with a glare.

His lips tip in a devilish smirk, and he gives me a careless shrug before looking back at Elliot.

My best friend is ruthless.

When neither of them speaks, Blaine turns his attention back to me. Gone is the nervous, stuttering mess he was less than a minute ago, having been replaced with the cocky, confident hockey player I met last night, making me wonder which one is real?

He rests his side against the counter, propping his elbow and forearm on the polished surface, and hits me with a dazzling smile.

"You must be tired…"

Umm, I'm what now?

He must pick up on my confusion as he continues, "Because you've been running through my mind since you left me last night."

Nate bursts into laughter beside me, and I snort. "Really?"

Blaine gives me a lopsided grin, completely unfazed by the cheesy pick-up line he just landed on me. "Yep! I have more for you. Wanna hear them?"

"Hit me with your best shot."

"Well, I'm here, so what are your other two wishes?"

I cover my face with my palm to hide my laughter. "You're ridiculous, you know that? It's astonishing how you get so much action."

I notice his cockiness falter for a brief second. "Well, you're the first person I've had to pull out these lines for. You're really making me work for it, Alex."

"Work for what?"

I know I'd told him he'd have to work beyond his charm for me, but I didn't think he would actually take my word for it. I didn't expect to see him again. I'd just put it down to one of those weird moments in life where you bump into a super hot guy once and then they disappear, like it was all an illusion, never to be seen again. A story to retell over drinks when you're old and wrinkly.

"I'd like to take you on a date."

Surprise chokes me. "A date?"

"Uhhh, yeah... You know, the thing you do when you want to get to know a person." He shifts from foot to foot, his hand going to the back of his neck again.

He's nervous.

"You want to take me on a date?"

Maybe he hit his head last night during the fight against that St. Louis player, because surely this isn't really happening right now.

Goose bumps ripple up my arms at Blaine's laughter. It's rich, slightly husky. It's pure sex, just like him.

My breath catches in my throat as he leans closer. "What do you say, Alex? Let's go out for dinner."

Seeing him again has completely thrown me, but him asking me out? Anxiety swirls in my stomach like a whirlpool as I try to read his face to pick up on any clues that he's joking around, playing me.

Is he only asking because I turned him down?

I'm not under the illusion that Blaine isn't enjoying the thrill of the chase. A fun game of cat and mouse. It's clear as a bright summer's day how attracted I was—and still am —to him, and I doubt many people would turn down a guy they're this into. Also, Blaine Olsen's been voted one of the sexiest men in the league on a number of occasions, so having to chase someone must be new for him.

And I'm not naive enough to think I'm special.

I want to say yes badly, but I also don't want to come off as easy.

Am I being cruel? Maybe. But I'm just trying to be cautious.

"I'll think about it."

His eyes go wide in surprise, clearly not expecting that answer. "Oh ... Okay."

Nate smothers his laugh with his hand. Over Blaine's shoulder, Elliot lifts his head, his eyebrows almost touching his hairline with shock as his mouth drops open.

"Can I at least get your number?" Blaine asks.

"Why?" Cocking my head to one side, I peek my tongue out of the corner of my mouth. "Did you lose yours?"

Another sheepish grin appears on his face. He has a good sense of humor, that's for sure.

"You know it, baby."

I roll my eyes, but I can't contain the smile that takes over my face. Holding my hand out for his phone, my inner cheerleader goes wild when he passes it over.

Blaine Olsen just asked for my number!

I fill in the blank contact page with my phone number, putting a fire emoji next to my name, then hand it back.

"Could I get some of the maple glaze donuts and a couple of the strawberry sprinkle cupcakes, please?" Zach's quiet voice distracts me.

For a big guy, he's incredibly gentle. I've heard him speak at interviews before, but didn't know whether his softer tone was from exhaustion after the game.

"Of course." I smile.

While I box up his selection and ring through his order, he thanks me endlessly, letting me know these are his favorite treats and how he often gets them delivered on GrubHub.

"Make sure to pop a note in your order next time, and I'll put in some freebies. We can have a code word or something, so I know it's you."

His face morphs into the sweetest smile I've ever seen. "Thank you, that's really kind."

Holding the two boxes close to his chest, like he's protecting precious cargo, Zach turns to the two brothers. "Are you two done? I need a nap."

Blaine blinks at the two of us. "How come he gets a code name, and I don't?"

"When you start ordering almost daily, you can have a code name." I grin.

He narrows his eyes and smiles. "You're on." They head toward the door, then he stops and turns to me, "I'll text you."

"Be sure to rack up those cheesy pick-up lines for me."

He winks. "You betcha, baby."

Six

BLAINE

Do you like raisins? How do you feel about a date?

ALEX

LOL. I really do like raisins, but I have to be in the mood for a date.

BLAINE

Did you know that I'm studying to become a historian?

ALEX

Oh really?

BLAINE

Because I'm really interested in finding a date.

ALEX

cry laughing emoji

BLAINE

:D

BLAINE

Am I making you laugh?

ALEX

I'm not sure if I'm laughing at you or with you.

BLAINE

I'll take that as a win.

BLAINE

I'll make you laugh a lot if you let me take you on a date.

ALEX

My answer hasn't changed since I saw you an hour ago, I'm still thinking about it.

BLAINE

I will get that date, Alex.

ALEX

We'll see ;)

BLAINE

Are you a broom?

ALEX

Umm what?

BLAINE

Because you've swept me off my feet.

ALEX

FFS *cry laughing emoji*

ALEX

I just snort laughed in the middle of Target.

BLAINE

:D

BLAINE

Go on a date with me, Alex.

ALEX

Hmm, still thinking about it.

BLAINE

Think about it harder then.

ALEX

You'd like that, huh?

BLAINE

No need, I'm already hard thinking
about you.

ALEX

Oh jeez *facepalm emoji*

ALEX

I walked right into that one.

BLAINE

Good morning.

BLAINE

I like that you already put a fire next to your
name.

BLAINE

Because I'm so hot for you.

ALEX

I don't know if you're being ridiculous or cute.

BLAINE

Can I be cute because I'm ridiculous?

BLAINE

Ridiculously hot for you ;)

ALEX

Please don't give up hockey.

BLAINE

Why is that?

ALEX

I don't think you could make a career out of cheesy greeting card slogans.

BLAINE

If I could rearrange the alphabet, I would put U and I together.

ALEX

face-palm emoji

BLAINE

Let me take you out on a date.

ALEX

You're relentless.

BLAINE

Is that a yes?

ALEX

It's a maybe.

BLAINE

Woohoo!

Seven

Blaine

The following morning is filled with practice, having our aches and pains taken care of by the team physical therapists and watching some video footage ahead of tonight's game against Detroit. It should be an easy win, considering we haven't lost a single game against them this season, and they're pretty much bottom of the league.

But even with those stats on our side, we don't let up on the preparation. You can never be too prepared for a game.

We listen intently as Coach goes through tape, pointing out Detroit's weaknesses in their defense and the textbook plays their offense always run.

The rooms set up like a mini movie theater. Black leather recliners embossed with the Thunder logo on the headrest, all facing a large screen with a small podium where Coach Harris and the video coach are sitting to the left.

I bounce my leg as anxiety creeps in, time ticking by slower than normal. I've got approximately an hour between the end of this session and needing to be home for my pre-game nap. I could get to Lincoln Park and back within that time.

I couldn't believe my luck yesterday when I saw Alex right there behind the counter at the dessert place Zach was craving. It was like fate was throwing the guy I couldn't forget about into my path again.

Leaning over to Elliot, I lower my voice so Coach doesn't yell at me for interrupting. "El, wanna come with me to that dessert place after we're finished here?"

His eyes narrow, a knowing smile creeping across his lips. "Why?"

I rotate my phone on the arm of the chair between my fingers as nerves bubble in my stomach. I don't want to admit that I'm itching to see Alex again. I've found myself reading through the texts we've exchanged in the past twenty-four hours, and I've had to mentally restrain myself from being too pushy.

"I don't suppose it has anything to do with the blond hottie? Alex?" Elliot's mouth twitches. "You gonna ask him out again?"

I shrug, hoping it comes across nonchalantly, and not wanting to tell him I've been doing that already. "I dunno? Maybe?"

He snickers. "You got it baaaaad," he sings.

I flip him off. "Shut up."

"Blaine's got it baaaaad."

"Tendy Olsen!" Coach slams his palm against his little podium, pointing his index finger at Elliot. "If you interrupt me one more time, I'm going to be benching you for the next three games, and no power break dancing for you."

Elliot mock gasps, his hand flying to his chest. "But you wouldn't *dare*, Coach!"

Coach raises a challenging brow, his silent glare screaming *try me*, and Elliot quickly holds his hands up in surrender.

Nobody can take Elliot's on-ice dancing away from him.

"Count me in. I could eat a donut or two right now," Zach whispers from behind.

Well, now that I've managed to find a way to see him without looking like I'm stalking him, all that's left to do is figure out how to get Alex to say yes instead of maybe.

When I push open the door to the bakery thirty minutes later, I freeze on the spot at the unfamiliar face behind the counter. He looks a little similar to Alex; same angelic features, but his hair is a darker blond, and he looks older. He flashes a smile, but it's not as gorgeous as Alex's.

"Hey, welcome! How can I help you?" he asks.

Zach goes straight to the glass cabinet, crouching down like yesterday, his gaze bouncing from all the different cookies, cupcakes, and donuts. I scan the shop, hoping Alex will appear, but he's nowhere to be seen.

Fuck. Did I miss him? Does he not work on Tuesdays?

"Is Alex here?" I blurt.

The guy's eyebrows go up. "Uh, he's just stepped out. Is there anything I can help with? Would you like me to pass on a message?"

Maybe fate isn't on my side after all.

I'm about to open my mouth to tell him not to worry about it when Elliot beats me to it.

"My brother here would like to court Alex."

My head snaps to my brother. Court? Are we in eighteenth-century England?

"The fuck, El?"

Elliot shushes me with a finger to his lips and waves his hand to be quiet. The guy looks kinda startled when he steps up to the counter.

"Blaine and Alex met a few nights ago, and when we came in yesterday, Blaine asked him on a date, but he said no." Elliot chuckles. "You should have seen his face; he was like a sad puppy. Anyway, my broski here would like to ask Alex on another date because it seems he's playing a bit hard to get."

The guy's brows drop into a deep frown. His eyes roam over me, but it doesn't feel like he's checking me out. It feels judgmental, like I'm under inspection.

"I can't answer for my brother, but I can let him know you've stopped by." His tone is a little dismissive.

Brother? Oh fuck.

Wow, way to make a good impression, Olsen.

My stomach churns with unease. If his brother doesn't like me—for whatever reason—this is going to ruin my chances. Alex isn't going to give me a second thought. I've gotta think fast.

"Can you give him a message?"

He nods.

"Can you let him know there'll be two tickets for tonight's game waiting for him at will call?"

I don't miss the way his eyes widen slightly before quickly schooling his features. "Sure, I'll let him know."

Once Zach finally chooses his two donuts, Alex still isn't back. It would be weird to hang around any longer, and I need my pre-game nap. Admitting defeat, we head back to my Range Rover, and I fire off a text to the Thunder's PR manager, Colleen, praying she sees it in time to help me out.

BLAINE

Col, babe, I need your help.

BLAINE

Can you leave two tickets at will call for Alex?

BLAINE

IDK his last name. Put Alex from Jacob's Delicious Desserts?

COLLEEN

No problem.

Then I quickly send a text to Alex.

BLAINE

Hey.

BLAINE

I stopped by to see you, I'm sad that I missed you.

BLAINE

I'm not stalking you, btw.

BLAINE

I mean, I had to go because Zach wanted donuts, and I don't wanna say no to the big guy because he can get a lil scary when he's hungry.

BLAINE

Anyway, I would love to see you tonight at my game. I've left two tickets for you at will call. Hope I see you later *kissing emoji*

Later, my pre-game nap is unsettled by anxious thoughts gnawing at me. Why do I want to see this guy so bad? Why is it bothering me the way it is? Why do I want him so badly?

I have no fucking idea. I can't quite put my finger on why Alex gets to me.

I haven't felt this off-center since the NHL draft, but I have to try and push him to the back of my mind because we've got a hockey game to win.

Eight

Alex

I'm pretty sure today is one of those days where the world is trying to fuck me over.

When we ran out of eggs this morning, I went to the store to find all of the shelves empty. After going to three different places, I finally struck gold at the fourth store, but at that point, I was already annoyed. Thinking my day couldn't possibly get any worse, I returned to my car to find it had a flat tire.

But what took the fucking cake? A fucking bird shat on me as I finished changing the tire.

Today can go fuck itself with a rusty spoon.

I push the door open to the shop and my frustration rockets at the bell chiming above my head.

"Ugh!" I grunt, throwing a glare at the object.

"What took you so long?" Jacob asks from behind the counter.

"There weren't any eggs anywhere," I reply, taking the bags into the kitchen.

"Wow, that's something I never thought would happen."

I set the bags on the counter with an irritated huff. "Me neither, but here we are."

I unpack the eggs, placing them carefully into the storage containers before disposing of the cartons in the recycling. "Then I had a flat tire."

"Ugh, you're kidding," he groans. "Really?"

"Yeah. Luckily, I managed to fit the spare, but I don't know how long it'll last. I'll ask Nate if his friend can look at it."

He rubs his hand over his face. Exhaustion is etched across his face, from his pale skin to the dark circles under his eyes. I know he's thinking the same as me—how are we going to be able to afford a new tire? But that's a problem for future Alex to figure out.

"The worst thing? I got shat on by a bird."

Jacob drops his hand, trying to suppress his laugh by rolling his lips together.

"It's not funny! I had to rush home and change my shirt because it was all down my back."

He holds his hand up. "Please, no grim details. You'll make me gag."

Rolling my eyes at my brother, I put my apron on and get back into work mode. We're nearly sold out, but we still have three custom orders to get finished today.

"You had some visitors while you were out," Jacob announces, leaning his shoulder against the door jamb. His head tilts to the side as he purses his lips.

"Oh?"

"Does the name Blaine ring any bells?"

My heartbeat speeds up at the sound of his name. I wasn't expecting to hear from him when I gave him my number. I just put it down to one of those experiences where you meet a hot guy and then never hear from them again. It becomes a story you tell your friends over drinks: *Do you remember that time an NHL player asked for my number? Ha, yeah, me too.*

But no, he proved me wrong. He's texted constantly, each time with a cheesier pick-up line than the last.

I can't deny that I feel giddy being the focus of his attention. That even with the number of people he could be texting, he seems to want to message me.

Maybe he's texting everyone else the same thing, too.

I grunt at my inner thoughts.

"He wanted to let you know that he's put two tickets aside for you at will call for tonight's game."

My mouth drops open, closes, then opens again. "What?" comes out a few octaves higher than usual.

Digging my phone out of my pocket, I see five texts from Blaine on the screen. A slow smile creeps onto my face. Why does he have to be so fucking irresistible when he's supposed to be a jackass? I don't know which side of him to believe is real.

Jacob lifts a shoulder. "That's what he said, but Alex?"

Looking up from my phone, I see my brother's forehead creasing in a deep frown.

"Be careful. He seems like trouble with a capital T, and I don't want to see you get wrapped up in whatever he's trying to lure you into."

Jacob's been there through every single one of my heartbreaks, so his concern is valid. He's always thought athletes are shallow, constantly looking for whatever greener grass is on the other side, regardless of who they have to hurt to get there. He went through so much in school, too, that I don't blame him for being jaded.

"I'll be careful." I give Jacob what I hope is a reassuring smile. "But if I'm gonna be getting out on time for the game, I need to get started on these orders!"

But first, I type out a reply to his texts.

ALEX

I'll be there. You better score a goal for me!

Nate lets out a low whistle. "Wow. I need to bag me a hockey player so I can get some free tickets."

After I replied to Blaine's text earlier, I sent one to Nate asking if he was free, since there was no way I'd be coming on my own, and Jacob hates hockey. Luckily, he works for himself, so he managed to shuffle his schedule around to get the night off.

We find our seats—a few rows up from the home bench—and get comfortable. We were late since I didn't finish as early as I'd hoped and ended up missing warm-up. I watch the Zamboni as it glides over the ice, chewing on the inside of my cheek as anxiety creeps in.

"Do you think any of his teammates wants a fuck buddy?" Nate asks.

I pinch the bridge of my nose, silently laughing to myself. He has no filter whatsoever.

"What?" He laughs between munching on some nachos. "I mean it. I could get used to this life. Hot sex, hot hockey player, free tickets." He shrugs. "Seems like a good time. Maybe that cute goalie would be down for some fun. Is there such a thing as a male puck bunny? Would they be like…" He waves his hand around, searching for the word.

"A buck?" I supply.

He hoots. "A puck buck."

I shake my head with a laugh. "You're ridiculous."

He blows me a kiss. "You know it, boo."

As the Zamboni leaves the ice, my phone vibrates in my pocket, and immediately my mind races to my brother. I left him to deliver the custom orders with that shitty spare tire that Nate has promised his friend will come and look at tomorrow, but the worry in my chest is replaced with surprise when Blaine's name appears on the screen.

BLAINE

Meet me outside the locker room after the game.

"He asked to meet after the game," I say quietly.

This feels like a wild dream, and I'm going to wake up soon.

"If he asks you on a date again, what are you gonna say?"

I chew on the skin around my thumb. "I don't know."

Nate angles his body toward mine, his usually playful tone suddenly turning serious. "It doesn't have to be something more. You can control it. Lay down the law and say you only want to go for dinner. If he's genuine about taking you out, he'll agree to just that." He muses for a bit. "It's kinda insane for a guy like him to be so persistent, considering his MO is fuck and chuck."

I've been thinking about it a lot because Blaine seems to have taken up permanent residence in my brain since the night at Gino's. I'd be an idiot to pass up dinner with him, right?

Can I protect my heart, knowing that whatever this is will probably be short lived, though?

Possibly?

But despite the heartache I've been through, I'm still in love with the *idea* of love, so it's hard for me to go into something without hoping it ends up in forever.

"Maybe," I say as the lights go down and the smoke machines start up. Red lights flash against the pristine white ice to match the beat of Thunder's signature entry song "Burn it to the Ground", and fans sing at the top of their lungs. I settle back in my seat, excitement thrumming through my veins for the game ahead.

The buzzer sounds, ending the game 5-0 to the Chicago Thunder. The team swarms onto the ice to celebrate their win, bumping helmets with Elliot.

My throat is hoarse from cheering and my hands sting

from clapping, and when the crowd disperses up the stairs toward the atrium, I turn to Nate.

"I have no idea how we get to the locker room."

He chuckles. "Maybe Blaine will find us with the little Alex-radar thing he's got going on."

Luckily, we're saved by a blond lady in a baby-blue tailored suit.

"Hey, Alex?" She looks between me and Nate.

Nate points to me as I say, "Hey, yeah, that's me."

Her face lights up with a smile. "Great! If you could both just follow me."

She begins to climb the stairs in her spiked stilettos at such speed that Nate and I have to jog to keep up with her. She leads us down some corridors, flashing a badge at the security guards as we go.

"Blaine was worried you wouldn't know where to go, so he asked me to come find you."

I swallow the lump in my throat. My palms are sweaty with nerves, and I subtly wipe them on the side of my jeans.

We pass through a final set of doors, stopping outside one with the Thunder's logo and *Locker Room* written underneath.

"If you could wait here, he'll be out shortly," she says before walking away.

Nate—being the mischievous fuck he is—goes straight to the door and gently pushes it open. The pumping sound of music and out-of-tune singing comes through the gap. He lets it close softly before turning to face me, wearing a wicked grin. "Wow, there's a lot of nipples in there."

My laugh is shaky, and I playfully swat his arm. "Stop it, you'll get us thrown out."

"Shame they had their towels on." He wiggles his eyebrows.

Forty minutes later, the door opens, and Blaine appears wearing a dark forest green suit that fits him like a glove. The color compliments his skin tone, and the crisp white shirt underneath is screaming for me to rip it off him.

His face lights up when he spots me. "You came," he beams.

"Yeah, thank you for the tickets. It was a really great game."

I really want to congratulate him and gush over his hat trick and assist, but I'm conscious that I don't want to seem like a fanboy.

"I know you asked for one goal, but I thought I'd give you three." He leans in, pressing a kiss to my cheek.

Holy shit.

Blaine Olsen just kissed me.

I sigh happily, my heart swelling in my chest as I practically melt under his touch.

"I was hoping that if I showed you how awesome I am, you might agree to go out with me."

His eyes twinkle, but there's a hint of uncertainty. This time, when he leans in, his voice is a seductive whisper. Deep and husky, and it goes straight to my balls.

"There's something wrong with my eyes." His lips tip up in a devilish grin. "Because I can't seem to take them off you."

A bark of laughter escapes me. "You're funny."

"I wasn't trying to be funny this time, but am I funny enough to go on a date with me?"

Yes, yes, yes!

But I can't give in just yet. I'm enjoying teasing him far too much.

"Why do you wanna take me out so bad?" I shove my hands into the back pockets of my jeans, trying to act aloof when all I really want is to kiss his gorgeous smile off his face. "You don't seem like the going-on-dates type."

He shrugs. "What can I say? You're hot, I'm hot, we've got some serious vibes going on, why wouldn't I?"

I tilt my head to the side.

Interesting. He oozes confidence, yet there are glimpses of vulnerability.

"He would love to go on a date with you," Nate interrupts. "His favorite kind of foods are Mexican and Italian, so if you take him for tacos, you're guaranteed a good time, but he also likes walks in the park and does this weird thing where he mixes M&Ms into his popcorn."

I glare at my soon-to-be ex-best friend.

"Nate," I curse under my breath.

He shrugs, not giving a shit.

Blaine looks between us, his brow furrowing slightly, like he is trying to work out some crazy mathematical equation. "You two aren't a thing, right?"

We both answer in tandem in a chorus of "Hell, no!" and "Fuck, no."

Blaine chuckles, the tips of his fingers rubbing over his stubbled chin.

"Good." He nods and looks back at me. "Let me take you out, Alex. I promise to keep my hands to myself." He wiggles his fingers.

I scoff in disbelief. "I don't believe that for a second."

"Okay, how about I promise to keep my hands to myself *during* dinner?" he counters.

I let out a sigh. What's the worst that can happen? Like Nate said earlier, I could be in control.

"Just dinner," I state.

Blaine nods fervently, as he moves closer to me. "Just dinner."

"Okay."

"Oh, thank fuck for that," Elliot wails, suddenly appearing behind Blaine and wrapping an arm around his shoulders. "Do you know what you've made us deal with for two days?" He steps around Blaine, shoving him out of the way to stand in front of me, hitching his thumb over his shoulder at his brother. "This guy has been crying into his cornflakes for fucking *days* about the cute guy who turned him down. Do you know how annoying it is to listen to him cry?" He looks exasperated.

"I was not fucking crying, El," Blaine glowers.

"You might as well have been!" Elliot spins on his heels to face Blaine. "Wah, poor me, this guy rejected me, and I thought he was really hot." He mocks with a roll of his eyes, then taps his temple with his index finger. "You forget that we're twins. We have that weird ass telepathic jedi juju thing. Everything you think, I hear! I feel what you feel! And fuck me, I thought I was gonna need to go and listen to some Lewis Capaldi while I sit in the shower to contemplate my life choices or something."

A bubble of laughter escapes my chest as the two brothers begin to bicker over whether or not Blaine was being annoying, completely unabashed by the fact that we're standing outside of the locker room with several people still milling around, including the media.

Looking at them, you wouldn't know they were twins—Blaine is bulkier, whereas Elliot is taller and leaner. Blaine's hair is a darker auburn, and Elliot's is strawberry blond, and his eyes are a pale green compared to Blaine's silver.

I try to contain my amusement, completely entertained by the two as they continue to argue.

Maybe this is the real side of Blaine Olsen. The guy with a great sense of humor who gets ribbed by his brother and gets nervous about asking guys on a date.

And shit, that scares me because that guy has the potential to hurt me.

My heart may be in a world of trouble.

Nine

Alex

"Just three more, Alex; you've got this."

I internally curse at Nate a thousand times over as I shakily push up the weighted bar on the chest press. I'm about to cry at how sore my body is already. In college, I used to hit the gym regularly with Nate, but since graduation, working out has been the last thing on my mind.

A few years ago, Jacob's baking business grew overnight. What started off as a small venture in our grandparents' kitchen soon turned into a full-fledged business. I put my business degree to use, and we started Jacob's Delicious Desserts together, taking on loans and investing everything into making it amazing.

But little did we know that luck wouldn't always be on our side and that we would make mistakes that cost us a lot of money.

Between the two of us, we're still trying to get rid of the

debt, meaning it's going to be all work and no play for us for a long time to come.

Thankfully, or thanklessly, depending on which way you want to look at it, Nate's persistence has kept me in shape, even if I only manage to get in a couple of workouts every week.

It's a good distraction from money woes and it keeps me healthy, and the fact he allows me to use the gym free of charge, despite his long waiting list of clients, is a major bonus.

With a final grunt, I hit the last rep, groaning with relief when he takes the bar from me. My arms dangle off of the bench like cooked spaghetti, and I lay there panting. Blood pounds in my temples, and sweat is literally dripping everywhere.

Nate hands me a towel and my water bottle from the floor. I take several greedy gulps before wiping my face.

"I feel so out of shape." I stand with a groan. My entire body feels like I've been hit by a Mack truck. "I wanna curl up in a ball on the floor right now. Why does wanting to be healthy have to be so painful?"

Nate chuckles. "You're doing really well. You'll get back to being fit, it just takes time."

"You've gotta say that since you're my friend."

"No, I don't. You've come so far since we started." He pokes my pec with his finger, causing me to wince and let out a little pathetic whimper. "Look at these! They're growing back!"

I rub my palm over the sore spot on my chest and pout, then follow him as he leads me to the mats. We go through our typical cooldown routine, and after the final stretch, I flop back onto the floor, closing my eyes.

"What's on your mind?"

I open one eye to see Nate sitting cross-legged beside me.

"I'm going out with Blaine tomorrow."

I still can't believe I agreed to a date with Blaine Olsen.

It's been a few days since I saw him after the game against Detroit, and I keep pinching myself because in what universe does someone like me, a *fan*, go on a date with a professional athlete who plays for the team they've supported since they were a child?

It just doesn't happen.

"Has he told you where he's taking you?"

"He said he's got a surprise activity, then dinner at Fire Garden."

Nate's eyes go wide, letting out a low whistle. "Boy is pulling out all the stops to impress you."

My cheeks heat.

Last night, I looked up the menu online and nearly passed out at the prices. Fifty-eight dollars for one dish—*that contained two tacos!*—which is more than Jacob and I spend on food for the two of us in a week. He had to calm me down because I was on the verge of a panic attack, then we sat on the couch with a spreadsheet and tried to figure out what my budget could be so I could have a nice night.

He may be a rich hockey player, but I don't expect him to pay for everything, and it's kinda overwhelming because Blaine and I live two very different lives.

"Why are you nervous? Just forget about who he is and see

him as any other guy. Yeah, he's got a cool job and more money in the bank than both of us will ever make in a lifetime, but he's still just a guy at the end of the day." He twirls his shoelaces between his fingers. "He's probably just as nervous as you, if the way he looked the other day is any indication. Also, he might be a complete loser and is actually really boring."

I chew on my bottom lip, remembering how unsure of himself he was when he came into the shop nearly a week ago and how awkwardly shy he was after the game the other night.

"Plus, you can put a good word in for me with the twin brother." Nate winks, slapping my shoulder before he stands, holding his hand out to help me up. "Come on, let's go get a shake."

X

Jacob is sitting at the dining table when I return home from the gym thirty minutes later. Paperwork covers every inch of the wooden table, the crease between his brows growing deeper and deeper as he reads through whatever document he's holding.

"Hey, what's that?" I ask, retrieving a glass from the cupboard to pour myself some water.

"The latest statements from the bank," he sighs. When he looks up, his eyes are puffy and red, his chin trembling.

"What's wrong?"

"Sometimes it just feels like I'm failing, you know?" he chokes out.

I place my glass in the sink and walk over to him. I wrap my arms around his shoulders, bringing him in for a hug.

"You are not failing! Look how far you've come. It all started in this very room, and now you have a shop with your name on the front."

He nods, letting out another defeated sigh. "I know. It's just overwhelming at times. I see the amount we owe, and while I know we've got the repayment plan in place, I just want it gone. I wanna be able to not worry about money and not feel guilty when I want to buy a new pair of shoes or takeout just because I feel like it." He presses his head against my stomach and lets out a small sob.

As kids, all I wanted to do was be like Jacob. Whatever he wore, I wanted to match. Whatever toys he played with, I wanted them, too. I was like his shadow; wherever he went, I would follow.

I wish I could wish all our problems away and allow the person he is to shine back through. He's exhausted, mentally and physically, and it pains me because I don't know what else we can do.

We can't afford to hire any staff right now, and while he's taught me how to decorate the less complex cakes, he's still working insanely long days to keep up with customer demand.

"We'll get through this, I promise," I murmur into his hair. "But you're far from a failure."

Unshed tears prickle my own eyes now.

Hoping to try and lighten his mood, I clear up the paperwork and stack it neatly to one side, as it will still be here tomorrow, but right now, my focus is making sure Jacob eats and gets a decent night's sleep before we do it all again tomorrow.

"Have you eaten?"

He shakes his head.

I retrieve a saucepan from the cupboard and bring some water to the boil to make a quick and easy pasta dish. Searching through the cupboards, I find a packet of chamomile tea and make him a cup, hoping the hot, calming drink will help ease his stress. Once the pasta is cooked, I serve it in two bowls and sit down at the table opposite him.

His voice is quiet and tearful as he thanks me.

"I think I'm going to let Blaine know that I can't make it tomorrow," I announce, voicing the worry that's been running through my brain since I got home.

Jacob's head snaps up, the firm shake tells me he doesn't agree. "No, don't do that over this." He motions to the stack of bills. "Cancel only if you genuinely don't wanna go. The money we've set aside for dinner isn't going to make a significant difference, and I'd rather you enjoyed yourself."

I chew on the inside of my cheek. I know I'm acting hastily on the anxiety whirling inside of me with a snap decision, and he's right—the money we set aside is less than a hundred dollars, so it won't be a game changer when the debt is eight hundred times more than that.

"Alex," Jacob sighs.

He leans across the table, his hand resting on my forearm. His smile is tired and sad, but his eyes are pleading. "Please go. Enjoy yourself. Don't let these opportunities pass you by; you will only live to regret it."

Ten

Blaine

Resting my laptop on the cushion in front of me, I wait impatiently for Hayden's video call. He texted me this morning to let me know he needed to talk ahead of my game tonight, and panic instantly zapped in my chest.

Is he going to call to say that I've gotta pack up my shit because I've been traded? I've done everything that's been asked of me and kept my name off of the blogs this past week—OK, that's not entirely true, because now my name is on there for a different reason. They are now discussing the fact that I'm *not* getting my dick wet.

Damned if I do, damned if I don't.

One thing I need Hayden to get in place is a no-trade clause in my contract, especially now that Elliot's here, and if things develop with Alex…

Fuck.

I'd hate for things to fall into place and then need to uproot my entire life to another city.

Thankfully, the chime of Hayden calling me echoes through the speakers on my laptop before I can spiral into a vortex of anxiety. His face fills the screen, his hair blowing in the sunny California morning breeze. Behind him, through the open patio doors of his beachside mansion, is the ocean.

I've been there once before, and it's gorgeous. He must be sitting at his dining table, which overlooks a wrap-around terrace and his own private beach.

It's definitely a life-goals kind of house for me.

"Hey!" I wave to the camera, then cringe at myself.

Hayden gives a throaty chuckle at my awkwardness. "Hey. How's things?"

"Good." I nod. "Really good, actually."

"And your hip? Still giving you trouble?"

After the hit during the St. Louis game, I've become a regular with Joe, asking him to relieve some of the discomfort. In each game since, it's been like the other team could smell that I'm a little sore and targets it on purpose. We've done a few scans just to be safe, and it was nothing more than a strain, but with the repeated hits to an already weakened spot, I'm really feeling it.

I move my hand from side to side. "So-so; it's feeling better every day. It's only a sprain. I was starting to worry it was going to turn into something more serious."

He nods. "Sprains are still serious, Blaine. Make sure you do as much recovery as possible. I'd hate to see it get worse."

I know he didn't call to talk about my hip, and the anticipation makes my mouth go dry. I take a sip of water and wait for him to get to the point.

"I'm just calling because I wanted to let you know what happened this week."

I squeeze the water bottle between my hands.

Here it comes.

"The team has done a great job at removing all traces of those photos, but one thing I noticed, which I'm pleased about, by the way, is that the media's now talking about how you've kinda fallen off the radar. Don't get me wrong, I'm stoked you've followed my advice, but they're saying they haven't seen you out with the team either." His head tilts curiously. "What's that about?"

This is either going to get me into a shit ton of trouble or it'll be the news Hayden wants to hear.

"I met someone."

Hayden stills. He's so frozen that I start to think maybe I've lost him. I move the cursor and check my internet connection. I'm still connected. I'm about to close the call so I can call him back when a rumble of laughter comes from him.

"Wait. Did I just hear that right? You've met someone?" His eyes are comically wide.

I nod, rubbing the back of my neck.

"Yeah, I actually met him that night after you visited." I smile when the image of Alex enters my brain—how shocked he looked when I knocked into the boards and spilled his drink over him.

Hayden leans closer to the screen. His brow furrows, his eyes searching. I have no idea what he's thinking, and the longer he remains mute, the more worried I get.

Is he going to tell me to call off my date with Alex?

My initial thought on that is "fuck no," but can I tell my agent to fuck off when he's working hard to make sure I don't end up on the trading table?

A whooshing breath escapes me when he lets out a laugh. A full-on belly laugh.

"Holy shit." He wipes his eyes with the heel of his hand. "I never thought I would see the day when Blaine Olsen met someone. So, are you going to do this properly?"

I nod. "Yeah, I'm taking him out tomorrow."

"And you're serious about him? You're not just using him to make yourself look good?"

I reel back as if I've been sucker punched. I want to be offended that he's insinuating I'd use Alex, but I can't because it is something former me would have considered.

Pre-Alex me.

I shake my head. "No, I'm not using him. I liked that he didn't just fall for my charms like everyone else. He's made me work. He was interested, but I'm sure my reputation made him question my motives. I haven't been able to stop thinking about him."

At all.

To the point where I haven't been able to think about anything else. All I see when I close my eyes is his shy smile, those sparkling blue eyes, his rosy, pink blush.

That fucking blush.

I can't put my finger on what it is that's drawing me to him.

Is it the chase? I don't think so.

Don't get me wrong, I dig the chase, but I want to get to know him. What makes him tick. What makes him laugh the way he does, which feels like silk caressing my skin.

I want to know everything about him.

Hayden's face softens. "Where are you taking him?"

"Booked to go to some crazy mini golf place, then out for tacos."

I spent yesterday afternoon searching for first date ideas. Some were kinda extravagant, like rock climbing or visiting ancient baths, none of which really seemed to pique my interest. Then Zach smacked the back of my head with his big, meaty paw and told me to stop overthinking it.

When I did, I found a glow-in-the-dark golf place that looks like a lot of fun and then made a reservation at Fire Garden, one of the best Mexican restaurants in Chicago, known for their exquisite tacos.

"Where'd you meet him?"

"Jeez, what's with the twenty fucking questions?"

Hayden glowers at my snarky response. "Because as your friend, I want to learn more about who the fuck has managed to capture your attention when you're usually like a kid in a candy store. As your agent, I need to know whether or not I should be concerned about what this may mean for your career."

I sigh. "I met him at a game."

"A game?"

I nod. "Yeah… He's a fan."

Hayden's eyes go wide. I can see the wheels in his head turning through the screen.

"Don't go there. If he wanted to fuck me over, he would have said yes the first time I asked him out, and he would have climbed into bed with me then and there. He'd have been like the rest of them," I say defensively. "I like that he was attracted to *me*, not just the hockey player."

"Well, from an agent standpoint, I have to say be careful, keep your wits about you, and please, *please* don't do anything stupid, but as a friend…" He smiles. "I'm fucking happy for you. I can tell that you really like him because you've lost that arrogant-as-fuck attitude you usually have."

I flip him off and laugh.

"Thanks, Hayden." I run my hand across my chest, rubbing my shoulder. "I just want it to go well, you know? I wanna show him that what he sees online isn't the real me."

"And I'm sure he will, but you need to remember that it will take time. He'll probably have some doubts, which is understandable, and he probably won't be sure which one is the real you, but if you like him as much as you seem to, he'll get there."

I can only hope.

Wanting to steer the conversation away from me, I ask, "How's everything back in Cali?"

Hayden sighs and runs his hand through his overgrown hair. "Stressful, to be honest."

"What's up?"

"She's making my life hell, arguing over silly things. Even my lawyer is getting tired of her."

I frown.

His wife was having an affair, and now Hayden is in the middle of a bitter divorce.

"I'm sorry, man. You know you're welcome here anytime you need an escape."

He chuckles. "Thanks. I might have to take you up on that. Is your mom visiting for Christmas?"

"Yeah, she is. You're welcome to come; you know she'll love fussing over you."

He smiles, but it doesn't quite reach his eyes. "Thanks for the invite, but I'll probably hide out here and go surfing for the day."

"Livin' the dream!"

"You bet." He grins.

I want to bring up the looming gray trade cloud, but I'm afraid of his answer.

"Just ask me whatever it is you're stewing about," Hayden prompts.

I take a deep, shaky breath and ask, "Has there been any talk about a possible trade?"

He sighs. "Other teams want you, but they haven't put a tasty enough offer on the table. I know Coach wants to keep you, so long as you keep your name clean, but it's not completely off the table."

My chest tightens as my heart rate increases. Getting traded is part of the game, one of the wild rides that comes with being a professional athlete, but for the first time in my professional career, I want to remain in this city more than I want my next breath. I have my brother. I have teammates who are more like family than linemates.

And if things go well, I'll have Alex, too.

"Blaine, just keep your head down. Put one hundred percent into every game and play your heart out. If it happens, it happens; there's no way we can control it, but we can make you so critical to the team that it would be a major loss for them to trade you."

Absorbing Hayden's words, I nod. "I will."

"Good." He smiles. "And in the meantime, I'll keep

working on securing a new contract that includes a no-trade clause."

I rub the ache in my chest, hoping with everything I have that he can make it happen. "Thanks, I really appreciate it."

He waves me off. "Don't let it eat away at you. Don't stress over things that are out of your hands; just make sure you do everything you can to make yourself irreplaceable to the GM."

"I will."

And I mean it.

I'm going to play the best fucking hockey of my life, so the big bosses at the Thunder HQ will never consider trading me.

Eleven

BLAINE

You should get two minutes for hooking.

ALEX

...

BLAINE

Because you've got me hooked on you.

ALEX

cry laughing emoji

ALEX

I'll happily serve that penalty.

ALEX

Good luck tonight.

BLAINE

Thanks! Will you be watching?

ALEX

I'll try and watch while I'm working.

BLAINE

I wish you were coming.

ALEX

I'm sorry, I wish I was too.

ALEX

But you'll see me tomorrow :)

BLAINE

I know but that's far away.

BLAINE

I wanna look up and see you in the crowd.

ALEX

Kick some Nashville ass!

BLAINE

I will, don't you worry about that.

ALEX

Are you gonna score another goal for me?

BLAINE

Baby, I'll win the whole game for you.

Twelve

Blaine

Going into this date tonight with Alex, I wanted to make sure I did it right.

I haven't needed to think about dating in a while—especially since the thought of going on one would make me want to run for the hills screaming—but with Alex, it's different. It's the thought of not seeing him again that makes me angry, like I want to Hulk smash everything in sight.

No one's ever had this kind of hold on me, and it's making me restless.

Back in college, when I was dating Kelly, it was easy. We'd go to a restaurant or bar near campus, nothing fancy because nine times out of ten we would bump into our friends, so it was never really just the two of us.

Thinking back, I wasn't exactly a picture-perfect

boyfriend. I'd often bail on planned date nights to stay late at practice or because I was too tired after a game.

But the one thing I do know is that I've never felt this excited about a date before. The only thing that comes close was when I lifted the Stanley Cup two seasons ago.

It was like seeing him at the bakery so unexpectedly was the universe's way of nudging me to follow Mom's advice. Not to mention the fact that Elliot wouldn't drop it in the car on the way back home.

I know I'm not supposed to get distracted, but can Alex even be called a distraction when I've been playing some of the best games of my career since that night I slammed into the boards in front of him?

It's like knowing I'll be seeing Alex tonight has empowered me.

Seven goals, five assists over the last four games, and the biggest shocker of all?

Zero penalty minutes.

Zero.

Zilch.

Yep, that's right. I've been such a good boy that even Coach has been in disbelief, but my game has been on fire, and I'm putting it down to Alex.

I slow down when I near his house. He's already standing on the porch outside a gray-clad house, a small lamp above the door illuminating him in a soft glow. The light bounces off the top of his blond hair like a halo, and my breath hitches in my throat as I take him in.

He's too fucking nice for me.

Putting my car into park, my stomach flutters nervously as he takes a few steps down to the sidewalk and heads toward my Range Rover. I wipe my sweaty palms down the front of my jeans, and I can't contain my smile when he opens the car door.

"Hey," he says, sliding into the seat. His cheeks and the tips of his ears are rosy from the cold. He puts his seatbelt on, then shifts in his seat, shoving his hands underneath his thighs.

"Hey." I chew on the inside of my cheek as I debate my next move. Do I kiss him? Do you kiss before a first date, or do you wait until after?

I should have Googled this shit.

"Fuck it," I mumble under my breath and lean across the center console. Placing my hand on his arm, a shiver runs down my spine as I kiss the corner of his mouth. His skin is cool beneath my lips, and my mind races, wanting to just slide my lips across and find out what his lips taste like, but a car blasts its horn, ruining the moment.

"Fucking asshole," I grumble.

Alex chuckles, biting his bottom lip. "You might wanna move; they get really angry around here when you block the road."

"No shit." I put my foot on the gas, glancing in the rearview mirror to see the angry driver behind me giving me the finger. I hope they hit every red light. "How's your day been?"

"It's been pretty quiet, which is good since we've had a lot of custom orders to get through, and we had another order from Zach."

I tip my head back and laugh. "That guy and his donuts. I have no idea how he stays in shape with the way he eats. He's like the donut monster."

Alex's laugh is like melted caramel, so smooth and soft. I want to make him laugh all night because the sound is fucking beautiful.

"Your game last night was incredible." He turns to face me, and a small crease forms between his brows. "I'm sorry, is it weird I just brought that up?"

"No, no." I shake my head. "Of course not."

He lets out a sigh of relief. "Oh, good."

"It was a really tough game for us, and I'll be honest, I don't like playing against Nashville. They're always pulling dirty tricks whenever they can, thinking that the officials won't see it."

I find myself telling him all about the game. How Zach was tripped, and it went unnoticed by the officials. The slashing, the heavy hits, the melon-sized bruise I now have on my ribs from being boarded, and how the pinching in my hip is keeping me awake at night.

Alex listens so intently. He's invested in everything I have to say, and I realize for the first time that nobody has ever really paid me this much attention before, outside of family and those who are being paid to. Nobody has really cared about my day.

Yeah, my teammates do, but that's because we're in it together. We have each other's backs, and we understand it better than anyone, but aside from that, it's only really my parents and my twin brother.

I can't remember the last time anyone new has given a shit about *me*.

And that's really fucking sad.

Alex fills me in on one of the custom orders they're

doing for a wedding when we pull into the parking lot outside of Neon Tee Party.

We head inside and check in at the front desk. The girl whose name tag reads *Maddie* lets us know the rules and hands over the putters. The entire place is completely dark except for the bright neon lights on the walls, lighting up each individually themed hole. There are dinosaurs, a circus, a forest, space, the ocean, and many more.

"Wow, this place is incredible!" Alex gapes, his eyes wide in amazement as he looks around.

I internally fist bump at the praise. "Yeah? I saw it online and thought it looked pretty cool."

He slips off his jacket to reveal a navy-blue ribbed Henley that accentuates his broad shoulders and slim torso, the color complimenting his fair skin tone. His skinny jeans sit low on his narrow hips, showing off his long, lean legs, and I nearly swallow my tongue at how hot he is. It takes me a minute to squash down the urge to pull him somewhere private and strip him.

Lord Gretzky, please give me strength.

"It's really cool. Do you like to play golf?" he asks as we head to the first hole.

This one has an underwater theme. Coral decorates the edge with a mermaid at the end, the hole situated at the end of her tail.

"Nah." I shake my head. "Some of the guys do, but it's not really been of any interest to me. I find it a bit boring, but this place looked fun." I come to a halt. "Shit, I should have asked if you liked golf."

"I like mini golf as it's less serious, but I find a driving range kinda boring."

I sag in relief and take a step to the side to let him take the first shot. He gets it really close, stopping only a couple of inches away from the hole. "Nice!"

When it's my turn, I end up hitting it so hard that it goes over into the next course, bouncing off the head of a T-Rex with a *ding*.

"Ugh! I'm terrible at this." I rub my jaw. "Here I am, trying to impress you, and I can't even hit a fucking golf ball right."

"You're not supposed to hit it like you're taking a slap-shot." He bursts into laughter. The motion exposes the slender column of his throat.

For fuck's sake.

I want to press my lips against it, hear his moans as I suck on his skin, and mark him as mine.

Mine?

Where the hell did that come from?

He fetches the wayward ball, and the smile he gives me does something weird to my heart.

I'm frozen in place. I'm unable to do anything except watch as he places it back down on the tee, then guides my body into position.

"You've gotta be a bit gentler with it."

He stands behind me, looping his arms around and placing his hands over mine. Goose bumps erupt over my skin from his touch. His scent fills my nostrils, like sweet apple and spice. My legs quiver from the soft thud of his heartbeat against my back, and it takes me by surprise how fucking good this feels. I have to stop myself from leaning into him, tipping my head back, and claiming his mouth.

He guides my hands, giving the ball a softer tap, and I watch as it travels up the course, bouncing off the mermaid's tail and coming to a stop not far from the hole.

"See?" His voice is like smooth whiskey, and my cock thickens in my jeans, pressing against my zipper as all my blood rushes south.

Squeezing my eyes closed, I take a deep breath through my nose before taking a step forward to remove myself from his embrace. If I stay that close to him any longer, I'll break my promise of keeping my hands to myself.

His eyes look heated when I turn, and that fucking bottom lip is caught between his teeth again. I close the gap between us, reveling in the hitch of his breath as I release his bottom lip with my thumb.

"You've gotta stop that if you want me to stick to my word and behave myself," I growl into his ear, rubbing my thumb over the pillowy flesh.

His pupils are blown wide. The blue of his eyes has turned dark with desire.

I want him to want me, just as much as I want him.

His nose brushes against my cheek, and he nips my thumb before whispering, "What if I don't want you to behave yourself?"

Fuck.

"I'm trying so fucking hard to be a gentleman, Alex. It's taking every ounce of willpower not to push you against this wall and fuck your mouth with my tongue. I wanna taste you so much it hurts, so please don't test me, because I'm holding on by a thread."

The sly grin that spreads across his lips completely

catches me off guard. The tips of his ears are still flushed, but he's showing me a more confident side of himself, and I fucking love the tease.

Thirteen

Alex

I have no idea what just came over me. It was like there was this little voice inside my head shouting *fuck it* when I wrapped my arms around Blaine.

Maybe I'm channeling Nate's carefree energy.

It wasn't that long ago that I was super confident, approaching guys in bars and grinding against them in clubs. I would be the one to make the first move on whoever was in my sights, but over the years, that confidence got knocked down, slowly chipped away by guys who didn't value me.

In hindsight, it was a *them* problem rather than a *me* problem, but hindsight is a wonderful thing. And sometimes it only takes that one person to reignite that confidence, and tonight, that person is Blaine.

He makes me feel seen. He makes me feel like I'm the

only person in this room. Hell, the only person in this goddamn *city*, and he makes me feel worthy.

That heat in his eyes every time he looks at me? It could burn this building to the ground. The feeling of loss is instant when he drops his hand and takes a step back. I follow him to fetch the ball, then we move onto the next hole. A bolt of electricity runs down my spine when he places the ball in my hand, and it takes everything not to melt into a puddle of goo.

I've never felt this kind of chemistry with someone before. So strong and great, like an intense magnetism. Just being around him gives me a dopamine rush.

Pull yourself together.

I let out a shaky breath, putting the ball down on the tee, and eye up the hole. This hole is a little more complex than the first, and I'm assuming the difficulty increases as we go. I give the ball a small tap and watch as it rolls toward the target. I hold my breath when it slows, waiting for it to go in, but instead, it settles on the edge of the hole.

"How are you so good at this?" Blaine cocks his head to the side. "Are you secretly a pro mini-golfer, and you were waiting for the perfect time to whip out your hidden talent?"

I chuckle. "No, Nate and I worked at one similar to this briefly in college. It allowed me to hone my skills." I wink before walking to where my ball stopped; it only takes a little tap now.

I retrieve the ball and head back to where he's standing. His eyes trail the length of my body before locking with mine. The look he's giving me is close to the one from that first night. Like he's starving, and I'm a feast. I'm pretty sure if we weren't in public, he would devour me.

"Have we found something where I'm better than you?" I tease.

"You're better than me in many, many ways," he admits.

I scoff. "I highly doubt that."

"Trust me." He steps forward, taking the ball out of my hand. "You're perfect." He presses a kiss against my heated cheek, then steps up to take his turn.

How is this guy real? It's hard to comprehend that this is the same guy who gets dragged through the dirt by the media.

I tug my bottom lip with my teeth, taking in how his broad shoulders fill out his dark green plaid button-down. Wide biceps strain against the material and rolled up sleeves showcase his thick corded forearms.

He's fucking hot.

And when Blaine bends slightly to take his shot, I internally groan as the dark denim stretches across the tight, rounded globes of his ass.

Hockey butts. They are the holy grail.

There's nothing I would love more than to drop to my knees, take those cheeks between my hands, and worship the most perfect creation that is a hockey butt.

"Are you checking out my ass?" Blaine asks over his shoulder, his brow lifted in challenge.

There's no point denying it, I've been caught red handed.

I give an unfazed shrug. "And if I was?"

He drops his putter to the ground with a thud, his turn forgotten as he stalks toward me like a predator would his prey. His eyes blaze with desire, and the closer he gets, the more I unconsciously step back until my back is pressed against the wall. My own putter ends up on the ground at my feet.

Blaine raises his hands, his palms flat against the wall on either side of my head and leans in, running his nose under my jaw. His warm breath against my skin sends shivers down my spine, and my heart beats wildly in my chest. The blood running through my veins is thrumming with anticipation.

"I told you I was trying hard to be a gentleman. I can't tell you how hard it is not to kiss the hell out of you right now." He confesses in my ear, his teeth grazing my lobe.

I swallow the lump in my throat as my words come out on a rasp, "Then stop resisting and just kiss me."

Our lips are only a breath away when he lifts his head. The soft fabric of his shirt brushes against the bare skin of my arms as I take a step closer. Feeling brave, I rest my hands on his hips, dipping my fingertips beneath the tails of his shirt to find the smooth, warm skin of his obliques.

He sucks in a breath at the contact. A ripple of pebbled flesh erupts under my fingers. His hand cradles my jaw, and I lean into the touch before my breath is stolen when his lips sweep against mine.

Holy smokes, Blaine Olsen is kissing me.

I was expecting hot and heavy, but instead it's tender and soft. A gentle caress of his mouth over mine, the heat from our tongues entwining, and it's like time has slowed. The world pauses as we lose ourselves in each other.

I'm lost in a fantasy world, and it's better than I could've ever dreamed of.

I'm having the best kiss of my life with *Blaine Olsen.*

He kisses me as though I'm a treasured prize. Like he's

scared if he goes too hard, too soon, he'll scare me away. He tastes of mint and perfection, and I let out a low moan when he pushes one thick thigh between my legs. I grind against him, aware that we're still in public, but nothing could stop me from kissing the most amazing man I've ever met.

When we part, we're both gasping for air. I gently tug his bottom lip with my teeth, and his gray eyes are stormy, completely blown dark with desire.

"What are you doing to me?" he whispers, resting his forehead against mine.

I dig my fingers into the firm flesh of his side, unable to form the words to describe the emotions I'm feeling.

He's surprising me at every opportunity, and it's dangerous. Dangerous because there's the potential I could fall, and that means I could get really hurt.

Blaine presses another kiss to my swollen lips, his thumb gliding in a smooth swoop across my jaw. "As tempted as I am to say fuck the golf and take you home, I promised I'd be on my best behavior, so you're gonna need to distract me."

A small bubble of laughter escapes me. "And how am I supposed to do that?"

He takes a step back and goes to pick up his discarded putter. "I dunno, ask me something you wanna know about me."

"Okay." A million and one questions run through my mind.

There's so much I want to ask, like why me? What made him want to slam into the boards that night? Why doesn't he date? Who hurt him?

But instead I settle on, "Tell me about your rookie year. You were drafted young, but stayed in college, right?"

I catch his eyebrows rising slightly in surprise before he nods.

"Yeah, that's right. I was drafted before I started college at eighteen, but I didn't sign a contract until the end of junior year, after we won the Frozen Four. So I didn't end up finishing college." He hits the ball, watching it bounce off the makeshift walls.

"What made you stay? I know it tends to happen, teams keeping players in for development, but did you have the option to sign there and then?" I ask.

"Yeah, they didn't offer a contract right away, so I played in the NCAA, using it for development, which also meant I could play with Elliot for a few years because he wasn't drafted."

For the next hour, he tells me stories from his school years to winning the cup, and I get to relive the moment from a different perspective from where I witnessed it while I sat on my couch. We settled into this comfortable place where we laugh and listen to each other's stories, exchanging subtle touches that light my skin on fire.

Once we're finished at the mini golf course, we make our way to the restaurant, but the closer we get, the more my nerves begin to settle in. Doubt is racing through my mind.

Will he still want to date me after he realizes I'm buried under a mountain of debt, and we're actually worlds apart?

Will he think differently of me, that I'm not as perfect as he thinks?

✕

Blaine

We managed to get through the mini golf course.

Barely.

Alex kicked my ass on each one, but being able to make him laugh has made me the real winner.

I should be freaking out that I feel so enamored by him, but I'm not. If anything, I'm freaking out more over the fact that I'm *not* freaking out.

Maybe this dating thing isn't as scary as I thought it would be.

Or maybe because it's Alex.

I can tell he's different from anyone I've ever met.

But when we pull up to the valet outside of Fire Garden, he goes eerily quiet. The shift in his energy is palpable. Did I make a bad call? Does he not like it here? Was the whole taco thing his buddy said just a joke when he actually hates tacos?

My mind goes into overdrive over what could have gone wrong. I really hope I haven't fucked this all up.

"Are you okay?"

He nods but doesn't look at me. He's gazing out the window at the restaurant, anxiously chewing on his lower lip.

The valet goes to open my door but I hold my hand up, letting him know we will be ready in a moment, and lean over to rest my hand on Alex's thigh. Taking his chin between my thumb and forefinger with my free hand, I turn his face toward me.

"If you don't want to eat here, we can go somewhere else. Hell, I'll be happy with a drive-thru at Portillo's or Wendy's. I just wanna get to know you; there's no pressure."

His breath comes out in a whoosh, freeing his lip. It's swollen and red, begging for me to suck it into my mouth. I manage to resist the urge and give him what I hope is a reassuring smile.

"Here is perfect, thank you. I've heard they make some pretty incredible tacos."

"That's what I've heard too." I wink.

Inside the restaurant, the low murmur of conversations mixed with the Tejano music playing creates a perfect, chilled ambiance. The walls are painted a deep red, and dark wooden stained booths and tables decorate the floor. It's not a fancy place, but it is on the higher scale. It's not quite suit and tie, but I'm not out of place in my relaxed lumberjack vibe. We're shown to our table, a private booth toward the back, keeping us away from any prying eyes that may want to intrude on our night. I ease myself into the booth opposite Alex, sinking into the soft red leather. The low lighting sets the mood, making it feel romantic and intimate.

"I'm James, and I'll be your server tonight. I'll give you some time to look over the menu and come back in a few minutes to take your orders," James says with a smile before pouring us some water.

I thank him without taking my eyes off Alex, noticing his forehead slightly creasing as he scans the menu, tapping his fingers on the table at an almost anxious rhythm.

A far cry from the confident Alex of only a short time ago.

"Is there anything that's tickling your tastebuds?"

And when he looks up, that's when I see it.

Worry. Concern. Panic.

Fuck, what have I done?

The blood rushing through my ears blocks out the noise of the restaurant, and my heart pumps a little harder in my chest. "Alex, have I overstepped?"

He shakes his head. "It's not you, I promise... I just..." He runs a hand through his hair. He looks lost, uncertain. "I feel really out of my depth here. I can barely afford anything on this menu."

I'm speechless because I didn't see that coming.

Even while I was growing up, I've never had to worry about money or prices, and now I have enough in the bank to last me a lifetime. It didn't even cross my mind for a second that this might be somewhere out of Alex's range... Not that I ever expected him to pay a dime tonight.

"I'm sorry. I didn't even think about this... but Alex, there's no way I'm letting you pay for anything tonight."

Alex shakes his head again. "You paid for golf; I can't let you pay for dinner too."

"I don't know what kind of assholes you're used to, but I invited you. It's my treat."

I know he wants to argue when I see his hands fiddling with the napkin in front of him, but I'm not backing down. He lets out a sigh, rubbing his face with both hands, then gives me a sad but grateful smile. "I'll owe you."

I wave him off and rest my forearms on the table to lean

closer. "One, you don't. But two, I wouldn't say no to another date." I grin widely.

The tension disappears from his shoulders when he laughs, and a sigh of relief escapes me.

"How about we have two of everything?" I suggest as I open the menu. "If you don't like it, I'll eat it. I'm a growing boy after all."

Alex raises an eyebrow, his lips twitching. "*Two?*"

There we go. My Alex is back.

"Yep. I'm going all in. It's the date to end all dates. All other men will pale in comparison to me."

Or I hope it will be.

"Trust me, that won't be hard."

"Tell me." I cock my head to the side.

He chuckles. "Ex talk isn't a good idea on a first date."

"Why not? I wanna know what kind of assholes you used to date."

He's silent for a moment, maybe trying to contemplate what to share with me, but either way, I'll be angry at whoever was lucky enough to be with him and at whoever hurt him in the past.

"I dated a couple of guys in college, it wasn't anything serious looking back, but I thought I was in love. They were good at pulling the wool over my eyes, telling me what I wanted to hear, giving me that false sense of security. It was only when I lost my grandparents that I realized it wasn't love at all." He shrugs. "But enough about that. I don't want to ruin our night, because it's been amazing."

I grind my molars. "Fuck those assholes. They didn't deserve you at all. And I'm glad you're having an amazing night, because I am too. I really like you, Alex. I hope you'll give me the chance to show you that you're worth the world."

Fourteen

Alex

I feel like an absolute idiot after Blaine witnessed my internal freakout over the prices here.

I knew what to expect. I shouldn't have been shocked, but still, it's wild. A completely different lifestyle from what I'm used to. From what I can afford.

But tonight, I've realized that Blaine definitely isn't the guy the media makes him out to be.

This entire night has been the best date I've ever been on.

He's attentive, funny, and confident, but there's something else underlying.

Something that makes me think the cocky playboy personality is all a front. He's been nervous all night, fumbling over his words, shaking out his hands when he thinks I'm not looking, and rubbing the back of his neck. It's like he's consciously making sure he puts his best foot forward. It's obvious he wants to impress me, and he did the second he picked me up earlier.

"So, do you really think you could eat two of each?" I ask.

He rubs the stubble on his chin as his eyes scan the menu, then looks up and gives me that wicked grin from the first night at the game. "I bet I can eat four."

My eyes widen. "What? There's like…" I scan the menu again, quickly counting the options listed. "Eight different tacos here."

His eyebrows lift in a silent challenge, giving me a *"Yeah, and? Your point?"* look.

I scoff, shaking my head in disbelief. "Hockey players and their crazy appetites."

"I told ya, I'm a growing boy." He winks, patting his solid abs through his shirt.

When the waiter returns to take our orders, his face is a mask of surprise when Blaine orders four of everything along with two beers, which he brings over straight away.

"So, have you always lived in Chicago?" he asks me once the waiter leaves.

I take a sip of beer and nod. "Yeah, born and raised. I went to college here, too. I didn't want to be too far away from my grandparents, though my grandma insisted I still experience dorm life, so I made sure I was only a bus ride away from them in case they needed me."

"You live with your grandparents?"

"I did, yeah. I lost my parents when I was seven, so my grandparents raised me and my brother."

"Fuck, I'm so sorry to hear that." Blaine reaches out to touch my arm.

"Thank you. Sadly, I lost both my grandparents two years ago, too. They passed away pretty close together, so it's just me and my brother Jacob now. The one you met."

I haven't talked about it in a while. We don't have any other family here, and our close friends know. My chest tightens as the emotions I'd buried deep float to the surface.

Blaine comes closer and takes my hand in his. The soft, soothing glide of his thumb across the back of my hand is comforting. "I'm so sorry, Alex. I can't even begin to imagine losing your family like that."

"It was really hard. It was four months before graduation, too. I'm still shocked that I managed to graduate, but Jacob needed me, so we kinda got through it together."

"You guys own the bakery together, right?"

I nod, impressed that he remembers. "Yeah, that's right. We opened the shop a couple of years ago." I smile at the thought of my brother. "He's three years older than me, but he's like my best friend."

"Elliot is my best friend, too."

"Is it true that twins have some kind of telepathic sense?"

He guffaws. "Yeah, we seem to feel what the other is feeling sometimes, like he was saying the other night. It happens even if we're not together. We have this thing as well where it's like we know what the other is thinking. It creeps the fuck out of Coach."

An image of Blaine and Elliot telepathically conspiring against Coach Harris enters my mind, making me snort. "I can imagine that would freak a lot of people out."

"He's just been the one person in my life who gets me, as weird as it sounds."

I shake my head. "It's not weird at all. He's important to you. Jacob is the same to me; he just gets me. Nate, too. We met in college."

"Would it be bad if I admitted I was a little jealous of him the other day?" he says coyly. His fingers trace idle patterns on my forearm, almost like a nervous tic.

The thought of Blaine being jealous makes me giddy. "Why?"

"Because I thought you were a couple, and I'd missed my shot with you."

I melt at how vulnerable Blaine looks. His playboy bravado has been replaced with boyish charm, and the sincerity in his stunning gray eyes makes me want to lean over the table and kiss him again.

But I don't.

Instead, a bubble of laughter escapes. "I can assure you there is nothing to be jealous of. Nothing has ever happened between Nate and me."

Blaine's eyebrows go up in surprise. "Really? Nothing at all?"

"Okay, maybe once, but I don't think making out in sophomore year really counts. We were pretty drunk, and soon realized it was like kissing your brother, so we didn't do it again."

He chuckles, shaking his head.

The waiter and two other staff members make their way to our table, carrying trays filled with tacos—chicken, fish, BBQ pulled pork, two variations of beef, veggie, lamb, and spicy bean.

I have no idea how we're going to eat everything because

the table is so full that they've had to pull up an extra one to accommodate the number of plates.

The final dish is put down, and there's tacos as far as the eye can see.

"Holy shit…" I whisper.

Blaine grins from ear to ear as he tucks his napkin into his shirt like a bib, then rubs his hands together eagerly. "It's taco time, baby!"

I take a bite out of the spicy bean taco, humming as delicious flavors take over my tastebuds, while Blaine eats his in two mouthfuls, licking his fingertips clean before going in for his second.

"When did you start playing hockey?" I ask between bites.

"I think I was about four years old. My dad grew up in Minnesota, and we used to watch the games with him. One of my earliest memories is of him telling us we weren't allowed to play football."

I chuckle. "What would he have done if you did?"

He shakes his head. "I have no idea, but El did show an interest, but my dad squashed that pretty quick. He used to play goalie for me in the yard before he started playing."

Blaine demolishes two more tacos before suggesting, "Let's play the quick question game. I'll ask some questions, and you've gotta give me the first answer that comes to mind. Kinda like speed dating, but you don't move on to another person." His smile is deviant. "Because you're on a date with me, and I don't wanna share you."

I roll my lips, trying to conceal the grin that threatens to appear. Inside, I'm still on cloud nine about being the main focus of his attention.

"Okay, then I'll ask you questions?"

He nods, picking up another taco.

I wipe my hands on the napkin and take a sip of my beer.

"Favorite movie?" he begins.

"Empire Strikes Back."

"Star Wars, huh?"

"Yeah, nothing beats the original trilogy."

He lifts his hand up, and we high-five.

"How about you?" I ask.

"Top Gun: Maverick." He leans forward. "Have you seen the beach volleyball scene? How can you not get a boner over that?"

"That's true, it's pretty hot. Pizza topping?"

"I'm all about Philly cheese steak covered in ranch."

My nose scrunches up at his questionable taste. "Pepperoni, but I kinda like anything as long as it doesn't have pineapple."

"Oh, the controversy," he chuckles.

"What about ice cream? This could be a deal breaker."

"Mint choc chip."

"Okay, I could get behind that. I'll be honest, I'm basic and love strawberry."

"Nothing basic about you, baby." He winks.

I laugh as my cheeks heat. Not from the compliment, but from the wink.

"Sex position?"

I choke on my beer and begin to cough. I hit my chest with my palm, trying to dislodge the fluid now stuck in my windpipe, and my eyes fill with unshed tears.

Blaine leans over the table, gently patting my back.

"Sorry…" He smirks, clearly not sorry in the slightest.

When the coughing subsides, I take a few deep breaths to regain composure, wiping my eyes with a napkin, and decide to pay him back with my own form of torture.

If he wants to play this game, it's on.

I take a careful sip of my beer, noticing his eyes latch onto the movement of my throat when I swallow. Placing my bottle back on the table, I move closer, and Blaine mirrors my movement.

I watch his tongue lick a path across his lips and I drop my voice a few octaves.

"I like my guy on his back, so I can see his face while I'm riding him. I like to be able to watch his face morph into absolute bliss when he comes so hard in my ass, and I get to cover his abs with my come." I pick up my beer again and take a sip.

I can't believe I've just said that, especially in public, but here we are.

Blaine squeezes his eyes shut. His teeth trap his bottom lip, and his hands clench into a fist on the table. His head hits the back of the booth with a thud, and when his eyes open again, fire is blazing in those stormy grays.

Need. Want. Lust.

All for me.

It radiates off him like a volcanic blaze, and my cock thickens in my jeans under his heated stare.

I don't miss his hand dipping under the table. Is he touching himself right now? I kinda hope he is.

"Fuck, you keep making me hard in public, and I can't do anything about it."

I smirk. "You shouldn't ask questions that put you in such a *hard* situation."

His nostrils flare. "My restraint is wearing thin, Alex."

My head tilts curiously. "And what are you gonna do about it?"

"If I had my way, I'd be getting these tacos to go and take you home to experience your favorite position in real life, except instead of letting you come on my abs, you'd come in my mouth so I could taste every sweet drop of you."

Well, fuck me. My plan backfired spectacularly.

I shift awkwardly in my seat, trying to ease the pressure of my achingly hard dick in the tight confines of my jeans.

Blaine leans forward, his tongue peeking out to swipe over his bottom lip. "Because believe me, Alex, when I get to taste you, once isn't going to be enough."

Our eyes flirt between mouthfuls of delicious food, allowing our imaginations to run wild after our heated conversation.

My dick settles down eventually, and I admit defeat after my twelfth taco. It lived up to the hype as the most amazing tacos I've ever tasted, and the side of guacamole, rice, and beans made my mouth water with every bite.

I relax back into my seat as Blaine, however, shoves more food into his mouth, and I'm amazed when he picks up what must be his twentieth taco.

He licks the tips of his fingers as he finishes chewing the last mouthful, then sits back in his seat with a groan, his hands holding his stomach. "Maybe I was a little too ambitious…"

I chuckle, balling up my napkin and dropping it onto my empty plate. "I'm very impressed, but I hope you've got an off day tomorrow because I'm pretty sure practice won't be fun when you've got that many tacos swimming around in your stomach."

He briefly closes his eyes, rubbing his hands in a circular motion over his stomach. "Thankfully, yeah. We leave for an eight-day-away stretch early Thursday, so there's morning skate, but it's only optional, so I think I'll skip it."

"Sounds like a plan." I laugh before asking, "Do you like road trips?"

I feel weird asking because it seems I'm back to being a fan, but it's clear Blaine has lived and breathed hockey since he was a child, and he didn't seem to mind talking about it earlier.

"Yeah and no. I like it because I love playing hockey. You could ask me to play in the middle of nowhere, and I'd still wanna do it, but I don't like all the traveling that's involved with long road trips. Going from time zone to time zone, it fucks with your system. You're exhausted from that, exhausted from playing, plus there's something about sleeping in hotel beds…" He starts to stack the empty plates, placing them in a neat pile at the end of the table. "I don't sleep well in hotel beds."

I'm a creature of comfort too, so hopping from hotel to hotel sounds like my kind of nightmare.

"Do you share a room with a teammate?"

"Not anymore. In my rookie year, I shared with Zach, and I wouldn't mind sharing with him now because I love the guy. He's so laid-back and chill that you don't really hear much from him. He's either engrossed in texting Carter or he's playing some game on his Switch. But I have my own room now, so whenever we're not together as a team, I usually just watch a movie on my iPad or I go out to find…" He trails off, but I can guess what he was about to say.

He goes out to find someone to fuck.

He shifts in his seat, clearly uncomfortable at having gone there. But I'm not going to hold his past against him. We all have one and it'd be unfair of me to judge him based on that.

It's how he treats me going forward that matters.

Just please don't treat me like the rest.

I swallow down the niggling feeling in my gut and change the subject.

"Is it nice having Elliot on the same team as you now? I read something that mentioned you've dreamed of being on the same team since you were kids?"

He nods, his face lighting up at the mention of his brother. "Fuck yeah, it's been our dream since we were like four years old. In all our school projects where the teacher would ask you things like 'what do you want to be when you grow up', we'd write 'hockey players on the same NHL team'. We even went to the same college because we couldn't bear the thought of being separated, but then I signed with Chicago, and moved end of junior year."

"That must have been really hard on both of you."

"Yeah, it sucked because it was the first time in our entire lives we had been separated, but we didn't give up hope. He signed as a free agent after he graduated and spent a few years in the AHL before moving up to play for

Vancouver two seasons ago, and when his contract was up in the summer, the Thunder snapped him up instantly." He snaps his fingers. "It was fate, in a way."

"Doughty retired last season, right?"

He smiles softly. "Good memory; yeah, he did, and Coach mentioned he'd been keeping an eye on Elliot throughout the years. He knew Elliot would be a great addition for the team, with it being a family-oriented head office and all."

I've read a lot about the Thunder organization being family-run and passed down through generations, so it was nice to hear they also took their players' family lives into consideration, even if Blaine and Elliot's situation is rare.

The waiter comes to clear the plates, asking if we'd like to order dessert. There's no way I can eat another thing, so I thank Blaine when he orders us another beer. Time slips away from us as we chat, and when the waiter returns again, he has a sheepish look on his face and is holding the bill. "I'm so sorry, guys, but we're closing now."

Blaine looks at his watch. "I'm sorry, man. I didn't realize the time." He places his card inside the binder and hands it over to the waiter.

"What time do you start work tomorrow?" he asks when the waiter disappears.

"My alarm is set for four, and I normally get to the shop around five to help Jacob with the prep for the day before we open at nine."

Blaine's face drops. "Fuck, it's past midnight. You're going to be exhausted tomorrow."

"It's okay, it's been worth it," I confess.

His face morphs into the widest smile. "Yeah?"

I nod, smiling. "Yeah, I'd say one of the top three best dates I've been on."

"Top three?" he practically growls. "I wanna be first. I'm gonna make the next one better."

The next one?

"You wanna see me again?" I don't mean for the surprise or slight insecurity to filter into my voice.

"Fuck yeah, I do." He pauses for a beat. "I mean, if you wanna see me again, that is."

Blaine Olsen, notorious playboy, suddenly becomes unsure and shy. It's fucking adorable.

I chuckle. "Yeah, I do."

He lets out a relieved breath, smiling shyly.

As the waiter returns for a final time with Blaine's card and the receipt, we thank him for the incredible food and service. I pull out my wallet to leave a tip, wanting to at least contribute something to this amazing evening. I scribble "cash" on the receipt.

"The next date will be on me," I smile.

The drive back home is over too quickly, and before I know it, Blaine is parking his Range Rover next to the curb outside my house. He unfastens his seatbelt and turns to face me. I mirror his position, butterflies swarming like crazy in my stomach.

"I've had an incredible night tonight," he states.

"Me too. Thank you for a great evening."

He rubs the back of his neck nervously, glancing out the window and then back at me again. "Can I see you when I get back from my road trip?"

"Yeah, I'd like that."

"Good, good." He nods several times, like he's reassuring himself. "Can I text you while I'm away, too?"

A breathy laugh escapes me. I'm loving his awkwardness. It's so unlike how he's perceived by the world.

"Yeah, you can talk to me whenever you like." I lean in. "In fact, I would be upset if I didn't hear from you. I've grown used to your cheesy pick-up lines."

When I'm an inch away from him, I stare into those gorgeous eyes, and my skin buzzes from the anticipation that's been building all night.

"Maybe we could even FaceTime, obviously when you're alone," I whisper.

A low growl reverberates from the depths of his chest, his nostrils flaring. His eyes drop to my mouth as I run my tongue along my bottom lip in a slow, teasing sweep, knowing it drives him wild.

I'm rewarded when it gets the reaction out of him that I was hoping for. His large hand grips the back of my head, pulling me to him, causing a bolt of desire to shoot through me. Blaine swallows my moan, our mouths crashing together in a hot, frantic kiss, pent-up sexual tension burning like a wildfire with every glide of his tongue.

Exploring.

Claiming.

He tastes like beer, tacos, and pure want.

I could get addicted to his kisses. They are absolutely intoxicating.

The hard planes of muscle beneath the soft fabric of his shirt feel delicious under my hands, and I want to explore him with my mouth. I wouldn't be surprised if the zipper of my jeans leaves indents on my shaft from how hard I am right now.

We're both gasping for air when we pull apart, pressing our foreheads together. His lips are swollen, and I can't help but drop my eyes to his lap, letting out a whimper when I see the outline of his hard cock bulging in his pants. As I move to touch him, he stops me.

"I want to do this properly, Alex. I want to date you, seduce you, treat you like the bright star that you are. I might not be any good at it, but you make me wanna try." His voice is deep and strained, like he's barely holding on. "But I need you to do something for me."

I give a shaky nod. At this point, I'd do anything he asked.

"I need you to go inside and get into your bed, completely naked. I want you to think of me while you touch yourself, and I want you to moan my name when you come," he demands. "And I want you to know that the next time you moan my name, it'll be because I'm so deep inside you, you won't know what fucking planet you're on."

I can't stop the rush of breath that escapes me. I press a hand down on my crotch, hoping that I can at least make it into my room before I explode.

I give him a small nod. "Okay," comes out in a whispered breath.

I steal one final kiss from those luscious lips, say my goodbyes, and head toward my house. Once inside, I quickly lock the door and head straight to my room. Thankfully, my brother is fast asleep, but I still slide the latch on my bedroom door because I don't want anything interrupting me.

I do as he instructed, stripping out of my clothes and climbing into bed with shaky limbs. Taking my cock in hand, I stroke it, twisting my palm over the sensitive head as I imagine him thrusting deep inside me. It only takes a few pumps of my fist for my release to hit. My balls draw up tight, and his name comes out in a hushed moan as I spill over my hand and onto my stomach.

While I lay there, trying to regulate my breathing, I realize that I might be fucked already.

Because Blaine Olsen might be trouble, but he might be the best kind of trouble.

Fifteen

Blaine

I've never been annoyed to see the team jet before.

Even though I dislike some aspects of road trip games, I'm usually filled with excitement over being able to play hockey and having the chance to hook up with new people in a different city.

My favorite duo for many years has always been hockey and hook-ups.

But now?

That favorite duo has now changed to hockey and Alex.

Now, I'm grumbling like a grumpy bear who lost his oatmeal as I step onto the tarmac at the private terminal at O'Hare International because I don't want to play hockey or hook up with people in another city.

I want to be able to play on home ice, ask Alex to come and watch me play, and see if he'll gift me one of his beautiful smiles.

The same Alex who left me so hard I could've put a dent in my car door if I'd whipped my cock out the other night. The sounds of his soft moans and whimpers as I took his mouth, the flush of his cheeks, and his lust-filled eyes… It was a fucking amazing feat that I didn't convince him to let me inside his house or fuck him in the back seat of my car.

I give my self-restraint a solid nine out of ten.

"Blaine Olsen, what are you wearing?"

I look up at the sound of my brother's voice. Elliot's standing by the open door of the team jet, holding up a phone, while the team's PR manager, Colleen, stands next to him, sporting a bemused expression.

I laugh under my breath and shake my head.

I don't think Elliot has a serious bone in his body aside from his pre-game ritual. Touch his pads or stick before a game, and you'll feel the wrath of Elliot Olsen.

He ambles down a few steps, still holding the phone out, obviously recording something, and waits until I start to climb the stairs.

He puts on his best David Attenborough impression and announces, "And here we have Blaine Olsen, the less attractive and talented of the Olsen brothers."

I scoff, flipping him the middle finger.

Elliot pushes my obscene gesture away with his hand. "Tell the fans what you're wearing and whether you're excited to head to the west coast?"

I climb the stairs slowly, mainly so he doesn't trip and hurt himself. I don't think I could deal with that on my conscience.

"I don't know what I'm wearing; I went to a suit store and got fitted, and yeah, I fucking love the west coast." I grin, knowing they won't be able to use whatever footage now because I cursed.

Elliot groans. "Fuck's sake, Blaine! Now Colleen's definitely not gonna include my parts on the team's socials."

He frowns and stomps up the stairs, handing the phone back to Colleen in a huff.

She laughs, rolling her eyes at his dramatics. "Don't tell him this, but I wasn't going to include it anyway."

"Sometimes you just gotta entertain him, kind of like you would with a child."

She lets out a loud hoot of laughter. We exchange a high-five, and I make my way onto the plane.

We have a routine on the jet—the same seat, same seatmate. Some of the guys play cards, some like to sleep, others watch movies or read a book. I like to use the time to take a nap or catch up on whatever series I'm binging.

I remove my headphones and iPad from my bag, dropping them in my seat before placing my bag in the overhead compartment along with my jacket, then sit down next to Zach.

He glances up from his Switch. His eyes are red, and the dark shadows underneath wash out his complexion. "Hey, man."

"Hey, bud. Are you okay?"

His blink is slow, and he gives me a tired nod. "I slept like shit last night. It's like my body knows that I'm gonna have to deal with hotel beds for the next week, so instead of giving me one night of blissful sleep, I'm tortured."

At six-foot-six, he often finds hotel beds too small, and his feet end up hanging over the end. He's even had a custom bed made for his apartment because nothing was big enough for him.

"That's the downfall of being a giant, I guess," I joke.

He gives me the finger and picks his Switch back up.

Zach's one of the best guys I've ever met. The kind of guy who deserves the world. Due to his size, he often gets shit on the ice as people try to pick a fight, but he's a big softie. He doesn't like to fight.

Whereas me? I'll happily pick fights any day.

Zach settles back into his seat, his thumbs busying away on his Switch. Slipping my phone out of my pants pocket, I read through the messages I exchanged with Alex yesterday.

To say I was shocked to hear from him after I dropped him home would be an understatement. I thought I might've scared him off with my parting demand, but no, it seems that he loved it.

I waited and watched in my car until I saw he was safely inside before I left. I made it as far as the parking lot, and my dick was in my hand before the engine was off. It only took a few strokes for me to spill my load, the evidence hitting the steering wheel and the window. I found some wet wipes in the glove box, and I cleaned up before anyone could see.

Bravo, hindsight of past-Blaine. Ten out of ten.

"How did your date with Alex go?" Ethan asks, sitting down in the row across from me.

"Really good." I nod.

When he doesn't respond, I turn to look at him. He's wearing a smug grin, and I know exactly what's coming.

I roll my eyes. "What? Spit it out!"

"I told you."

"Yeah, you did. Well done! The great Yoda Ethan comes through with solid advice. Gee, you should become a captain or something," I say sarcastically.

He punches my shoulder. "Fuck off with that Yoda crap."

"Hey, don't call Yoda crap," Zach pipes up, scowling at Ethan.

"Whatever." Ethan waves him off.

Zach harrumphs.

"Blaine, I'm proud of you. It's like you've finally leveled up to maturity. I never thought the day would come."

I narrow my eyes at Ethan, trying to pretend that he's starting to piss me off, but inside I'm fucking buzzing.

Praise from Ethan is like catnip. We all fucking want it, and when we get it, we're high as fuck.

"Thanks, man."

"Are you going to see him again when you get back?"

The plane doors close once the final person steps on board, and the flight attendant begins to run through the safety procedure.

I lower my voice so I don't interrupt. "Yeah, I hope so. I'm just worried I'm going to fuck up somehow." I sigh, smoothing my hand over my bouncing knee. "I'm not good at this shit."

I want to be better.

I will be better.

Ethan nods understandingly. "What about something casual? Go for a walk on the pier before it gets too cold, get a hot dog, sit in the park, cook dinner for him. Just get to know each other, spend time together. It doesn't have to be big, grand gestures every time, because that gets old fast.

Dating is about getting to know one another, developing that connection."

I make a mental note of everything he's just listed. That's doable. I can do that. It wouldn't be flashing my bank balance in his face, and I can still make it feel special.

"Are you sure you're not Yoda, oh wise one?"

Ethan chuckles. "Secret, shall I tell you? Grand Master of Hockey Captain Order am I." He winks before opening his book, letting me know that he's done with this conversation.

⚒

The whistle blows for a TV timeout and the ice crew appears with shovels to clear the ice. I squirt some water into my mouth, and, at the sound of cheers and claps, I glance over my shoulder toward Elliot as music filters through the sound system.

I know what's coming.

The fans know what's coming.

We all know what's coming because this is what he's known for.

It all started in senior year of high school when he completely forgot where he was and started dancing to the music between plays, and ever since, it's become iconic. Every game—home and away—fans wait in anticipation to see what Elliot will dance to next or serenade his goal posts to—he's been known to crouch down and sing a bit of Taylor Swift to the iron—and they will send him endless song requests on social media.

A bubble of laughter escapes me as Elliot shimmies his

shoulders under his pads as "Da Ya Think I'm Sexy" echoes through the arena before removing his mask and placing it on top of the net. He was always a dancer as a kid, dancing to commercials on TV, or begging our mom to let him go on those dance machines whenever we passed an arcade.

The crowd gets louder as Elliot places his stick, glove, and blocker on top of the net, and then starts to dance. We crack up laughing on the bench, his bright smile visible as he gyrates his hips the best he can with his pads on and places his hands on the back of his sweaty head.

"We think you're sexy, Elliot!" one fan screams.

I shake my head, my cheeks aching from laughing.

Once the song changes to another, he waves at the crowd and skates over to us, shimmying his body to the music. I slap him on his padded shoulder and pass him a drink when he reaches us.

Coach is trying not to laugh, but the way his lips keep twitching is betraying his usual stoic facade. "Olsen, I'd say let's not give up the goaltending gig just yet. You might be popular with the crowd, but I'm not sure you'll make it onto Broadway."

Elliot grins, squirting some water into his mouth before he flicks some in the air, his eyes trailing every droplet. "No problemo, Coachio. Between the posts is where my heart lies, and where it shall remain, 'til death do us part."

The game in Anaheim ends six to one. A major win for us.

The locker room is buzzing with electricity as we enjoy our post-W singalong and hit the showers.

It's always good to start a long stretch on a high. We'll be heading to Los Angeles next, before San Jose, Seattle, and then Vancouver before making our way back to the windy city. We load up our bags onto the waiting coach and make the drive to Los Angeles for the game tomorrow night. Once we're checked in, some guys head to the bar for a drink, while others head straight to their assigned room. I flop down on the bed, groaning into the sheets. Damn, my body aches. Kicking off my shoes, I slip my phone out of my pocket and text Alex.

BLAINE

Hey, are you awake?

His reply is almost instant.

ALEX

Yeah, I am.

ALEX

Congrats on the win! :)

BLAINE

Thank you! It feels good to start the road trip with a win.

BLAINE

Can we FaceTime?

ALEX

Yeah, of course.

I hit the FaceTime button, and it only takes one ring before his gorgeous face fills my phone screen. His bright smile lights up my insides like never before.

"Hey, great game tonight!"

I preen like a peacock. "Thanks, hot stuff. I dedicated my goal to you."

"Wow, thank you, I'm honored." He laughs, his bare shoulders peeking into view as he lays back onto what looks like a pillow.

"Are you in bed?"

He nods, his teeth grazing over his bottom lip. "Yeah, I just got out of the shower."

"Fuck, Alex," I groan, hitting my head back against the headboard. "You can't just say that. I can't stop thinking about you. I keep wondering what you must have sounded like the other night when you moaned my name when you came. I bet it was fucking amazing."

I palm my thickening cock through my pants. Even with the low lighting from his bedside lamp, I see the soft flush of his cheeks. That tongue that I can still taste from two nights ago sweeps across his lower lip, and I wish I could take that lip between my teeth and drive him wild.

"Tell me how your day's been because if you don't distract me from being pretty much naked in bed, I'm gonna want phone sex, and I'm trying to be good here."

His laughter coats me like a warm blanket. "It's been busy; we almost had another sell out today and finished up a custom order, then went to the gym to work out with Nate."

Fucking Nate.

I hate that I'm going all green-eyed monster over the fact

that he gets to spend time with Alex when I'm over two thousand miles away. Spotting him while he squats, watching that peachy ass stretch his shorts, seeing those biceps pop.

Ugh!

A weird sensation bubbles up in my stomach. I've never experienced this kind of jealousy over someone.

And the fact that I'm not freaking out about it is making me freak out a little, which is becoming a common occurrence.

"I want to work out with you," I grumble.

"I wouldn't be able to keep up with you." He grins, clearly picking up on my jealous streak. "I lost a lot of muscle mass after college. I'm trying to build it back up again, so I think you would destroy me."

"Fuck yeah, I would, and I don't mean in the gym." I wiggle my eyebrows, a wicked grin spreading across my face.

Alex tries to hide his shy smile, the tips of his ears turning the deepest shade of pink. He raises his hand to cover a yawn, and once again I feel like an asshole for keeping him awake knowing how early he gets up for work.

"I'll let you sleep; it's like one in the morning there." I chew on my bottom lip, not wanting to push my luck but knowing I don't wanna wait another week to see his face. "Can I call you again tomorrow night?"

"Yeah, I'd like that." He smiles. His eyes grow tired as another yawn escapes him. "Good luck for the game tomorrow."

"Will you be watching?" I hold my breath as I wait for his answer.

"Yeah, I will. Goodnight, Blaine."

Pride blooms in my chest.

"Goodnight, Alex."

The call disconnects, and I rub at the weird knot in my chest.

Part of my brain is screaming at me to run. To end things before I develop feelings and have my heart broken again when Alex leaves me.

Because it will happen.

But for now, as I get undressed, settle into the hotel bed and close my eyes, listening to the soft sound of sirens in the distance, I realize that Alex might be worth the risk.

Sixteen

BLAINE

<photo of Blaine climbing a taco statue outside of a restaurant>

ALEX

Is that supposed to be a taco?

BLAINE

Yes! He was holding a sign saying, "lettuce celebrate."

ALEX

LOL!

ALEX

How's LA?

BLAINE

Nice and warm! Makes me miss Cali when I see the beach.

ALEX

I've never been to California.

BLAINE

I'll bring you one day.

BLAINE

I'll even take you to Disney.

BLAINE

Could go and visit Daddy Vader.

ALEX

…

ALEX

Did you just call Darth Vader…

ALEX

… Daddy?

BLAINE

Yeah, he gives major Daddy vibes.

ALEX

I…

ALEX

I genuinely have no idea what to say right now.

BLAINE

Do I give off Daddy vibes?

ALEX

Ummm

ALEX

No?

BLAINE

NO?

ALEX

I'd say if anyone on the Thunder gave Daddy vibes, it would be Ethan.

BLAINE

I AM HURT, ALEX.

BLAINE

HURT.

ALEX

cry laughing emoji

BLAINE

ETHAN?

ALEX

Yeah, he's got that dark and mysteriously broody vibe, kinda like if you didn't behave yourself, he'd bend you over his knee and spank your ass.

BLAINE

I... I'm kinda uncomfortable right now?

BLAINE

I just snort laughed and he looked me in the eye, and now I'm envisioning him spanking my ass, and I don't like it.

ALEX

You're welcome :)

BLAINE

angry emoji

ALEX

You won't stay mad at me for long.

BLAINE

Damnit, you're right.

BLAINE

I'm still hurt though.

ALEX

I will kiss it better when you're home.

⚔

BLAINE

We're not socks, but I think we'd make a great pair.

ALEX

Oh wow.

ALEX

That one was really bad! :D

BLAINE

I'm still hurt you don't think I've got Daddy vibes.

BLAINE

I could spank you just as well as Ethan.

ALEX

I didn't say you wouldn't.

BLAINE

Good.

BLAINE

Because I will.

ALEX

Spank me?

BLAINE

Fuck yeah I will.

ALEX

smirking emoji

BLAINE

Wait... did you only say that to get a rise out of me?

ALEX

angel emoji

BLAINE

Oh, you're getting it now!

ALEX

I nearly cried during that shoot-out.

BLAINE

Me too.

BLAINE

I genuinely thought we were a goner.

ALEX

Elliot has some insane skills.

BLAINE

He's milking it, that's for sure.

ALEX

He deserves a big reward.

BLAINE

He's being rewarded with an ice cream sundae lol.

BLAINE

<photo of Elliot with ice cream and chocolate sauce smeared down his chin>

ALEX

LOL looks like he's really enjoying that.

BLAINE

I'm really enjoying the fact that you were watching my game.

ALEX

I try to watch all your games.

BLAINE

I want you at all of my home games.

BLAINE

I want to look up and see you there. Know you're there for me.

ALEX

<photo of a hockey-themed birthday cake>

ALEX

Finished this custom cake today for a six-year-old's birthday. He's a big Thunder fan.

BLAINE

Holy shit, that's incredible! You really did that?

ALEX

I did! It took me about six hours to get it how I wanted it, but I'm happy with it.

BLAINE

I just showed the boys. They said it's fucking amazing.

BLAINE

Can you make one for us?

BLAINE

We'll pay you, obviously.

ALEX

Sure :)

ALEX

I'll pencil you in. We're nearly fully booked with the run-up to the holidays.

BLAINE

What are your plans for Christmas?

ALEX

My brother and I haven't really celebrated it since we lost my grandparents, so we'll probably just chill on the couch and watch some movies.

BLAINE

This is probably a bit weird because it's so soon but...

BLAINE

Wanna come to mine? Your bro too?

ALEX

Really?

BLAINE

Only if you want to, but I'd like you to come.

ALEX

That would be really nice, thank you.

BLAINE

My parents are coming to town.

ALEX

You want me to meet your parents?

BLAINE

Um... yeah?

BLAINE

Is that weird?

BLAINE

Yeah, that's kinda weird isn't it?

ALEX

Not unless you don't mean it.

BLAINE

I mean it.

Seventeen

Blaine

We're at the halfway point of our eight-day road trip, and the moment the plane touches down in Seattle, I'm ready to go home. But we still have another four days before we head back to Chicago.

Thankfully, we have practice later this afternoon, followed by a team dinner, which means we can get an early night.

And that also means I can spend some quality time on FaceTime with Alex.

Once the seat belt sign is off, we all get up and begin to redress. There's nothing worse than sitting in dress pants on a flight. It's a mandatory league rule to wear suits while traveling, but once those plane doors close, the suits come off and sweats are on. It just means getting dressed again before we exit the plane.

"I'm ready to nap," Elliot says as we board the bus to the

hotel, where we'll have some downtime before we head to the practice facility.

"Me too, but I wanna call Alex more than anything. I feel like a dick for always keeping him up late."

I've been feeling guilty that by the time I'm able to call him, it's usually past midnight in Chicago. He gets up at 4 a.m. for work, and when I spoke to him last night, the lack of sleep was evident on his gorgeous face.

"You gonna take him out when we get back?" We take a seat, and Elliot presses his forehead against the window to watch our equipment get loaded into the bus.

"Yeah, I just don't know where to take him yet."

Elliot turns to face me; his eyes go wide, and his eyebrows nearly touch his hairline. "You could take him to the zoo!"

I snort a laugh. "We're not seven, El. I wanna impress him, not make him think I'm taking him on a school field trip."

He flips me off. "I think the zoo is a fun date. You can bond over the cute animals, and the zoo in Lincoln Park is free, *and* they have otters!" He gives me a pointed look. "Also, if he doesn't like otters, then, I'm sorry to say, he isn't cool in my book."

I pat my brother on the shoulder. "Okay, I'll consider it, 'kay? I'll look it up later."

Elliot grins, satisfied with my answer. "Cool. I'd love for someone to take me to the zoo on a date, but then there's the risk that I would get arrested for kidnapping an otter, and I don't think my bathtub is big enough to accommodate an otter..."

As he rambles on to Kendrick about how many otters

could fit in a bathtub, I take my phone out of my pocket and pull up the texts with Alex. He sent me one this morning on his way to work, wishing me a good flight. As the bus departs for the hotel, I type out:

BLAINE

Hey, I'll be at my hotel soon. Will you be free to talk in about an hour?

His reply doesn't come until we reach the hotel thirty minutes later.

ALEX

Yeah, I'll be around. I'll still be working, but you can call.

I sigh. The hours he works is insane,

We get off the bus and collect our luggage, while the team's designated travel coordinator goes to check us in and collect our key cards. The lobby's crowded while we wait, and my phone is burning a hole in my pocket.

"I'm gonna drop my bag and go for a walk," Zach says.

I look up at my best friend, his hair a mess from where he fell asleep on the plane. We usually hang out before practice, but I have a feeling he's just as eager to get to his phone as I am.

"That's cool. I'm gonna FaceTime Alex for a bit, then take a shower before we have to go."

Zach's about to respond when Elliot comes rushing through the crowd. "Guess who is your next-door neighbor, broski!"

I groan. "Please don't sing obnoxiously loud in the shower. You know hotel room walls are thin."

Elliot gives me a devilish grin, tapping his chin with his finger like he's deep in thought. "I wonder what the first song for shower-time karaoke should be?"

"Have fun with that one," Zach laughs, slapping my shoulder.

Once we have our card keys in hand, we head up to our rooms for an hour.

Kicking off my shoes, I take off my dress pants and hang them in the closet before unbuttoning my shirt and hanging that too so it doesn't crease. I climb onto the bed in just my black boxer briefs and socks, and press the camera button on Alex's contact card.

My heart skips a beat when his face fills the screen. He's in his state-of-the-art kitchen at the bakery, surrounded by stainless-steel equipment, and wearing his signature apron. In front of him is a row of at least two dozen cupcakes.

I'd like to see him in nothing but his apron.

I groan internally, pressing down my cock that also likes that thought.

"Hey!" he says. "How was your flight?"

"It was good, thanks. I'm so ready to go home, though."

He frowns. "Are you worried about the game tomorrow?"

"No." I shake my head. "I like playing against Seattle, they play a good game, I just…" I drift off, rubbing the back of my neck. I'm conscious it's still early into our "relationship", but my mom taught me to be honest and open. "I just wanna get back to Chicago so we can go on another date."

Nothing could prepare me for the wide smile on his face.

"I'm looking forward to it, too."

"Really?"

He nods. "Yeah, I've had some ideas where I could take you."

It's my turn to grin. "Oh yeah? Where are you gonna romance me up then?"

He tips his head back and laughs. "Depending on the weather, I thought we could go to the zoo."

Elliot would be over the moon.

"I've never been to the zoo in Chicago…" I admit.

His eyebrows lift. "How long have you been here?"

"Six years." I grimace.

"Blaine Olsen, I am disappointed," he chuckles, shaking his head.

I'm about to open my mouth when the sound of Elliot singing—off-key—at the top of his lungs interrupts me. My eyes go wide at his awful rendition of "Never Gonna Give You Up".

Alex rolls his lips, trying to stop himself from laughing, no doubt. "Who's that?"

"Elliot." I answer as Elliot sing-shouts the iconic chorus. "Fucking hell!" I drop my head into my palm and laugh.

Alex bursts into laughter, wiping his eyes with his hand. "Your brother's just Rick-rolled you."

"He's doing it on purpose."

"Your hotel must have really thin walls."

"True, but it doesn't matter where we are—if Elliot's singing, everyone will hear it. It's been like that since we were kids."

"He sounds like a lot of fun."

"He'd love the fact you're thinking about the zoo."

Alex's eyes sparkle. "Yeah?"

I nod. "He was talking about it on our way to the hotel. He really likes otters," I chuckle. "How's your day been anyway? What are you making?"

Alex looks down at the cupcakes in front of him. He's holding a piping bag filled with pink frosting. "We had someone cancel their order last minute, so they've lost their deposit, but we had these cupcakes baked ready for decorating, so I'm going to do it and take them to Nate's gym for their receptionist's birthday."

"That sucks. I hope they gave a valid reason."

He nods. "Yeah, they did. These things happen, it can't be helped, it just sucks that it's money we lose, you know?"

There's a tug at my heart at the defeated look on his face. If I were home, I would go in and buy everything. It's on the tip of my tongue to ask if there's any way I can help when he speaks.

"Nate's lined up some freelance graphic design work for me, though, so there's always that."

"Tell me more about that. Do you want to start your own business?"

He nods and begins to decorate the top of the cupcakes

with delicate frosting swirls as he speaks. "Yeah, that's the plan. I got a degree in business because I wanted to help Jacob out, but I've always loved graphic art. I used to create my own comics and stuff, so now I do the occasional job for Nate's gym friends, like designing their website and ads."

I'm absolutely fascinated when he lifts the frosting bag, his fingers tightly wrapping around as he squeezes with such precision. All I can think about is those fingers wrapped around my shaft, working it deliciously. My cock starts to thicken in my briefs, tenting the material. I don't realize I'm staring until he clears his throat. When I look back at his face, his lips are tilting up in amusement.

"See something you like?"

I swallow, trying to wet my suddenly dry mouth. "Your hands are sexy."

He glances down at the frosting bag. "My hands?"

"Yeah." I nod. "I may have… uh… just had some inappropriate thoughts when you were squeezing that thing."

He smirks, picking up the piping bag and giving it a squeeze. "Really?" Frosting oozes out of the top of the piping bag onto his finger before his tongue licks it off. "And how do you feel about frosting?"

He has me captivated, unable to take my eyes off of him or the way his tongue curls around his finger. "You're such a tease."

Alex bats his eyelashes innocently. "Me? Never." He grins.

"I know this is probably too soon, and I don't want you to think that I'm a stage-five clinger, but I can't wait to see you again."

"I'm looking forward to seeing you, too."

The bell over the bakery door chimes, and Alex disappears from view, returning moments later. "I have to go; Jacob's just got back from the wholesaler, so I've gotta get back to work."

The selfish part of me doesn't want him to go. I want to talk to him until the very last minute, but he has a job to do, and I have to shower and wash away the plane stink.

"Can I text you later?"

He nods, giving me a soft smile. "Yeah, I'd like that."

And just like that, I went from loving away games to counting down the hours and minutes until they're over.

Eighteen

Alex

It's been a bit of a whirlwind since our date ten days ago.

I'm exhausted from how crazy work has been, and the lack of sleep has finally caught up with me. I have no idea how I managed to get through classes in college on only an hour's sleep not so long ago.

Blaine ended up FaceTiming me nearly every night, even if it was only a quick ten-minute call before both of us ended up yawning non-stop. I wanted more, but by the time he'd done his post-game routines, eaten, and showered, it was always past midnight.

He texted throughout the day—the odd message here wishing me good morning or a photo of something that made him laugh or think of me.

I told my brother and Nate that if he continued like this —and didn't get bored of me—I could see myself really falling for him. Every time I see his name on my phone screen, my heart pitter-patters. Even when I had to work late and couldn't watch the game, I found myself grinning like an idiot and feeling all fuzzy inside every time his name popped up on my notifications for a goal or assist.

The pull in my chest is growing stronger every day, and I know I have to keep myself protected, just in case his interest in me is only temporary. It's becoming harder, though.

But right now, I have to put Blaine in the back of my mind because Jacob needs me.

He was pale as a ghost when he came home last night from delivering an order. He put it down to exhaustion, but by the time he showered, it was evident it was more than that when he struggled to eat a sandwich. I'd woken up shortly after midnight to the sound of him coughing and made him some hot tea with honey and lemon.

I was kind of thankful that Blaine was on his flight home because I barely slept.

When my alarm went off at four this morning, I poked my head through Jacob's door and was relieved to see he'd finally fallen asleep. I tiptoed inside and turned his alarm off because there was no way he was fit to work, at least not for the next few days. Taking a super quick shower, I got dressed and left him a note on his bedside, along with a cold bottle of water, and made sure the heating wouldn't switch off.

Little did I know that a few hours later, I'd be questioning whether ten in the morning was too early to have a breakdown.

I thought I could manage on my own, but in reality, I really, really can't.

The line seems to be getting longer, which on the one hand is amazing for business but on the other hand means I simply can't keep up with the demand.

I'd baked and decorated all of our staple bakes just in the nick of time before unlocking the door, and despite posting on our social media that we would be running a limited selection to try and ease some of the pressure, I'm working as fast as I can, on the verge of tears, and I can't remember the last time I had a drink.

I box up the six red velvet cupcakes and ring through a customer's order when the bell chimes above the door. I glance up to say a quick hello, but the words get lodged in my mouth.

The last person I expected to see walk through the door was Blaine.

Dressed in black sweatpants and a light gray hoodie, his eyes widen in surprise when he sees how busy the store is and how alone I am.

Some of the waiting customers go silent in awe, before congratulating him on the wins over the last eight days. He's the poster boy of a polite and friendly pro athlete when several ask for a selfie before his attention lands on me again.

"Do you mind if I jump in for a minute?" he asks the lady next in line.

"No, no, of course not. Go ahead." She flashes a seductive smile, flicking her luscious brunette curls over her shoulder.

Jealousy bubbles inside me, and I have to suppress the snarl that threatens to escape at the playful wink he throws at her, but my anger soon fizzles out as he comes up to me.

He's so fucking gorgeous, even with his forehead creasing with a frown, eyes filling with concern.

"Are you okay? I saw your text after I got out of physio." He looks around the bakery, searching.

I sent him a text on my way into work letting him know Jacob was sick and I wouldn't be able to meet him for coffee during my lunch break like we'd planned.

"I know you said you couldn't meet me for coffee, so I bought coffee for you." His nervous smile warms my heart.

He's trying so hard, it's cute.

He holds up a cup from a coffee shop just around the corner, a paper bag, and a small bouquet of white tulips. "These are for you. I picked up a mozzarella and tomato panini; the barista said that you could reheat it in the microwave for twenty seconds and it'll make the cheese all gooey again."

I spot one girl filming on her phone, but it doesn't seem to faze him that he's showing this display of affection so publicly. His eyes remain focused on me.

If I wasn't already close to crying from the stress of not wanting to let my brother down, I would break down from his kind gesture alone.

Nobody has ever done something like this for me before.

So thoughtful.

And I'm already falling, hard.

"Alex?"

His words break my train of thought, his eyebrow slightly quirked as he waits for an answer. "Is it okay if I help you out?" he asks.

Would that be okay?

Sure, he could help with serving or boxing up the baked

goods. It's not a difficult task, and I'm sure the customers won't mind having to wait to be served when they have one of Chicago Thunder's finest behind the counter.

Can I really ask that of him, though? A fucking NHL All-Star working behind the counter?

But I cave at the sight of his pleading eyes.

"Yeah, that would be amazing, thank you." I nod quickly. "There's an apron in the kitchen."

He grins and makes his way around the counter, but before he can go through to the kitchen, I stop him with my hand on his arm. I give his very solid forearm a small squeeze, trying to let him know how much this means to me.

"Thank you for thinking of me. For the coffee and the flowers and the sandwich and…" I rapidly blink away the tears forming. My voice shakes as I whisper. "Thank you."

His eyes light up as he smiles. "You're welcome."

A few minutes later, Blaine joins me behind the counter wearing a white apron with *"Jacob's Delicious Desserts"* embroidered on the front in pink cursive lettering. He ties it behind his back and rubs his hands together. "Now, who wants some cake?"

Everyone cheers.

I chuckle under my breath, quickly going through where the boxes and paper bags are kept, then get back to serving. The line keeps getting longer when word gets out that Blaine Olsen, star forward of the Chicago Thunder, is behind the counter boxing up cookies, cakes, and donuts, and within a couple of hours, we are completely sold out. I flip the closed sign, sending an apologetic smile to everyone who comes to the door, trying not to feel guilty from their disappointed faces.

After I flick the lock, I sag against the glass, letting out a heavy, tired sigh as I close my eyes.

"Wow, that was hard," Blaine says from one of the booths.

He's eating one of the strawberry vanilla cupcakes he must have set aside when I open my eyes. He's got frosting stuck in his stubble and a tiny bit on his chin. He licks off the frosting from his fingers, his tongue curling around the digit before disappearing between his lips. My cock jerks excitedly behind my fly.

Thank God I'm wearing an apron.

"That wasn't a normal day," I say, dropping down opposite him.

I rest my head back on the pink leather and close my eyes again. We have never sold out before lunchtime.

Yeah, I had a limited selection on offer, but I still baked the same quantities.

"You really do this seven days a week?" Blaine asks.

"Yeah, it wasn't the plan originally, but at the moment…" I keep my hands busy by folding a napkin several times. "We opened the shop about two years ago, and things were going really well… Until they weren't. We ended up having to replace equipment, then we had things go wrong in the house that weren't covered by insurance." I sigh. "We took out a few loans, maxed out credit cards… It's been tough, and Jacob's taking it really hard."

Blaine's expression softens, and I want to argue when pity filters into his eyes.

"Sorry, you didn't come here to listen to my woes."

His brows furrow. "Alex, I want to hear anything you

want to tell me, whether it's happy or sad. I'm sorry you're in such a shit position; is there anything I can do?"

I shake my head. "I couldn't ask that of you, but thank you."

He opens his mouth, then closes it again. For a moment, he just stares at me, his eyes searching for something.

"Your grandparents would be so proud of you."

My breath gets lodged in my throat.

They were my rocks throughout the grief of losing my parents, the agony of my teenage years, and realizing I was gay. I was worried about their reaction, but they just sat me down, opened up their arms in a hug, and told me how much they loved me, how proud of me they were, and that all they wanted was for me to be happy.

"I hope they are. They passed shortly after we opened. My grandma had been sick for some time, and was taken to the hospital after a blood test. We found out that she had leukemia, and she passed away three weeks later. Then, within a week, we lost my grandfather. The doctor couldn't give us a reason behind his sudden passing, the only thing they said was it was more than likely from a broken heart."

My voice cracks. My chest tightens, like the weight of an anvil pressing against me, and my vision blurs. Jeez, I'm really freaking emotional today.

Blaine takes my hand, the warmth of his skin against mine startling me from my thoughts. He rubs his thumb in soothing circles over the inside of my wrist, supporting me as I go on.

"They'd been together since they were fifteen. Seventy years together is a lifetime. I can't even begin to imagine losing someone who has been by your side your whole life."

"Fuck, I'm so sorry for your loss, Alex. I know it's only words, but I'm so sorry." He squeezes my hand, his eyes brimming with sympathy. "You two are doing incredible. They'd be so fucking proud of you and what you've achieved. Yeah, it probably feels like shit at times, but I mean it—if I can help in any way, I'd be happy to."

Taking a deep breath, I blink away the tears. "Thank you for today. I didn't realize how much I just needed someone to be there for me." I give him a small, shaky smile.

His face lights up, but he downplays it by giving a sheepish shrug of his shoulders. "I think I aced it, to be honest."

I laugh, grateful that he's trying to lighten the conversation. "You did."

"Those people loved me, and I think I look pretty fucking sexy in an apron."

"Yeah, you do."

He'd taken his hoodie off within ten minutes of being behind the counter, and the white apron against his gorgeous, bronzed skin. His thick, corded forearms and bulging biceps that looked ready to burst the seams of his athletic-fit Chicago Thunder tee.

Yes, it was very distracting, and oftentimes I found myself wanting to stand and stare, possibly drool a little. The thought of how he would look wearing *just* the apron ran through my mind a lot.

A dark brow kicks up. "Bet you're wondering what I'd look like in nothing but an apron."

I roll my lips to stop the laugh from coming out. "You got me."

"I knew it!" He grins, stretching his arm across the back of the booth. "You think I'm hot, and you want to see me naked."

Heat floods my cheeks. I raise my hands to cover them, and my skin is hot to the touch.

I can't deny it. I really do.

Who wouldn't want to see this Adonis of a man naked?

"I can't confirm or deny that accusation."

"I can honestly say I've wanted to see you in only an apron before, so it's only fair." He winks.

My earlier conversations with Nate and Jacob come flooding back into my mind. It may be too late to keep my defenses up, because if today's act of kindness has proven anything to me, it's that Blaine isn't here just to get me in bed.

I think he actually *cares* about me.

If I was just a meaningless fuck, he wouldn't have gone out of his way to bring me lunch when he knew I was busy. He wouldn't have stepped in to help, and he wouldn't still be sitting here, just holding my hand, after I opened up about my struggles.

"Is there anything else you need me to do?" he asks.

Stop being so damn dreamy!

"No, I couldn't ask any more from you. I need to get started on some custom orders; I've only got two, so it shouldn't take me long, then I'll get cleaned up and check on Jacob."

"I can help clean if you tell me what to do," he suggests.

"Are you sure?"

"Of course. Perhaps I can come over and make you dinner tonight?" He rubs the back of his neck. "Like, if you don't mind? I don't want to intrude, especially with Jacob being sick. I just thought maybe—"

"That sounds great." My heart squeezes at his nervous ramble while I toy with the napkin again. "You know, you're nothing like I expected you to be."

"Um…" he chuckles. "Is that a good thing?"

"Yes." I snort. "I had this impression that you were a cocky and arrogant playboy." I sigh, feeling awful for even voicing this now that I'm starting to see what I think is the real side of Blaine. "I'm sure you know the image painted of you on the internet isn't a nice one, but nobody has seen this side of you, have they? This unsure, almost anxious side?"

He lets out an unsteady breath, then shakes his head. "No, only my brother, Ethan, and Zach." His eyes darting everywhere except on me.

"When I signed my contract with the Thunder, I had a lot of growing up to do. I got my heart hurt in college, and figured the best way to get over it was to get with other people. I basked in the attention I was getting, and it worked for a while. Then I tried relationships again…" He trails off, dropping his chin to his chest. "People didn't want to be with me for me. They wanted the status. It made me feel kinda worthless, like if I wasn't in the NHL, they wouldn't give a shit. I was just a trophy to brag about."

The vulnerability behind his confession is evident—the crease in his forehead, the perspiration around his hairline. The way he anxiously rips up the cupcake wrapper into small pieces.

"Until I met you. You challenged me to look at things differently. There was something about you that I couldn't get off of my mind. Something that made you special." He laughs, but it lacks humor. "I sound so fucking cliché."

When he finally looks at me, that's when I see it.

Insecurity.

Fear.

"Alex, it fucking terrifies me that I can already see myself handing my heart over to you, and that you have the power to crush it."

"But I wouldn't…"

"You don't know that. You can't promise me that, and I wouldn't expect you to. I get nervous around you because you scare me. Because of how much I want you, and it's more than just sexual attraction, which scares me even more. Because the last time I felt even an iota of this, I had my heart torn to shreds."

There's a sting in my chest. A dull ache for him and for the younger Blaine, who was thrust into the spotlight while trying to come to terms with his emotions. It's soon replaced with rage. How could people not see the incredible person he is?

"I'm not gonna pretend I'm a saint because I'm not, but the media control the narrative. Some of what you read is true… There are guys who aren't loyal, they'll cheat whenever they can. Some take advantage of the sex readily available to them, using it to feed their egos, but then you've also got the guys who are silently pining for their best friend or too afraid to let love in in case it hurts them."

Another heavy sigh leaves him, his wide shoulders slumping, his upper body folding in on itself.

"At the end of the day, we're still normal guys. Yeah, we've all got massive fucking egos like every other professional athlete on the planet, but we still have feelings. We still have trauma we're dealing with; we just have to do it behind closed doors because society has made us feel like we've gotta be tough off the ice, too. A lot of us play into the narrative by letting the world believe we're these cocky, arrogant assholes, but in reality, we can be awkward as fuck. We devote so much of our lives to the sport that sometimes we struggle off of the ice, and they're not kidding when they say hockey players are weird." He taps his temple with his finger, a shy smile playing across his lips. "We're weird up here too."

I swallow the lump in my throat that's formed from his sad admission. Slipping out of the booth, I sit next to him and take his face in my hands. The soft stubble grazes the palm of my hand as I lean in and press my lips to his in a tender kiss.

His hand curves around my neck and his tongue runs across the seam of my lips, sliding into my mouth. The kiss is gentle, unhurried, and I melt into the moment. When we part, I rest my forehead against his and give him a small smile. "I'm sorry for thinking negatively of you."

Blaine holds my face in his hands. "I don't really care about what the rest of the world thinks of me, but I want you to see the real me. I did hook up a lot; my headcount is higher than I'd like to admit, but it was more because I didn't think I was worthy of anything else. You make me want to be better."

"You are worthy, Blaine. You are so worthy."

Nineteen

Blaine

The packets of pasta shells are mocking me. I know they are because I feel so out of my depth it's unreal.

Me? Cook? It's a disaster waiting to happen, it's a miracle if I don't burn toast, let alone manage to cook a full meal. I once managed to set the fire alarm off at the practice facility when I attempted to toast a bagel.

But I want to do something to help Alex. Hearing his heart breaking story earlier had my mind racing of ways I could help, especially knowing he wouldn't take any money. My mom always told me that sometimes, a heartfelt gesture can mean the world to someone, so I wanted to do just that.

Except now I'm wondering what the hell I'm gonna cook without setting both Alex's kitchen on fire and potentially making him sick.

I scan the aisles in the supermarket, wondering if there is something easy but fulfilling I can whip up for Alex and his brother, but the longer I stare aimlessly at the rows of food, the more nervous I get.

"Maybe I should just order takeout," I say to myself.

And great, I'm now talking to myself in the middle of Whole Foods.

I look down at the sad bottle of wine in my basket and sigh. Maybe takeout will be the best option. Admitting defeat, I pay for the bottle of wine and head back to my car, ramping up the heat as a cold shudder takes over my body. Winter in Chicago is brutal for my Californian roots.

I scroll through the various options on GrubHub and settle on a place the boys and I order from all the time. I order a mix of dishes: noodles, rice, dim sum, a few different chicken and beef dishes, a couple of sides and a soup for Jacob. Once I've set the delivery to Alex's address, I drive to his house and park down the street.

Alex opens the door with a bright smile on his face, and my heart somersaults in my chest. Seeing him smile doesn't get old. I still feel that same warm fuzzy feeling in my chest every single time.

"Hey," he greets me with a kiss before stepping aside to allow me in.

"Hey, beautiful." I grin when his cheeks flush.

I toe off my sneakers while Alex takes my coat to hang up, and when he turns around, I wrap my arms around his waist and bring him close to me and claim his lips with mine. He sags against me, his warm, soft hands cradling my face.

Pressing a kiss to his nose, I rest my forehead against his and lose myself into those bright blue eyes. "How's your day been?"

"It's been good. This really hot guy came to help me out today."

"Oh, yeah? How hot are we talking?"

"Super hot. Like I'm surprised the room doesn't go up in flames because he's *that* hot." His eyes sparkle with mischief.

"Well, baby," I begin, taking his hand in mine and lacing our fingers together, "you're so hot, you'd make the devil sweat."

His blush travels up from his neck to the tips of his ears as he ducks his chin against his chest. I place a finger under his chin and lift his head to face me again, "Honestly, you're that hot I'd walk into traffic if you were on the other side of the street."

Pressing another kiss to his lips, I hold up the wine. "I thought I'd cook but then remembered I suck at cooking so I've ordered takeout which should be here in forty minutes. I ordered Jacob a chicken noodle soup, is that okay?"

Alex's eyes soften. "That's really kind of you, thank you." He then glances around, chewing nervously on the inside of his cheek. "I'm… I'm sorry about the state of the house. We haven't been able to decorate since my grandparents passed, it's kinda dated."

I take in the decor for the first time, having not even noticed when I walked in because all I could see was Alex. Yeah, it's a little dated. Cream walls, rich mahogany wood, and a lot of floral patterns. It's definitely not the kind of decor you'd associate with two guys in their twenties, but I'm not one to judge.

I'm about to open my mouth to offer to help with

getting it redecorated when his finger lands on my parted lips.

"Whatever you're about to say, no, but thank you." He removes his finger and replaces it with his lips, then takes my hand to lead me further into the house. We stop in the living room where the Edmonton v Dallas game is playing on the television.

"I need to take a shower before food arrives," he says. "Make yourself comfortable, I won't be long." He plants a kiss on my lips then disappears down the hall.

I gaze around the living room. There are framed photos on the wall, along with a bookshelf overflowing with old paperbacks. One of the photos catches my attention. It's of a couple with two kids. They must be Alex's parents. All four of them are wearing bright smiles. Alex's mom has her arm around his middle, he looks maybe four or five years old, that smile is wide and cheesy, covered in the ice cream he's holding.

My heart pangs in my chest. For Alex and Jacob having lost their parents so young, and for his parents not being able to see the incredible people they've become.

There's another photo from what must have been Alex's graduation, Jacob standing proudly beside him, but the sadness is evident in their eyes.

The heartfelt conversation we had earlier solidified the fact that Alex is different than people I've dated before. He isn't with me for the money, or the status, or the fact I'm a hockey player. He likes me for *me*, and damn, did it make me feel like King of the fucking world that this beautiful guy, who has been through so much heartbreak in his life, sees me as someone he wants to spend his time with.

Taking in all the photos, I wind up wandering down the hallway. Stopping at every photo to take it in, then I come across his room. My eyes landing on his unmade bed, and my thoughts going back to that night after our first date where he fisted his cock until he came with my name on his lips. I sit on the edge, smoothing my hand over the cover before leaning in and inhaling his scent on the pillow. My dick gives an excited twitch against my fly, and as I sit upright again, I notice a puck on his bedside table.

The warmup puck from the night we met.

I grin, picking up the rubberized disc in my hand and toss it in the air. I can't believe he kept it.

"Be careful with that, it's my favorite puck."

His voice startles me. The puck drops to the floor with a thud and my head snaps up, and when I see him, my tongue lolls out my mouth like a dog. He's standing in the doorway in just a towel.

Just a towel.

Water droplets run down his chest before disappearing beneath the terrycloth. I watch in avid fascination as he walks to his dresser and pulls out some briefs.

"You're killing me here!" I groan.

Alex looks over his shoulder, a playful smirk spreading across his lips. "You're the one who came in here, I can't just stay in a towel."

"I wouldn't mind if you just stayed naked."

He snorts and shakes his head as he drops the towel, exposing that perfect, peachy ass and I let out another groan, pressing down on my throbbing erection in my jeans as he pulls on the tight black briefs in his hand.

"You're such a tease, how do you expect me to get through dinner now?"

Alex walks over to me once he puts on some sweatpants and stands between my legs. Placing my hands on his waist, I slide my hands around to grab a handful of that peachy ass he teased me with, then I practically purr like a cat when he runs his fingers through my hair.

My head tilts back, closing my eyes as the sensation of his nails against my scalp causes tingles to travel from my head to the tips of my toes, the hair on my body standing to attention like I've been shocked.

"I'm sure you'll manage." He leans down to kiss me, threading his fingers through the strands of hair on the back of my scalp.

I grip hold of his waist and pull him onto my lap before laying back on the bed. We make out like we've got all the time in the world. My hands exploring the soft skin of his back, feeling the curve of his spine and teasing handfuls of his ass. I could kiss him forever and I still wouldn't feel satisfied.

The food arrives shortly after, and we feast on the most delicious food, then lay on the couch to watch the last of the hockey game. Alex curls into me, his head resting on my chest, his hand on my hip. His soft snores fill me with so much happiness, the back of my eyes burn.

He's so fucking special.

I want to do everything with him. I want to give him the world. I'd do anything he asked of me and more. Anything as long as I get one of his smiles and see those blue eyes sparkle.

I would burn the world for him and walk right into the flames.

Twenty

Blaine

"That was good, but it can be a lot better. Do it again." Coach blows his whistle, and we skate back to our positions.

This morning's practice consists of running through power play and penalty kill drills ahead of tomorrow night's game against New Jersey.

There's always a lot of penalty minutes accumulated whenever we play against them. I don't know whether it's because Zach's older brother, Brody, plays for them, and they purposely try to get under our skin, but whatever it is, it works. But it also means Coach is putting us through our paces to ensure that they don't get an advantage by sending our asses to the box and that we monopolize every power play opportunity we get.

"That's it! Great job!" Coach blows his whistle again.

We skate over to him and take a knee, forming a semicircle around him. He gets out his whiteboard and pen, explaining what was good and what needs improving and drawing different plays on the board.

"We need to be more available here." He circles an area on the whiteboard by the blue line. "And let's work on our speed back to the defensive zone. We're leaving it way too open."

Everyone nods in understanding.

We all stand and run through it again and again until our bodies begin to ache. I let out a groan of relief when Coach blows his whistle, "Good job, boys. Hit the showers; we've got tape in fifteen."

We make our way down the tunnel, handing our sticks over to Jordan, our equipment manager, on the way back to the locker room.

"Anyone wanna hit up Gino's for some wings after tape?" Zach asks.

A murmur of yeses echoes through the locker room as we begin to undress. I can't wait to hit the showers and stand under the warm spray. My thighs throb under my pads, twinging from the strenuous workout.

"Nah, I gotta go shopping for Katy's birthday present," Jonathan Peyton sighs, running a hand through his shaggy hair. "She told me that if I don't spend at least five thousand dollars on her, it means I don't love her."

I lift my head. "What the fuck, man?"

"I know." He sounds defeated.

I've only met Katy a few times. She's often given the impression she's only with Peyton for his paycheck, but I haven't had the heart to tell him that. Plus, we're not as close as some of the other guys on the team.

Since there are at least twenty of us, it's hard for us all to get along off the ice. With so many different personalities in the locker room, you're not going to be best buds with everyone, so more often than not, we run in different circles when we're out of skates.

But the most important thing is that we gel on the ice.

And luckily, we do.

"I never knew having a wife would be so fucking expensive. Every month, she maxes out a minimum of two credit cards, and I have no fucking idea what she spends it on." He throws his jersey into the laundry basket a little harder than necessary. "Like last night, she yelled at me because I didn't notice this new vase on the coffee table in the living room. Like, it's a fucking *vase*? I don't give a shit."

Kendrick chuckles from his cubby. "I'm so glad Maria isn't like that. The most money she spends on is food, and that's only because I fuckin' eat all the time!"

The locker room fills with raucous laughter.

Kendrick and Zach are the biggest guys on the team, which means they have the appetite of a pack of rabid wolves. I feel for Maria; it must cost a fortune to feed him. Good thing he earns a lot.

I hook my skates in my cubby and glance over my shoulder, catching Brian Petford glaring at Peyton. He's grinding his teeth so hard I'm surprised his molars haven't turned to dust, and he's giving him some serious stink eye, like he wants to Superman-laser beam Peyton into tiny atoms.

What the heck is that all about?

The guy was traded here last season and has failed to make an effort with any of us. We invite him for food, he declines. We suggest drinks after a game, he always passes.

Kendrick's his linemate, and says Petford never engages in conversation; he simply grunts.

I tilt my head to the side like a curious owl, and when he catches me watching him, his upper lip curls in disgust. He throws his pads into his cubby before stomping into the shower.

"So, wings, you say?" I pipe up, wondering if anybody else saw Petford's childish tantrum parade.

"Yeah, you in? Or you gotta go run to see lover boy?"

A few of them start making smoochy kiss noises, and then Mitch starts to moan. "Ooohhh, Alex! I love you, Alex!"

I fling my sweaty sock at Mitch, hitting him in the side of the face, and he gags before flipping me off.

I snicker. "Yeah, count me in. Alex is working 'til later, so I'm cool to hang out for a few hours."

After reviewing some tape, we're chowing down on the best bourbon wings and fries while recapping last night's Minnesota and St. Louis game.

"Did you see that hit from DeLuca?" Kendrick lets out a low whistle. "I don't know how that dude hasn't received a suspension; the guy's dangerous."

"It makes me question how far it's gotta go before something's done." Ethan shakes his head. "I would hate to see someone get badly hurt for him to receive the ban he's overdue."

"Are you excited to play against your bro tomorrow?" Mitch asks Zach around a mouthful of fries.

Zach gives a small shrug. "Yeah, I guess so. His team-mates are dicks, though."

"Amen to that," I scoff.

We high-five across the table.

"He isn't happy there at the moment; there's some internal drama going on, and I think his coach is worried, too, because he'll be an unrestricted free agent at the end of next season, and he doesn't want to lose Brody."

"It would be super cool if he came here." Mitch's eyes go comically wide. "Team of bros."

"No way." Zach quickly shakes his head. "I love my brother, but we're better separated. We clash too much, and it's not good for team dynamics when you've got two players constantly at each other's throats."

"Talking about teammates being at each other's throats, did you see Petford giving the evil eye at Peyton earlier when he was talking about Katy?" Elliot chimes in. He's got sauce all around his mouth, even a bit on his forehead. I've no idea how my brother can rival a toddler with the mess he gets into when he eats. "He was looking at him like he had kicked his dog."

"Yeah, I have no idea what that's all about," I sigh.

"Do you think he's just jealous? I mean, who would want to marry *him*? The guy's a douche canoe," Mitch says.

Ethan slaps his hand around the back of Mitch's head. "You don't talk like that about your teammates, no matter what their problem is. I'll deal with it."

From Ethan's tone, he's putting an end to the conversation, and while I trust him to dissolve any bad blood before it can escalate, there's something about Petford that makes me uneasy.

One bad apple can make a bad bunch, and Petford is just that.

Nobody trusts him on the ice. He's unpredictable and doesn't seem to work well with his linemates, no matter how hard Coach tries.

Let's just hope he pulls his head out of his ass soon, because we can't afford to make any mistakes. The playoffs are in our sights, and we can't allow one person to diminish all the hard work we've put in this season.

X

Hopping from skate to skate, I drop down into a few squats to keep my thighs warm. At the end of the tunnel, bright lights glisten against the ice, and that's our cue. It's warm-up time.

We slap hands and trade fist bumps and ass slaps as we make our way down the tunnel. "Thunderstruck" blares throughout the arena's sound system, and fans cheer and bang their palms against the boards when we jump onto the ice.

If there's one feeling I'd like to bottle up for others to experience, it would be this.

The fan's sheer adrenaline and excitement. Their passion, their love for the sport, for the team. Their need for a win is just as prominent as our own.

It makes me feel alive, and I'm the luckiest motherfucker in the world to be able to live my dream—to play my favorite sport with my best friends in the best league.

Pucks are knocked off the bench wall, and I take one on my stick, bouncing it a few times on the blade before shooting it at the empty net. I run through my routine; three laps clockwise, behind the goal, then take a slap shot. I finish it off by skating to the blue line to stretch. Resting my stick down on the ice in front of me, I get down onto my knees in a frog pose to stretch my groin, kicking my legs out to stretch my hips, then lay on my back to work on stretching my glutes.

When I hop back onto my skates, I scan the crowd to look for the face that has been at the forefront of my mind for the last three weeks, and the second I see him, I skate over to the boards. It's like deja vu. I pick up some speed, then turn on my blades, slamming my body sideways into the boards. He laughs, tipping his head back and exposing that silky-smooth column of his throat that's begging for my lips.

I want to mark him as mine.

Because he is.

I texted him yesterday morning to let him know I'd put two tickets at will call for him, but he wasn't sure whether he was going to make it with Jacob still sick. He's been manning the bakery single-handedly the last few days, with Nate stepping in to help on occasion to ease some of the pressure.

As much as I want to hate the guy for being able to spend more time with Alex than me, I've got to hand it to him: he's a solid friend.

I also feel a tiny bit guilty that since my appearance in the hot-as-fuck apron the other day, word has spread, and Alex said there's been an actual line of people down the street waiting to get their hands on the baked goodies.

I'm really happy it's brought in more business, given

what Alex mentioned about the money struggles he and Jacob are dealing with. It's just unfortunate that it comes at a time when they're short-staffed.

If it had been anyone else, alarm bells would have been ringing like crazy in my mind, thinking Alex was only interested in me for my money, just like the rest. He's not like them, though. His reaction to me paying for our date snuffed out that worry, and I want to help them. I just don't know how.

Because I have a feeling that if I offered to help them with money, Alex would shut down that suggestion quicker than I could say the word "please".

"How are you?" I shout through the boards.

"Good!" He smiles. "How are you feeling?"

I raise my hand, tipping it from side to side like a scale. "Better, now that you're here, but it's going to be a tough game."

He gives a nod of understanding.

This is something I didn't know I would appreciate when it comes to dating a fan.

He *gets* it.

He gets my schedule. He gets my different moods depending on what team we're playing. He gets my diet and how I have to take naps and stick to a grueling routine because he's been watching the team for decades.

I'm about to tell him how hot he looks when I catch the "*C*" on his jersey.

Again.

Um, what the fuck?

Why the fuck is he not wearing *my* name?

"Why the fuck are you wearing that for?" I point an accusing finger.

He looks down at his jersey, and when he lifts his head, he's wearing a mischievous grin as he shrugs. "You haven't given me one of yours."

I open my mouth to argue, but he has a point. Taking off my glove, I hold up one finger, letting him know I'll be back in a minute. I quickly skate over to the bench where the team's equipment manager, Jordan, is organizing her case of blades.

"Can you arrange for one of my jerseys to be delivered to my seat, please?" I point over to where Alex is sitting.

Jordan gives an exasperated sigh. "What am I? Your PA?" she snorts. "Sure, you got it."

I thank her and skate back over to where Alex is waiting with a beer in hand. This time I don't slam into the boards with my body, but I slap the plexi with my hand to get his attention.

"I don't fucking like you wearing another man's jersey."

"And why is that?" I know he's baiting me.

"I want you to wear my name because you're *mine*. I want everyone in here to know you're here with me. For me."

Twenty-One

Alex

"He's got it baaaaad!" Nate sings as we watch Blaine skate away to join the team for the rest of warm-up after his alpha-possessive moment.

My knees feel weak, and my dick is hard.

Blaine texted me yesterday morning saying he really wanted me to come to his game tonight, and he'd left two tickets at will call again, so I knew he wanted me here. I just didn't know how bad.

Or maybe I did, which is why I wore this jersey.

He's been so attentive since we met. Nothing like the guy that's plastered over the bunny blogs, labeled a man-whore and selfish. Saving my ass when Jacob was sick, constantly checking in to see how I am, how Jacob is, what he can do for me, inviting us for Christmas—it's like online Blaine Olsen is a mere illusion compared to the person he is in real life.

Part of me thought going over for Christmas was too soon, and I thought he'd forget once he got home from his road trip. But he proved me wrong, asking what we like and dislike so he can pass it onto his mom and whether our family has any traditions.

The thought and effort he's putting into this, into *us*, is making it hard not to fall head over heels for him.

We take the same seats as before, two rows behind the home bench. Blaine said that every player gets a number of seats for each home game, and usually his seats remain empty unless his parents visit, or he gives them to a charity he's an ambassador for to auction off.

My heart swells at the thought. He really is a good guy.

"I still don't believe this is really happening to me."

Nate looks at me over his beer. "What's that?"

"All of this. Dating Blaine, being invited to games." I shake my head. "It doesn't feel like this is my life. It feels surreal, like I'm a fraud."

"A fraud? Why? Because you're a fan?"

I nod.

"But you're not a fraud, Alex. You deserve all of this. You deserve to have someone who's so smitten with you that they will do everything to make you happy." He takes another sip of his beer. "And someone who will throw down the possessive gauntlet when you're wearing another man's name on your back." He winks.

We both laugh.

The buzzer sounds, signaling the end of warm-up, and despite pretending to scowl, Blaine skates over to the boards and blows me a kiss before skating back to the bench. His eyes stay locked on mine until he disappears into the tunnel.

"Wow…" Nate says with a wistful look in his eyes. "I'm pretty sure if you weren't in public, and he wasn't on the ice, he'd have you bent over and made sure you knew exactly who you belong to."

I snicker, recalling our texts while he was away about spanking, but that fire in his eyes just then? I have no doubt that if we were alone, I'd have a handprint on my ass. He's intense, and I love it.

"Excuse me, Alex?"

I turn around at the familiar voice.

Standing on the steps is the same woman who took us to the locker room after the last game, this time dressed in a gray tailored suit and wearing yet another pair of tall, pointy stilettos. She's holding a bag with the team logo printed on the front.

"Hey, is everything okay?"

She hands over the bag. "This is for you. Blaine was adamant that I tell you he needs to see you wearing this when he comes out for the national anthem." Her mouth tips up in a wide grin as she leans in and lowers her voice. "I must say, it's a breath of fresh air to see him so hung up over someone. I never thought I'd see the day that Blaine Olsen would find someone he's head over heels for."

On that mind-blowing note, she turns on her heels and heads back up the stairs, leaving me speechless. Taking a look inside the bag, I pull out a jersey with "B. OLSEN" stitched across the back, along with his number, 80.

I quickly stand up, pulling my Parkes jersey over my head, and carefully fold it up, slipping it inside the bag. It's a few sizes bigger than I'd usually wear, so when I pull it over my head, the bottom hits mid-thigh, and I need to roll up the sleeves slightly.

It smells like him. His aftershave and a slight undertone of sweat. I bring it to my nose, taking a deep inhale of his scent.

This is *his* jersey.

My heart squeezes in my chest, and goose bumps tickle across the back of my neck.

I look over to Nate. His eyes crinkle at the sides from the shit-eating grin he's wearing.

"What?"

He shakes his head. "Nothing. It looks good on you."

I smooth my hand across the front of the embroidered Thunder logo as I sit in my seat, just as the lights go down and the iconic Thunder intro begins.

Blaine steps out onto the ice, and I can't hide my smile when he immediately looks at me, a wide grin spreading across his face.

Little did I know that I'd end up sitting next to Blaine's parents. They must've flown in from California this afternoon, and I've been on edge throughout the entire game that they'd pick up that we're in Blaine's seats. I recognized them instantly because Blaine looks just like his dad, whereas Elliot is more like his mom. Seeing his dad and getting a glimpse of what Blaine might look like in twenty years makes my stomach swoop.

He'll be fucking handsome.

"Shove that in your five-hole!" his mom bellows as Blaine scores on New Jersey's goalie.

Nate chuckles next to me, throwing more popcorn into his mouth. She takes her seat, clapping excitedly as Elliot removes his mask to take a drink.

"Well done, El!" She looks over to me and says proudly, "They're my boys."

I can't help but smile. "I thought they might be."

She giggles. "Was it obvious?"

I hold my forefinger and thumb up. "Only a little."

But before she could say any more, the official blows his whistle, and her attention is back on the ice.

Thankfully, his parents were too engrossed in the fast-paced game to pay more attention to me, and they went absolutely wild when the Thunder won in overtime six to five.

I think I may have lost some of my hearing from his mom's screaming.

You could sense the frustration bubbling on the bench, especially when Blaine snapped his stick in half after the officials didn't call an obvious hooking call and New Jersey ended up scoring on Elliot. Blaine's face was so red with anger that I thought he was going to drop the gloves, but what surprised me most was seeing Ethan do it instead.

He's never been a fighter in all the years I've been watching him play, but he was pissed tonight after Zach took a nasty hit from one of New Jersey's wingers. I watched with worry when he was slow to pick himself up off the ice.

"You don't have to stay if you need to get home," I suggest to Nate while we wait by the locker room after the game.

It still feels so weird being able to come back here, and even weirder that I haven't seen Blaine's parents since they disappeared into the crowd.

"And miss out on hot hockey players in suits?" Nate tsks. "Don't deprive me of that beautiful sight."

I shake my head, chuckling.

He leans back, propping one foot on the wall behind him. His arms cross over his chest, and he keeps his eyes locked on the door to the locker room.

Thankfully, we're not in a rush to get home this time. I've been burning the candle at both ends, and with Jacob still sick, I need a break. So the shop is closed tomorrow, and I'm taking a day off.

The last thing we need is for me to end up sick, too.

I'll need to bring it up with Jacob when he's better because working seven days a week while there's only two of us isn't manageable, debt be damned.

When I told Blaine I was taking the day off, he invited me to stay at his place tonight. If he'd asked me a week ago, I would've said no, but things have changed since he came into the shop the other day.

At least for me.

My worries over him only wanting me for the chase have evaporated.

The door to the locker room opens, and the first person to appear is Blaine, wearing a light gray suit and crisp white shirt.

Jeez, he's so goddamn hot.

I salivate at the sight of him. Thick thighs look ready to burst from the seams of his pants, the fabric tightly cradling an impressive bulge between his legs. His jacket sleeves display strong forearms and wide biceps. The white button-down shirt gives a sneaky glimpse of the muscles that lay underneath as he moves. Within seconds, he's standing in front of me, his arms tightly wrapped around my waist, pulling me close to his chest, and kissing me like his life depends on it.

Where did that come from?

Not that I'm complaining.

Reaching up, I wrap my arms around his neck, leaning into his embrace.

"Stop groping your boyfriend, Olsen!" someone cackles.

He lets out a low groan, his hands still fixed on my ass when we pull apart.

"I'm so happy you're here," he whispers, his eyes sparkling. "And I fucking love this." He tugs on the hem of the jersey I'm still wearing.

His jersey.

"I fucking love seeing you wearing my name." He presses a gentle kiss to my cheek. "Can I take you home?"

I nod.

We walk Nate back to his car to fetch my overnight bag from the trunk. We say our goodbyes and head to Blaine's Range Rover in the players' lot. His apartment is only a fifteen-minute drive from the arena, and the second the elevator doors close, Blaine's lips are on mine.

Hot, wet, needy kisses.

My bag drops to the floor with a thud. I wrap my arms around his wide shoulders, my fingers threading through the hairs at the back of his neck. His hands smooth down my spine, over the curve of my ass, and when he squeezes the globes, my toes curl in my sneakers.

My dick throbs in the confines of my jeans, begging for more, and my wish is granted when Blaine rolls his hips, his moan muffled by my mouth as our dicks rub against one another.

"Fuuuck," he groans against my mouth.

The elevator dings once we reach the sixty-ninth floor—something I'd joke about if I wasn't so high on sexual adrenaline. He takes my hand and collects my bag from the floor, then practically sprints down the hallway to his apartment. With a quick swipe of his door key, we're inside, where my bag is swiftly dropped again by an end table.

A sigh escapes me when a warm hand cups the side of my neck. I close my eyes and lean into his touch, reveling in how good his fingers feel against my skin.

"I want you, Alex." He rests his forehead against mine. Our chests heave as our lungs try to take in as much oxygen as possible. "I want you so fucking much, I might crawl out of my skin if I don't get to have you soon."

"I want you, too." I press my lips against his, loving how desperate he is.

Quickly toeing off my shoes, I barely notice the stunning view outside his window or his impressive apartment when Blaine leads me down the hallway. His bedroom is on the corner of the building; floor-to-ceiling windows take up two sides, allowing a cinematic view of Navy Pier and Lake Michigan, with the moon and stars sparkling on the still lake like a mirror.

It's beautiful, but not as stunning as the man in front of me, slowly and teasingly unbuttoning his shirt.

"You're so beautiful." His words are soft, almost in disbelief.

He steps forward, allowing his shirt to fall open, and takes my lips in a slow, tender kiss.

Gentle.

Savoring the feel of my lips. The taste of my mouth with his tongue.

Pushing the shirt off his shoulders, my hands explore his chest. Grazing over inches of hard muscles and warm skin.

I drop my head back between my shoulder blades, exposing my throat when his lips trail down my jaw to my neck. Hot, open-mouthed kisses trail along my throat, over the pulse that's fluttering wildly, before moving down to the collar of my shirt.

"I want to fuck you while you're wearing my name, but not tonight," he admits, running a finger down my chest. "Tonight, I want to see you. I want to see how far down this fucking blush runs, and I want to kiss every part of you."

He takes a step back to strip out of his pants, and I follow, removing my clothes and dropping them in a pile on the floor.

Once I'm down to just my boxers, Blaine's eyes roam my body, leaving a path of fire on every inch of my skin. And fuck, he is perfect. Endless muscles, abs carved like stone. A small smattering of hair across firm and sculpted pecs. Biceps flex as he palms his steel-hard length tenting the front of his black boxer briefs.

My cock kicks against the material of my underwear, wanting to be touched.

"Take them off for me, Alex. Show me that beautiful dick of yours."

I swallow my nerves, hooking my thumbs into the waistband of my boxers, and step out of them. My hard shaft hits my stomach, leaving a smear of precome against my skin.

"Fuck," Blaine groans. "Can I taste you?"

I nod shakily, my eyes widening when he slides his boxers down his legs and drops to his knees in front of me.

His hands look huge as he strokes up the front of my thighs, moving up until he reaches my dick. He runs his tongue slowly up my shaft, teasing me, and I can't help but moan. When he finally opens his mouth, taking the head of my cock between his lips and flicking his tongue over my slit, a broken cry escapes me.

It's too much, but it's not enough.

I want it all, but not too fast.

Blaine wraps his thumb and forefinger around the base of my cock, playing with my balls with his fingers while stroking his own dick. It's hard to keep my eyes open, but I fight against closing them as he looks up at me, not wanting to miss a single second of this.

"Mmm…" The vibrations at the back of his throat resonate through me, and I almost lose it.

I lace my fingers through his slightly damp hair, combing my fingers through the curls beginning to form. My toes curl into the plush carpet when he sucks me to the back of his throat before tracing his tongue down from tip to root.

"Ah! Blaine!" I gasp.

He pulls away, resting my cock against his cheek. His hand dips between my legs, his fingertips lightly caressing my taint. "I love hearing my name on your lips."

My head rolls to the side. It's been so long since I've

been touched like this. My body's trembling with the need for release, tingles rushing down to the base of my spine.

I'm so close, and we've only just begun.

He pumps his thick shaft with his fist, his hand running over the precome beading at the head. A whimper escapes me when he strokes it back down his length.

I can't wait to feel the weight of it against my tongue.

Wrapping my fist around the base of my dick, I teasingly push it through his lips once, twice, then step away to climb onto the bed.

Blaine remains kneeling on the floor, looking at me through hooded eyes. The moonlight casts a perfect glow over the curve of his wide shoulders, highlighting the strong muscles on his back, emphasizing the sheer strength of his body.

A body that I want on top of me.

"Get over here," I groan.

The only sound in the room is our heavy breathing. Blaine stands and retrieves a condom and lube from the bedside table. He rolls the condom onto his length, then crawls up onto the bed, stopping between my spread legs.

My dick twitches, begging for his attention, when the bottle of lube lands on the bedspread. Blaine shoves a pillow under my ass and shuffles down the bed, lifting my legs and pushing them back toward me before leaning in, licking a wet stripe with the flat of his tongue across my exposed hole.

The sound that leaves me is wild, animalistic. "Fuck!"

He begins to lick, suck, and eat my ass like it's his favorite meal. The sensation from his moans cause my stomach to clench. I hiss between clenched teeth when he pushes one thick finger past the tight ring of muscle, stretching me.

I whimper and groan, melting into the mattress, losing myself as he slides the digit in and out, grazing my prostate on every other stroke. By the time he adds a third finger, I'm so close that my legs are shaking.

"Blaine," I pant, squeezing my cock to stop myself from coming. "I need you inside me."

The sense of loss is instant the second he removes his fingers, and my chest heaves, gasping for breath.

My feet are tingling, my toes aching from curling. Another sharp breath leaves me when I feel the cold lube around my hole, and I close my eyes at the pressure of his thick head.

Even though I had three fingers inside me only seconds ago, his cock feels huge.

Moving my legs to wrap around his waist, I open my eyes to see Blaine leaning over me. The muscles in his arms quiver, his neck straining like he's barely holding on. Sweat beads at his hairline, and I lose myself in those gorgeous silver eyes as he sinks inside me.

Twenty-Two

Blaine

People often say that when you have sex for the first time with that special person, it's like your brainwaves are altered. There's a shift in the force, and it changes you.

The second I was inside Alex, as soon as I felt him around my cock, it all made sense. My body count is high—extremely high—but it has never once felt like this.

Nothing could ever compare to this.

Not even lifting the Stanley Cup.

It's like he was made for me.

I piston my hips, my cock brushing his prostate. That fucking blush stretches down his neck to his chest, spreading across his porcelain skin. Dipping my head, I nuzzle my face into the crook of his neck, pressing wet kisses under his jaw before sliding my lips over his.

"Touch me, please," he begs.

Bracing my weight on one arm, I reach down to take his

cock in my hand. He's like steel wrapped in silk. He's leaking, causing my hand to become slick with his precome as I coax him with jerky strokes.

I nearly blew my load when I had him in my mouth, loving the weight of him on my tongue. He tasted like perfection.

He feels like perfection.

I think this is my new favorite place, and I don't ever want to leave.

"Fuck," I grunt, mentally running through my stats to ward off my release.

"Blaine," he moans, his legs squeezing my waist. "I'm so close."

"Come for me, baby."

I let go of his cock and place both hands on either side of his head, my thrusts turning frantic as the skin slapping skin fills the room. My balls are drawn up so tight I can't hold back anymore. I come with a wild cry, releasing into the condom, while Alex moans with his own release.

His moans are like ecstasy, and I'm addicted.

His come lands on his stomach and chest, and I collapse on top of him, both of us gasping for air.

I'm lightheaded, dizzy from the most incredible orgasm I've ever experienced.

I don't think I've ever come so hard in my life.

My body melts as Alex runs his fingers through my hair, his nails scratching my scalp. I'm aware his come is currently squished between us, but I'm unable to move, my body trembling with post-orgasmic shakes.

"As much as I don't want you to move, you're kinda heavy," Alex says with a strained laugh.

I roll off of him, running my fingers through the remnants of his release on my chest, and bring it up to my mouth to lick it off.

"Mmm."

He tastes so fucking delicious that my spent cock gives a tired but appreciative twitch.

When I can finally feel my legs again, I head into the bathroom and retrieve a wet washcloth. Realization hits me, knocking the breath from my lungs like I've just been boarded by a two-hundred-and-forty-pound D-man.

I brought him to my room.

I had sex with him in *my room.*

Nobody ever comes into my bedroom. This is my safe haven. All my hookups have happened in my spare bedroom, so I can keep things separate. But what shocks me most of all is how it doesn't bother me.

Looking over at Alex, I like the sight of him in my bed. How the bright moon shines through the windows, highlighting the soft features of his face, cascading down that exquisite body of his. And I really like how he looks tangled up in my sheets.

I should be freaking out and thinking of ways to ask him to leave, but instead I'm hoping this isn't the last time I see his blond hair in a blissed-out mess against the pillow.

I absentmindedly rub the pleasant ache in my chest when his voice pulls me out of it.

"Blaine?"

I carry the washcloth back into the room, wiping away the come that's starting to dry on his stomach and the lube from between his cheeks. I quickly swipe it over my abs before I toss it onto the bathroom floor and crawl back into bed.

He curls his body into mine, his head fitting perfectly beneath my chin, and it almost makes me burst with emotion.

"This is probably a really inappropriate time to bring this up, but... I met your parents today," Alex quietly announces.

I'm startled by his admission. "What? They're not supposed to fly in until tomorrow."

Elliot didn't mention they were coming, but they've done this before and snagged tickets through Coach to surprise us.

He chuckles. "They must have come early to surprise you or something, but I instantly knew who they were. Your mom was screaming about staying away from her son, and whenever a puck got past Elliot, she would shout that it was goalie interference."

I laugh because I know exactly what my mom's like. She's been the same since we started playing hockey.

"Oh yeah, my mom gets very invested. Was she arguing with every single call the officials made?"

I feel him nod against my chest. "Yeah, especially that hooking call. I thought she was going to run down and jump over the boards at one point. She was going on about how they need to go get their eyesight checked because even the astronauts in space could've seen that was hooking."

"Yep, that's my mom; she lays into the officials pretty hard."

"They seemed lovely, though."

"Did they not realize it was you?"

He shakes his head.

"She's gonna go crazy when she finds out she sat next to you the entire game and didn't get to quiz you." I can just picture my mom's face when she sees Alex on Christmas Day.

"She's going to quiz me?" Alex lifts his head, his eyes wide in horror.

Another bubble of laughter escapes me.

"Maybe; she's super eager to meet you. She's been asking a lot about you."

Because she wants to know all about the guy who captured my attention and may have captured my heart.

And I know he's going to capture hers too.

The following morning is spent in bed, exchanging lazy kisses and mind-blowing hand jobs.

I can't remember the last time I felt so content. Watching the December sun trying to peek through the clouds over Lake Michigan, all while being wrapped up in the most incredible guy I have ever met.

His fingertips idly trace shapes over my abs while his head rests on my pec. His soft breaths against my skin give me goose bumps all over.

"I've been thinking about what you said the other day, about how you had your heart broken." He looks up at me with kind-hearted eyes. "Will you tell me about it?"

I swallow the lump in my throat.

I haven't spoken about it since I was drafted, when

Ethan pulled me to one side, as he must have picked up that something was troubling me.

"I met Kelly in freshman year. She was the girl every guy wanted and everyone wanted to be friends with. I met her at a frat party, was instantly dazzled by her, and as soon as she found out I was on the hockey team, she was all over me." I rub my jaw, feeling my palm begin to sweat. "I was too dumb to see it then, high on the fact that I got the girl. I thought I was in love, thought she was gonna be my end game, but as time went on, the cracks began to show. She'd yell at me for the smallest things, like being late to meet her because I got caught up in practice, or how people would look at me in bars. Like I could control that; I was on the hockey team, of course people were gonna look at me. I tried to make it obvious I was only interested in her, but she wouldn't have any of it. Every away game, she'd blow up my phone, asking me who I was hooking up with, even though I wasn't and hadn't given her any reason to doubt me."

I look out the window at the lake, trying to fight off the tightness in my chest from reliving feelings from years ago.

"I was arriving home from an away game; we'd just had our asses kicked big time, and all I wanted to do was lose myself in my girl and forget about it, so the second I was off the bus, I dumped my stuff at home and rushed over to her house. She didn't hear me arrive. She was in the living room with her friends, and I heard her…" My teeth clench, and I swallow the bitter taste in my mouth.

I tell Alex what I heard her say that night, running my fingers in soothing circles on his arm when he snarls. "What a bitch."

"She was also cheating on me with a guy from the

basketball team, so all the times she was bitching at me for cheating on her, she was pushing her guilt onto me to make herself feel better over the fact that she was the cheater."

"I'm so sorry, Blaine. Being cheated on can really damage your self-esteem and make you doubt your self-worth."

I shake my head. "After her, there was David. We met at a club and we hit it off. I thought I'd found someone good, but turns out he lied the whole time. He told me he was a lawyer, but he was actually a journalist. He used me to get a promotion…" I sigh. "I would've helped him if he'd been honest, y'know? But they made me feel worthless. That the only good thing about me was my pay check or that I'm a hockey player. I don't think I'm all that, but I fucking cared about them, and all they cared about was how many dollars were on my contract."

He sits up, his eyes are earnest as he cups my face between his warm hands. "I hope you don't think that's why I'm interested in you, especially after what I said about the debt Jacob and I are dealing with, because I would never, ever, be that shallow."

I mirror him, sitting up against the pillows and pulling his face toward mine, pressing gentle kisses against his lips.

"I don't think that at all; if anything, I want to help you and Jacob."

He shakes his head vigorously. "No, I wouldn't let you do that. Your money is yours, it's for your future. We couldn't accept that."

I open my mouth to argue, and he presses his finger to my lips. A sad, soft smile appears on his face. "Thank you, though. It's an incredibly generous thought, but I like you for *you*. I don't care how much money you've got in the bank or that you're a hockey player; I just like you."

Biting the inside of my lip, I try to ward off the smile that's threatening to take over my face. "You like me?"

Alex chuckles, nodding his head. He leans down and kisses me a few times before saying, "Yes, I do. Isn't it obvious? And not just that amazing butt of yours." He winks.

I pump both fists in the air. "Fuck yeah!"

A whirlwind of butterflies swirls in my stomach as Alex laughs, his cheeks and the tips of his ears turning my favorite shade of pink. I tackle him on the bed, smothering him in kisses before his stomach rumbles loudly.

We erupt into a fit of laughter. "Let's get you fed."

Once breakfast has been consumed and we make out like horny teenagers in the shower, we fall back into bed and nap for an hour, only to have our nap interrupted by my brother blowing up my phone.

ELLIOT

DUDE!

ELLIOT

Did you know mom and dad flew in yesterday & got tickets from Coach?

ELLIOT

Send help, mom's organizing my socks.

ELLIOT

How can you organize SOCKS?

"I should probably go home and see how Jacob is," Alex says, slipping those luscious long legs into his jeans.

I don't want him to go. I want him to stay with me and get naked on the couch and make out while watching movies. But I don't want him to think I'm needy, so I reluctantly nod.

Plus, I'm pretty sure if I don't show my face at Elliot's soon, he's going to be using the key I'm going to end up regretting giving him.

I fetch my things and put on my sneakers. Taking Alex's hand in mine, we head out to the elevator.

"Huh?" I wonder as the elevator stops on my brother's floor.

I groan at the sound of my mom's voice filtering through the doors before they slide open to reveal my parents.

My mom's eyes light up when she sees me, then flick to Alex. Her hand flies to her mouth, and next thing I know she's jumping her way into the elevator like a happy kangaroo.

"Please don't jump in the elevator, Nicola," my dad grumbles, holding onto the bar. He looks a little green when he greets me. "Hey, kid."

Alex rolls his lips together; his eyes are comically wide as my mom throws her arms around his shoulders and pulls him into a tight embrace.

"ALEX! I'm so happy to meet you! SO happy!" she squeals.

His hand squeezes mine. I should have warned him that her mouthing off at the officials is just a snippet of how wild she can be.

"Mom, can you not be so embarrassing?"

Her head whips toward me, glaring as she points an accusatory finger. "Why didn't you tell me we would be sitting next to the lovely Alex all night? Now I feel rude!"

"Why didn't you tell me you were flying in a day earlier? Maybe then I could have told you that you would meet Alex." I cock my head to the side in challenge.

She purses her lips, knowing I have a point.

"Tough game last night." My dad breaks the mother-son glare off, color coming back to his face now that my mom has stopped bouncing.

"Yeah, it's always shit against Jersey. I don't know what their issue is."

"Jealousy." My dad nods confidently. "Their offensive line is weak, and their D? Pfft. Their goalie couldn't catch snow in a blizzard."

Alex chuckles nervously next to me.

"Mom, Dad, I would like you to meet Alex." I turn to him. "Alex, this is my mom and dad, Nicola and Graham."

He holds his hand out to my dad. "It's a pleasure to meet you, sir."

"None of that sir bullshit, I'm not seventy." He shakes Alex's hand.

Alex turns to my mom next, "It's a pleasure to meet you, ma—"

She points a red-painted nail at him as the elevator doors open. "Don't you dare ma'am me. If you ma'am me, I might have to start jumping again."

"You won't hear a ma'am from me." He winks.

My mom wraps her arms around him, and over his shoulder, she mouths, "I like him."

Me too, Mom, me too.

Twenty-Three

Blaine

We're on fucking fire tonight.

Montreal doesn't know what hit them. Their goalie must have holes in his pads because his five hole is wider than the Grand Canyon.

Leaning in for the face-off, I rest my stick against my thighs as I wait for the Montreal center to take his position. He's been smacking his gums at me since the first period, probably thinking it's going to put me off, but he has it all wrong.

It's only spurring me on.

I give him my widest grin.

"You getting a little tired there, bud? Looking a lil' slow."

"Fuck you, Olsen," he snaps.

"Aw!" I scrunch up my nose. "I don't think my boyfriend would like that, but I'm flattered, thanks."

He grunts some derogatory slurs, but while he's sprouting off, he misses the official dropping the puck.

Chuckling under my breath, I win the face off. Zach gets the puck and passes it to Ethan. He's already past the blue line, and I follow him into the offensive zone. Montreal is as slow as molasses as they play catch-up.

A quick flick of his wrist, the puck hits my blade, and I wind it back.

Whoosh.

Back of the net, baby.

BUHHHHHH, sounds the horn. Our standard goal song, Nirvana's *Lithium*, blasts through the arena, and fans are up on their feet going wild.

I fucking love how enthusiastic our fans are.

Raising my hand in celebration, I exchange a high-five with Ethan, then Peyton, Kendrick, and Zach skate over for a group hug before we skate past the bench, trading glove fist bumps.

"Nice! Good job, boys. Keep it up," Coach says when we sit back on the bench.

I squirt some water in my mouth, then wipe the sweat from my visor with a towel.

My focus is primarily on the game, but every now and again, my mind will drift off to the man who is sitting two rows behind me, watching my game with my parents. Maybe it's that thought that keeps me so fired up. I've been on top of my game recently, playing some of the best hockey of my life, and maybe it's the standard hockey player superstition, but I'm pretty sure it's because of Alex.

He's like my lucky charm.

"Atta boy, Mitchy!" Ethan shouts as Mitch dekes a

Montreal d-man whose face is getting redder with every passing second. He passes the puck to Tait, and it's like watching magic happen. Tait passes it back to Mitch, who one-timers the puck right into the back of the net.

"Fuck yeah!" I holler, banging my stick against the boards.

The rookie's wearing a shit-eating grin when he skates back to the bench.

I give him a noogie with my glove. "What a shot, bud! That was beautiful."

He dips his chin in embarrassment, trying to hide his bright pink cheeks, squirts some water in his mouth, and then shoos me away. "Your turn now!"

I hop over the boards for my next shift and line up for face-off, biting my lip to suppress my laughter when Middleton's sour face appears.

"You know, maybe it's that lip lettuce you've got going on. It's hindering your game, bud." I wave my gloved hand in front of my mouth, referring to the handlebar mustache he's rocking.

He glowers at me, his nostrils flaring like a crazed bull.

I snicker, focusing on the puck. I win again and pass it back to the boys. This time Montreal is a little more awake; they've clearly faced a grilling from their coach, but it's not enough. Even with bodies in front of the net, Zach sinks one between the tendy's legs, and the thousands of excited fans roar.

By the time we're back out for third, we're up six to one. The one goal that slipped past Elliot's defense was unlucky as it bounced off of his pad.

It's like Montreal have given up; we sink two more into

the net—one being a power play goal after one of their defensemen cross-checked Zach, and another was an empty net goal scored by ...

Elliot!

The horn sounds, and we've won eight to one. I skate up to Elliot, dropping everything on the ice, and he's jumping into my arms, trying to wrap his padded legs around my waist.

"I fucking scored a goal!" he screams, and when I catch a look at his face through his cage, his eyes are filled with tears.

"It was fucking amazing!" My voice croaks with emotion.

The rest of the team joins us, congratulating Elliot with helmet taps, and when I skate over to Middleton, I roll my lips.

"Good game, but seriously, dude. I think that lip foliage is slowing you down." I grin.

He rolls his eyes, but I can see the corners of his lips twitching. "Thanks for the advice, Olsen; I'll take it into consideration."

I place my hand over my heart, "I'm so happy to have such a positive impact."

He scoffs as we shake hands.

Before I step off of the ice, I glance up to my seats. Alex's smile is wide and proud, and when our eyes lock, I blow him a kiss. He catches it and holds it over his heart.

Back in the locker room, Elliot is swinging his jersey around his head like a lasso while he tries to ride one of his leg pads like a horse.

"Watch out, broski, I'm gonna be in contention for the Maurice Richard Trophy soon. Better watch ya back!" He suddenly stops, and his face drops. "I don't have a goal song… I'm gonna need a goal song. Reid, find me a goal song! It's gotta be iconic! Think like ABBA or Taylor Swift…"

I laugh as he rambles on to a terrified-looking Zach.

Who knew one goal would make him this cocky?

Placing both hands on my hips, I watch my twin bundle his jersey up into a ball and shoot it into the laundry hamper. "If you beat me, El, I'll be more ecstatic than if I win it myself."

And I mean it.

Just playing my favorite sport with my brother is the biggest award for me; everything else is a bonus.

And playing my favorite sport with my favorite guy watching me in the crowd makes me feel like the king of the fucking universe.

✕

"Are you sure they won't mind me coming?" Alex twists his hands in his lap, chewing on the inside of his cheek.

"Of course not." I shake my head.

We're on our way to Gino's to meet up with a few of the guys to play pool and enjoy some wings, and because Alex finished work earlier than expected, I asked him to tag along. It'll be the first time they'll meet him outside of the arena.

"If anything, they'll probably give me shit to try to embarrass me in front of you."

He grins. "Now that I'd like to see. I can't imagine you get embarrassed easily."

"When your ass has been plastered online, it's hard to be embarrassed about anything. I own everything I do, but maybe I'll remind my mom that baby photos are strictly forbidden."

"What?!" He playfully slaps my bicep with the back of his hand. "You can't take away baby photos from me, it's like… mandatory at Christmas!"

I shake my head, laughing under my breath, but honestly…

I'd do anything for Alex.

He wants to see my embarrassing baby photos? He can see every single one if he wants.

I park my Range Rover in the lot behind Gino's and we head inside, weaving through the crowd, to find the boys at the back by a pool table.

"Here he is, mister lover boy!" Elliot wolf whistles, then picks Alex up, swinging him around in a circle. "Welcome to the best boys' club *ever.* We eat wings and drink beer and play pool and it's great fun."

Once he's back on his feet, Alex looks over at me, the apples of his cheeks turning a deep shade of pink.

"Twinny, go get the drinks in; Alex is going to be on my team." Elliot wraps his arm around Alex's shoulders and guides him over to the high table where Zach and Ethan are sitting, sipping on a beer.

I do as instructed, placing our food order and return with beers, handing one to Alex, who's looking at Ethan with a somewhat stunned expression.

"Why are you looking at Ethan like that?" I say teasingly in his ear.

His head swings to face me. "I… uh… I…" he sighs, letting out a small, deprecating laugh. "It's just a little surreal for me. I'm sitting in a bar next to a guy I've watched play hockey since I was in high school. I'm sorry, I didn't mean to be weird."

I shake my head. "It's not weird. I was the same when I first came to Chicago. I had no idea Ethan was picking me up from the airport, and you wanna know the first thing I said to him?"

Alex nods, his eyes sparkling with glee.

"I said, 'Holy shit, you're Ethan Parkes; I've jerked off to your Sports Illustrated cover'…"

His body shakes with laughter. "Are you kidding?"

"Nope, totally serious. That's probably the only time I've been embarrassed. Twenty-one-year-old me, wet behind the ears, came face to face with my idol, and that was the first thing I said."

"What did he say?"

"He just blinked at me, then scowled and told me to put on my big boy pants because I wasn't in college anymore."

Alex glances back over to Ethan, chuckling quietly to himself, before Elliot comes over, armed with a cue.

"Ready to help me kick Zach and Ethan's butt?" Elliot hands over the cue to Alex with a grin, then turns to me. "Broski, have you ordered food? Because I'm famished."

"Famished? You ate like an hour ago."

He pats his stomach. "I'm a growing boy, and I'm gonna be burning a lot of cals kicking some grumpy ass." He points to Ethan, who is, of course, scowling.

"Are we getting this game started or what, Olsen?"

"Ooohh," Elliot chuckles, "don't get ya panties in a twist, Cappy; I'll even let you break."

Ethan rolls his eyes and breaks.

I lean back in my seat, watching in contentment. Alex fits in so seamlessly, like he's been around them for years, when really, we only met three weeks ago. The initial nerves disappear, and soon he's teasing Elliot and joining in ribbing Ethan. All while I notice Zach frowning at his phone between turns, his shoulders hunching up to his ears.

When he glances up from his screen, I give him an upnod, asking if he's good. He nods back jerkily, then steps up to the table to take his turn.

Hmm, odd.

"You trying to wipe us out of wings, Blaine?"

I turn to see Dylan transferring the order of wings and loaded fries from his tray onto the table.

"Yeah, we'll still be hungry after this, I'm sure." I laugh.

Dylan shakes his head, putting the final dish on the table. "Let me know if you need anything else." He gives my forearm a gentle squeeze before disappearing into the back.

"Grub's up," I say, and my mouth goes dry when I see Alex's face. His eyes are locked on my arm where Dylan touched me, a slight confusion marring his brow.

Elliot deems the game paused while we eat, and I make space for Alex to sit next to me. He thanks me when I hand him a plate, but the silence is killing me.

My mind races back to when I was with Kelly, to the times I was accused of cheating and flirting, and I really hope that's not what Alex is thinking.

"It didn't mean anything," I say quietly, so only he can hear.

"What?"

"Dylan… We hooked up a long time ago, but nothing has happened since."

His brows furrow. "Do you think I'm mad because he touched your arm?"

I nod. "Yeah?"

"I'm not mad at you, Blaine. I'm not going to doubt you unless you give me a reason. I know you've been with a lot of people, but I'm not going to hold your past against you…" He sighs, then gives a small smile. "I was just taken aback by how jealous I felt about him touching you, that's all."

My heart leaps in my chest, and my words come out more gleefully than I expected. "You're jealous?"

"Yeah," he laughs. "I was tempted to come over and stake my claim on you, but then I realized I don't need to do that."

"Why not?"

Alex leans over, pressing his lips to mine, and ignores the heckles from my brother. "Because you staked your claim on me the other night in front of an arena full of people."

Twenty-Four

Alex

"I'm really glad you're feeling better." I smile at my brother.

Jacob's finally up and about. He's gotten some color back in his cheeks, and thankfully, the wicked cough has gone.

"I never want to feel like that again," he admits.

I'm not sure how he's going to take this, but considering how sick he's been from stress and burnout, I'm hoping he'll take the suggestion I'm about to make seriously.

"About that... I've been doing some thinking..." I rub the back of my neck nervously, hoping he doesn't immediately veto my idea. "I think it'd be a good idea to close the shop one day a week. It's not healthy to work the hours you've been doing seven days a week. It's not sustainable, and I don't wanna see you get sick again."

Jacob sighs, wrapping his hands around the hot cup of tea I made.

"We've been so busy this past week that I think we'll be able to manage without losing too much income. We're pretty much booked up for custom orders until after Valentine's, and the demand's been insane since Blaine helped out."

A small smile plays on his lips. "I still can't believe he stepped up like that."

I laugh.

I'm still in disbelief that he didn't hesitate to throw on an apron and jump around the counter.

"I know! That was some seriously good marketing, even if it was unplanned."

He smiles, and I can tell he's mulling my suggestion over as he takes a sip of tea.

"You need a rest, Jake, or you'll burn yourself out again, and I don't think I'd cope with seeing you hospitalized."

"I know, you're right." He sighs. "I do think it would be a good idea; maybe we could do a Sunday or something?"

"That would work, plus it's always the quietest day of the week."

He nods. "Thank you for everything, for holding the fort while I was out. I don't know what I'd do without you."

I take his hand across the table, giving it a gentle squeeze. "I love you. You mean the world to me, and I wanna take care of you. I know we've got shit to deal with, but we've got this, I promise. Your health comes first."

Jacob's smile is sad, but I know he means it wholeheartedly when he says, "I love you too, Alex."

"Good, because I've offered to bake a cake to bring with us for Christmas."

"You didn't." He rolls his eyes lovingly. "How many are going?"

"Um, Blaine mentioned it was him, Elliot, his parents, Zach, and the two of us."

When I told Jacob that Blaine had invited us both to his place for Christmas day, I could tell he was hesitant.

"They're good guys," I say reassuringly.

"I believe you; I just… I still get a bit nervous."

A couple of guys from the football and hockey teams made Jacob's life miserable in high school. Years of bullying had left their mark on him, even a decade later, so I understood his natural reluctance around jocks, but I knew he'd eventually see these guys are different from those douchebags from school.

When the timer pings, alerting me that dinner's ready, I serve up the chicken alfredo and hand a bowl over to Jacob.

"How are things going with Blaine?"

"Good, really good," I say between mouthfuls. "I ended up telling him about our situation the other day, and he wanted to help us out."

Mirroring my own reaction, Jacob shakes his head. "We couldn't ask that of him."

"That's exactly what I said."

"It's kind of him to suggest it, but it's too much."

I nod in agreement, waving my fork around as I finish chewing. "I don't think he realizes the incredible impact he's had just by showing his face in the shop. He's been mentioning us on Instagram, and Zach's been posting photos of his orders. It's brought in a lot of new customers, so that in itself is a big help."

"Wow."

"Yeah, it's been crazy, but I have a good feeling about it."

Not just about the shop but about the developing relationship with Blaine, too. I'm still nervous as fuck because Christmas is only a few days away, but I find myself counting down the minutes until I get to spend time with him. This isn't how I envisioned my life, but they always say sometimes the best things in life are unexpected.

X

A couple days later, Christmas Eve is upon us, and my nerves are running wild. Blaine offered to pick us up, and since he's arrived, he's been checking every photo in the living room, and asking questions.

"Is this you?" Blaine asks, pointing to a framed photo on the wall of me with my grandfather.

I walk over to stand next to him, a smile appearing on my face at the memory.

"Yeah, I was in ninth grade, and it was 'come as your hero' day, so I went as my grandpa."

I chuckle to myself, remembering his face when I came down the stairs in stone khakis and a sweater vest. My grandma even managed to find some glasses similar to his, and he was rendered speechless for possibly the first time in his life.

Blaine's face softens. "Will you tell me more about him?"

"He was such a prankster. Always telling jokes and pulling pranks on people. There was this time he installed this small speaker thing in the cupboard, like the kind you get out of greeting cards where you record your own message. Anyway, he recorded himself saying, 'Margaret, bring me more snacks', so whenever my grandma would open the cupboard door, that message would play out and she couldn't figure out where it was coming from." I laugh, remembering how mad she would get. "You would hear her shouting, 'Ernie, get off of your ass and get your own damn snacks!'"

Blaine laughs. "Ha! I'd never have thought to do something like that."

"Me neither." I walk over to the couch and sit down, tucking my feet under me. "When I was about five years old, he blew up his vegetable patch. I'd come here during summer break while my parents were at work, and one day we were playing in the yard with this science experiment kit I'd gotten for my birthday, but he decided to take it a step further. I can't remember what he used exactly, but cabbage ended up all over the yard. He claimed it was an accident, but I think he knew exactly what he was doing."

Blaine's eyes are wide, a matching smile on his face. "Wow, he sounds like a really fun guy."

I nod. My grandfather was an incredible man.

"He was so much fun, but he was so caring, too. He was besotted with my grandma. Every Thursday, without fail, he'd go to the store and bring home a bouquet of flowers, and Sunday was the day they always had a dance."

"A dance?"

"Yeah, he loved Elvis. He used to say to me, 'Alex, if there's only one thing I can teach you, it's that the King is the King of music, not just rock and roll, and don't let anyone tell you differently.'" I shake my head to ward off my emotions as my heart starts to feel heavy in my chest. "I still have all of his vinyl. We'd sit and listen to them together, and we'd both sing along as I did a jigsaw or some coloring. He and my grandma would dance to 'Can't Help Falling in Love' every Sunday after dinner, and he'd sing along to the words to her. They used to say it was their song."

Jacob and I used to stand by the door and watch. Even as kids, we knew their love was special. We were so lucky to have them in our lives, helping us through the grief of losing our parents and grow into our identities as we became teenagers and into adulthood. Giving us the space to be who we wanted to be with no limitations. We owe them every-thing, and it still hurts, even after two years, to know that I'll never get to hear my grandfather's cackle when he pulled another prank or my grandma complaining when he'd leave his dirty socks on the stairs.

A lump forms in my throat, and I blink away the tears forming in my eyes. I miss them so fucking much.

Fingers gently tip my chin up, and my heart clenches. Blaine's face is filled with so much love that a stray tear falls down my cheek.

"He sounds like an incredible man. I'm sorry that I won't get to thank him for raising such an amazing guy." He presses a soft kiss against my lips.

"He would have loved you," I admit.

Blaine's eyes widen slightly in surprise. "Really?"

"When you were drafted, he was all, 'This Blaine Olsen kid is going to be great for the Thunder; he's fast, he's nimble, he's got a killer wrist shot. I have a really good feeling about this.' He was in awe of you, thought you were incredible."

He gives me an aw-shucks grin, tucking his chin to his chest, fiddling with the strings on his sweatpants.

"He would have been so honored to meet you. He might have talked your ear off and given you some pointers from his armchair, but he would've loved you." I smile. The last game he watched before he passed away was the night Blaine scored his very first NHL hat trick. He jumped from his chair, pumping his fists into the air with joy.

It feels like kismet to be sitting here in this living room with Blaine, talking about my grandpa, when he was the one who spoke so highly of him for years at this exact place.

He sits down next to me, wrapping an arm around my shoulders and pulling me into him. I rest my head on his chest, listening to the soft thud of his heartbeat, and wrap my arms around his waist.

"Thank you for sharing him with me," he murmurs into my hair.

I press a gentle kiss to his pec through his t-shirt.

"Will you tell me about Christmas with your family? Is there anything I should be prepared for?"

I feel his laugh vibrate through his chest. "Christmas has always been pretty chaotic. We'd have both my grandparents over, my mom's sister, and my cousin. Usually, Elliot and I would be running around the house with our new hockey sticks, and most of the time we'd be wearing full gear, too. You could guarantee that we'd end up breaking something, no matter how much my mom yelled at us to be careful."

I look up at him. The image of a young Blaine and Elliot dressed head to toe in hockey gear, surrounded by broken vases and ornaments, runs through my mind. I can't help but laugh.

"Didn't you go to the same college, too? What did your parents do then? You weren't able to travel with hockey, right?"

He nods. "My parents would visit us on campus for Christmas; they would rent a house or stay in a hotel, but once we went pro, Elliot was in Vancouver and I was here in Chicago, so they would alternate… One year they would visit El and the next they'd visit me. We usually get a couple of days off for Christmas, but we'd be exhausted, so we settled for FaceTime."

"That sounds tough on your parents… I bet they're excited to be able to spend it with the both of you for the first time in a few years."

"Yeah it was. They often felt guilty about whichever one of us was on their own, but we would spend it with our teammates or something. Like with Zach—his parents do the same with his brother, Brody, so they'll alternate between New Jersey and here, but he's lucky that his parents live in Chicago, so it's not as bad. He'll be coming tomorrow because his parents have gone to Jersey, but yeah, being able to spend Christmas with both my parents and my brother for the first time in like, six years, is pretty cool."

We both look up when Jacob walks in holding his overnight bag. He's dressed in navy chinos and a light gray knit sweater decorated with white snowflakes.

"I'm ready." His smile is shaky from nerves.

I peel myself away from Blaine's warm embrace and walk over to my brother, giving his elbow a gentle squeeze in reassurance. We're staying at Blaine's apartment tonight and tomorrow night—at Blaine's request—so we can have a few drinks and not have to worry about anything. It took some convincing, but as soon as Blaine mentioned that his apartment building has a spa, Jacob quickly agreed.

I pass by him to slip on my shoes and collect my own bag, and when I turn to face the door, Blaine's standing there with a wide grin and rubbing his hands together.

"Are you ready for a crazy Olsen Christmas?"

Twenty-Five

Blaine

"Blaine! I need your muscles!" my mom shouts from the kitchen.

I came home from collecting Alex and Jacob to find my mom had taken over my kitchen, and it's been like a whirlwind since I walked through the door. Elliot's standing next to her, dipping his finger into the bowl of cookie dough whenever she's not looking or busy talking to Jacob. My dad's at the breakfast bar on his iPad, and Alex is decorating the cake they brought with them.

My kitchen has never looked so busy, and there's currently stuff out on the countertops that I didn't even know I owned.

"I need you to knead this for me." She steps out of the way and points to a large mountain of wet dough on the counter.

"Knead it?" I ask.

Um. What the fuck is kneading?

I ball my hands into fists and start slamming my knuckles into the dough.

"No, no, no!!" Mom wails, flapping her hands in the air like a little bird.

"Let me help, Nicola." Jacob appears at my side, shooing me out of the way with his perfectly manicured hands, and starts doing something with the dough, which I assume is kneading.

"Thank you, Jacob, honey. I've always tried to get my boys to be more responsible in the kitchen, because it's not a good look to be twenty-seven and not know how to boil an egg." She throws a glare over her shoulder at me.

Jacob laughs, and it's the first time I've seen him relax. Those soft, delicate features often turn hard whenever me and the boys are around. Alex told me his brother had a tough time in school with some guys on the hockey and football teams but didn't elaborate. I hope he can see that we're not like the douche canoes he knew years ago.

After being banished from my own kitchen, I take a seat next to my dad at the breakfast bar and watch as Alex adds the finishing touches to the cake.

My heart fills at the sight. Could this be a new tradition? It should scare me that I've known Alex for less than a month and I'm already envisioning him as a permanent fixture in my future.

Christmas, Thanksgiving, birthdays, and weddings.

He fits in, like a piece of a puzzle that I didn't know was missing.

"You okay there, kid?" Dad says quietly, bumping his shoulder with mine.

I turn to the man everyone says I look like. "Can I ask you something?"

He nods.

"How did you know Mom was the one?"

My dad glances over at my mom and smiles. The content, happy-as-fuck smile of someone who is deep in love. "She made me feel like I could be myself without fear of judgment. She made me laugh, always listened to me, and supported me without fail, and when we were apart, it was like I didn't feel whole. Like I was missing a part of myself. It was also like she was in tune with me; she could pick up how I was feeling without me saying a word, and there was a level of trust that I hadn't felt with anyone else before."

I look over to Alex, taking in his bright smile and the way his blue eyes sparkle when he laughs. I absorb my dad's words, thinking back to my previous relationships. I didn't feel an ounce of any of those things. I didn't feel like they listened, supported me, or that I could be my true self. Alex saw right through the playboy bravado I was showing the world from the very first moment. He always listens so intently to everything I have to say, even when I'm complaining about some nonsense on TV or a shit play that happened during a game. He makes me laugh, and there's never once been that feeling of distrust.

My stomach begins to knot at the thoughts running rampant in my mind.

Am I falling for him?

The thought doesn't make me feel as anxious as it once would have. If anything, it makes my chest warm.

Hours later, our bellies are full of my mom's signature Christmas Eve meal of honey glazed-salmon, potatoes, and vegetables, and we laze on the couch and watch movies. Elliot and my parents head back to his apartment with the promise they'll be back bright and early, and Jacob heads off to one of the spare rooms. I switch off the Christmas tree lights and the TV before taking Alex's hand and leading him down the hallway to my room. The moon shines bright in the sky, casting a perfect glow through the floor-to-ceiling windows. Alex walks over to stand in front of them, staring out at the lake. The water is calm and peaceful, a far cry from the rabid beat of my heart.

"It's so beautiful up here," he whispers.

I walk up behind him, wrapping my arms around his waist, and rest my chin on his shoulder.

"Yeah, it was my favorite view... Until you."

He turns his head, his cheek brushing against mine, our lips only a breath away.

"Yeah?"

"Yeah." I kiss him, loving how his body melts back into me. I bask in the feel of his pillowy lips, how his tongue meets mine stroke for stroke. The warm heat of his mouth.

He turns in my arms, and a low groan rumbles from the depths of my throat as his erection rubs against mine.

We stand there in the moonlight, a collision of desperate tongues and roaming hands, separating only briefly to remove our shirts before our mouths crash together again.

I reach down to cup his ass, giving the perfect globes a firm squeeze, making him moan.

"I need you naked," he demands.

I simply nod.

Because I'm unable to deny the most amazing man I've ever met anything he wants.

Maybe I'm already way past falling.

Twenty-Six

Alex

Blaine Olsen is the sexiest man I have ever seen.

He's got muscles on top of muscles. The way his biceps flex as he pushes his jeans down, taking his boxers with them, makes me want to get down on my knees and worship him. His thick cut thighs and strong calves are covered in a dusting of hair, and the light from the moon creates the most exquisite shadows in the grooves of his abdomen.

It's like every single time I see him naked, my mind short-circuits.

And his cock?

Fuck, my mouth goes dry at the sight.

I want to explore every inch of his body with my lips, my tongue, my hands. I want to lose myself in him, and only come up for a gasp of air so I can dive right back in.

"You're unreal," I confess.

Blaine's lips twitch, morphing into a sexy grin. His

fingers wrap around his hard length, giving it a slow, sensual pull.

"You're still wearing too many clothes, Alex."

I glance down at my jeans, where the visible outline of my own erection is straining against the denim, and a small wet patch is beginning to form from where I'm leaking. I make quick work of shedding the rest of my clothing, leaving them in a pool by my feet.

Blaine's eyes trail the length of my body. His stare warms every inch of my skin, making me feel like I'm on fire, and when his gaze stops on my cock, it gives an excited twitch.

I lick my lips with the tip of my tongue, watching his hand continue to tease what I so desperately want. I take a step forward, stopping in front of him, and drop down to my knees.

My hands run up over the curve of his calves, my thumbs kneading the strong muscle before moving up to ghost over the delicate skin on the back of his knee. The hitch of his breath causes my cock to give another excited twitch, but I continue to ignore it.

Because delayed gratification can be a magical thing.

My hands make their way up higher, moving around to touch the front of his thighs, gliding over the smooth skin covering defined muscles, watching as they flex and tense when my thumbs meet his groin. I dig my fingers into the side of his glutes, gently brushing my thumbs over the sensitive skin of his tight sac.

"That's not enough, Alex, I'm going to lose my mind if you don't touch my cock soon," he growls, his fists are clenched at his side, like it's taking every ounce of strength to stop him from grabbing me.

I lean in, flicking the tip of my tongue teasingly over the slit on the angry, plump head, lapping up the small, pearly drop of pre-come from the tip. A satisfied hum rumbles in my chest from the heady taste, and when I look up at Blaine, his nostrils are flaring and his jaw is clenched. His eyes are filled with so much heat, like I've just poured gasoline on the inferno that's currently burning wildly inside of him.

Wrapping a hand around the thick base of his cock, I take the swollen head into my mouth, swirling my tongue around and massaging the sensitive glans.

"Fuck, Alex. Your mouth is heaven," Blaine moans.

So is your dick, I mentally reply.

I respond by humming, relishing as the vibrations cause another moan to escape Blaine's lips.

Stretching my lips wide around him, I take him as deep as I can before pulling off with a wet pop. I do it over and over again while gently cupping his heavy sac.

Blaine's fingers grip my hair tight, and I relax my jaw as his hips begin to thrust, allowing him to fuck my mouth, not caring about the saliva starting to seep from the corners of my mouth or the water leaking from my eyes.

"Fuck!" he yells.

He pulls out and pinches the head of his cock with his fingers. "Your mouth is too good, but I want to be inside of you when I come. Get on the bed."

With a satisfied grin, I do as instructed and settle on my stomach, pushing my ass up teasingly in the air and giving it a little wiggle.

I wince slightly when his hand connects with my ass,

hard enough to leave a mark, and then gives my cheeks a firm squeeze before spreading them apart.

"Your hole is one of my favorite places to be," he admits, and the next thing I know, his tongue is tracing the puckered skin.

"Blaine," I whine, pushing my hips up to try and get closer.

Thwack.

Another crack of his palm meets my flesh.

"Stop rushing me. I wanna take my time so I can enjoy the taste of you," he demands.

I grind my achingly hard length against the sheets, seeking relief. My eyes roll to the back of my head from the rough sensation of his stubble against my skin and the sheets against the underside of my cock—combined with Blaine's wicked tongue spearing inside my hole, I'm on the edge of oblivion. His grumbling voice sends vibrations up my spine while murmurs a mix of *fucking delicious, my favorite, this is mine, you are mine.*

And I am his. Completely and wholly.

Gripping onto the bed sheets, my body trembles at his heavenly assault.

"Please, Blaine," I moan. "I need you."

With his fingers still buried deep inside me, he moves up my body and flicks his tongue over my ear lobe, tugging it between his teeth as his cock grinds against my crease.

"You want me to fuck you?"

I give a shaky nod. "Please."

"You want me to fuck you so hard you can barely sit tomorrow?"

I nod again, whimpering.

"My fucking pleasure," he growls.

He removes his fingers, and I let out a cry at the loss.

My entire body quivers with need. I'm so desperate for release, but at the same time, I want this heightened sensation to last forever.

The crinkling sound of foil ripping followed by the click of the lube bottle cap opening filter through the blood pounding in my ears. He applies the lube to my hole and then yanks my hips up, pulling me onto my hands and knees. I bite down on my lower lip to stop myself from moaning too loudly when the thick head of his cock is met with resistance from the tight ring of muscle.

Blaine smooths his hands up my spine as he pushes in inch by slow inch, pulling out before pushing back in again, making me feel everything as he eases into me. When he's deep inside to the root, his balls pressing up against my taint, he leans over me, his hot breath panting in my ear causes me to shiver. It feels amazing.

"I love being inside of you, how you take every inch of me so perfectly. It's like you were made for me."

I angle my head up to face him, taking his lips in a desperate kiss. Our tongues tangle in aggressive strokes as he begins to piston his hips, his cock hitting my prostate with perfect precision, causing my toes to curl up tight. I can feel every inch of him pulsing inside of me.

The room fills with the sound of his balls slapping against me with every thrust and our ragged breaths between ravenous kisses.

There is nothing, and no one, that could diminish the sizzling chemistry between us.

Blaine moves to take my cock in his hand, stroking me.

Sweat trickles down my neck, and my orgasm sizzles at the base of my spine. "I'm gonna come," I moan.

Blaine presses his lips against the shell of my ear, his tickling breath only adding fuel to the fire when he whispers, "Come for me, baby."

I don't need to be told twice.

My balls draw up, and with a strangled moan, I spill into his hand and onto his sheets. My muscles ripple around his solid flesh.

"Fuck! Alex!" Blaine roars.

His thrusts become unsteady, and another wave hits me when he comes.

I'm gasping for breath, and my heart is beating like a crazed drummer in my chest. Blaine falls next to me; one strong leg lays heavy across mine. I open my eyes to take in this gorgeous man, his chest rising and falling in quick concession, his arm covering his eyes. His lips part as he, too, tries to retrieve as much oxygen as possible.

How is this man real? He's fucking perfect.

"Alex?"

I look up at him.

He takes my face between his palms. His eyes are filled with something that looks a lot like love before he says with a bashful grin, "You should get two minutes for tripping, 'cause I've fallen for you."

And my heart melts because only Blaine could confess his feelings with a cheesy line.

This perfect man, with the kindest heart. And I think I may have fallen too.

Twenty-Seven

Alex

Blaine wasn't kidding when he said Christmas with his family was chaotic.

His parents and Elliot arrived Christmas morning at nine, armed with a mountain of gifts and singing Christmas carols at the top of their lungs—badly. Jacob and I helped his mom with the food while Blaine, his dad, Elliot, and Zach watched the football game.

It turned out Zach's best friend, Carter, was the defensive end for Denver, and the big guy sat there anxiously chewing on his nails whenever the defense was on the field. By the end of the game, his hair was sticking up all over the place from the number of times he'd run his fingers through it.

Blaine had absolutely spoiled us with gifts, my favorite being a beluga whale experience at Shedd Aquarium, but the biggest surprise was the photo Blaine insisted on doing.

As he didn't want to be in the photo, Jacob did the honors, and we all stood in front of the perfectly decorated Christmas tree, his parents standing to Blaine's right while he wrapped his arm around my shoulders, and Elliot and Zach were next to me.

He posted it on his Instagram with the caption:

Happy Holidays! I had an amazing day with my loved ones. Hope you all had a great day, see you on the ice!

He also included a silly outtake Jacob had taken where his dad was dipping his mom like in a ballroom. Blaine must have said something funny because I was laughing and he was wearing the biggest smile, while Elliot jumped on Zach's back, his hand to his forehead like he was looking in the distance, and Zach stuck his tongue out.

The most special thing in that photo was the way Blaine was focused only on me as he held my hip protectively. His smile was soft, and his eyes sparkled with love.

I find myself staring at the photo on several occasions throughout the day, still unable to believe this beautiful man wants to be with me.

It had been such a nice day, and the first time we'd celebrated the holidays since my grandparents passed.

But now the festive cheer was coming to an end, and so was the high I've been on as my phone vibrates.

"I've just received another one," I sigh, tossing my phone down on the counter.

"What? Another message?" Jacob asks from the other side of the kitchen.

I nod and read out one of the many Instagram DMs I have received since Blaine tagged me in the photo. "This one says, 'Do you realize he's only with you because you're shiny and new? He will soon get bored.'"

Jacob scowls. "What the hell is wrong with some people?"

I click on the profile and the bio reads *Caitlin, Chicago Thunder #80. CEO of the Blaine Olsen Fan Club* with a bunny emoji. The photo shows the back of a red-haired girl wearing a B. OLSEN jersey.

"They're apparently fans."

"That's no excuse; Blaine's personal life is none of their business."

Another defeated sigh escapes me as I block yet another account.

I know he's right. Do they think they can pretty much bully me into breaking up with him or something? It's borderline harassment.

"Have you told him?"

I shake my head. "He's about to go on a road trip, and won't be back until late on New Year's Eve. I don't want to risk ruining his game."

My brother frowns. "He needs to know, Alex."

"I know, and I'll tell him at some point, but it's not something I wanna mention when he's about to go on the road."

Plus, maybe it's naive of me, but I'm hoping the messages are just a fluke, and these people will soon get bored when they realize they're not getting a rise out of me.

I don't want to worry Blaine for nothing. They must know how pathetic they look sending abusive messages to a player's other half.

Jacob gives me a pointed look, letting me know he's not buying it, but thankfully drops it. We have a busy day ahead with custom orders for birthdays, a wedding, and several new year's parties, and the moment we open the bakery, it's non-stop. People line the streets to get their hands on our Christmas-themed menu before it disappears in a few days, and when my best friend walks through the door, I'm overcome with joy.

"Ho, ho, hoes, baby!" He grins, holding his arms out wide.

I walk around the counter and wrap my arms around him in a tight hug.

"How was your Christmas?" I ask.

"Good, me and my sister didn't kill each other, and my mom didn't burn down the kitchen, so I'd say it was a success."

I chuckle at his unabashed grin.

When we were in college, Nate would return to campus after the holidays with so many stories. Most of them involved his mom setting something on fire, whether it was food or a dish towel, and it didn't help that Nate and his sister Sophie had quite a rocky relationship. He once returned home with a black eye after she'd thrown something at him in a fit of rage.

"But how was your Christmas with the Olsen clan?" Nate rests his forearms on the counter. "I saw the photo he posted." He wiggles his brows.

"It was really nice. His parents are great, they made us

feel welcome".

"And Blaine?"

I tuck my chin to my chest, trying to hide my flushed cheeks as I remember his admission on Christmas Eve: *You should get two minutes for tripping, 'cause I've fallen for you.*

My heart swelled to triple its size in my chest. It was cheesy as hell, but it took me back to all those cheesy pick-up lines he used on me when we first met. So now every time I close my eyes, I'm reminded of his face. The way his eyes crinkled at the side; his smile so wide from joy, I would be surprised if his cheeks didn't ache.

"What?" Nate asks with a bright smile. "Tell me what just made you smile like that, 'cause I like it. I fully support whatever it is."

I chew on the inside of my lip, my stomach twitching with nerves. "He told me he's fallen for me."

My best friend's face lights up.

"Shut the fuck up, are you serious?" He wraps his arms around me again in a tight hug, lifting me off my feet. "I'm so fucking happy for you."

I thank him, suddenly feeling shy.

"So, are you two official now?"

"I don't know, we haven't said the words or put a label on it, but I'm not seeing anyone else, and I don't think he is either…" My words drift off.

Is putting a label on it important? My gut feeling says we're exclusive and given how smitten and possessive Blaine seems to be, I doubt he'll be seeing anyone else.

"So now that you're like a WAG or a HAB or whatever it is, you can hook me up with the cute goalie." He rubs his chin as his head tilts to the side, drifting off into his thoughts. "I bet he can do the splits… I've never had sex with someone who can do the splits."

I snort. "You're impossible."

"You love me." He winks.

X

The mid-morning sun casts a warm glow through the full-length windows, gently waking me up as I try to stretch my aching body without waking Blaine, who's snoring softly beside me. His thick arm lays heavy over my stomach, like a protective band restricting my movements.

I turn my head on the pillow to take him in. His full lips are slightly parted, his brown lashes fan across the top of his cheeks, his hair is a wild mess of curls against the crisp white pillowcase.

He's beautiful.

Beautiful might be the wrong word for someone like Blaine, but he is. He's beautiful in a rugged way.

Carefully lifting his arm so I don't wake him, I slip out of bed, retrieving and putting on my discarded boxers in the process, before gently tiptoeing into the bathroom to do my business. I take in my appearance in the mirror; a big purple love bite sits at the crook of my neck where it meets my shoulder, my skin flushed with a post-orgasmic glow.

I look *happy*.

I haven't looked like this in a long time.

Blaine's still fast asleep when I step out of the bathroom, his arm raised above his head on the pillow, showcasing his wide biceps and the hair of his armpits. I just wanna go over and shove my face in them and inhale his delicious, manly scent. The sheet rests just above his hips from where he's rolled onto his back, displaying those magnificent abs. His broad chest rises and falls lightly as he breathes.

He's a sight to behold, and I have to physically pinch myself to remind myself this isn't a dream.

I leave him to sleep for a little longer and head into the kitchen to make coffee and investigate the contents of his fridge. Eggs, bacon, mushrooms, tomatoes, Swiss cheese… An omelet is healthy for an athlete, right?

Finding a chopping board, I begin to prep the ingredients, stacking them neatly on a plate before working on whisking the eggs.

"Why didn't you wake me?"

The gravelly voice makes me jump, causing the egg I was about to crack into a bowl to fly out of my hand and splat against the wall.

"Shit, I'm sorry," I apologize, quickly grabbing a wet cloth to wipe down the wall before turning back to Blaine. "You were exhausted and I didn't want to wake you. I figured it's not often you can get to sleep in during the season."

His sleepy face fills with a soft smile, and he rubs his tired eyes with the heel of his palm as he pads toward me barefoot and naked as the day he was born.

I take in his god-like form. His long, thick cock is half hard, hanging heavy between his legs and slapping against his equally thick thighs as he walks closer to me.

"Good morning, gorgeous!" He tilts my head up with two fingers beneath my chin and closes his mouth over mine.

A low moan escapes from deep in my chest as our

tongues collide, wet and hot. I wrap my arms around his neck and hear the chopping board being pushed across the counter before he lifts me up to sit on the cool surface. He stands between my legs, his fingers digging into my ass.

"Mm, I love mornings with you," he murmurs, nipping my bottom lip with his teeth.

He raises his head to reveal that delicious smirk across his lips as he taps my hips. "Lift."

I place my hands on the countertop to push myself, and he pulls my boxers off, tossing them over his shoulder. He runs his warm hands up the front of my thighs, his thumbs getting dangerously close to my erection before moving back down to the inside of my knees. "You're fucking sexy."

I practically beam under his praise, feeling my cheeks heat.

He crouches down so he's level with my crotch, his breath teasingly ghosting the head of my cock.

"Please," I gasp between labored breaths.

Blaine licks a bead of precome from my tip, looking at me with hooded eyes, the corner of his lips tilting up. "Please, what?"

"Please suck me."

"Mmm," he hums, leaning in and lapping at my balls with his talented tongue before licking a strip from the base of my cock to the swollen head. "Seeing as you asked so nicely."

Blaine lifts both of my legs to rest over his shoulders and brings my hips closer. A strangled moan escapes me when he takes me into his hot mouth, hollowing his cheeks as he sucks and takes me to the back of his throat.

"Holy fuck," I grunt when he swallows around me.

My head falls back, hitting the cabinet doors behind me, fingers gripping onto the edge of the countertop so tightly that I'm sure my knuckles are turning white. The vibrations of his moans are making me lose my mind. He continues to bob his head, lavishing at my cock like he's a starved man.

There's no way I'm going to last much longer. Not with the way I keep hitting the back of his throat or how his fingers knead my heavy balls.

"Blaine!" I gasp.

Our eyes lock, and I trace my fingertips over his stretched lips, over his cheekbone, and push away the hair that's fallen on his face. My body begins to tremble from the pleasurable onslaught, my balls drawing up tight, and Blaine's name echoes through the otherwise silent room on a moan. My release hits the back of his throat, and he swallows every last drop.

"Mmm," he murmurs, lazily licking the remnants of my come from the head of my cock. "My favorite kind of breakfast."

When he stands to full height, he wraps his arms around me, pulling me close and holding me as I regain my composure.

"I wish I didn't have to leave you," he whispers. "I don't wanna go to this team-building thing, and I don't wanna go on the road. I wanna spend every minute of every day with you."

I press kisses to his lips, letting him know without words that I feel the same, even though it terrifies me.

Twenty-Eight

Blaine

There are around twenty of us gathered in a conference room, each wearing a slightly concerned expression.

"Do you know what this is about?" I ask Ethan.

He shakes his head. "No, I asked Colleen, but she's being very tight-lipped about it. All she said was that it's going to be fun."

I narrow my eyes. "Fun for Colleen could be anything."

Hell, we could be going shopping for all we know.

His lips twitch, fighting off the laugh that I know he's holding back. "Let's just wait and see, eh?"

We received an email last week from the Thunder PR team stating that we'd be filming a segment for the 'Off the Ice' series on the team's YouTube channel, and to ensure we wear comfortable team attire, but that was it. There was no information on what it was, where it would be, or what we would be doing. Just what to wear and to be in this conference room after morning skate.

We're heading off on a five-day road trip tomorrow, so the last thing any of us want to do is spend more time away from our loved ones.

Hell, I've never grumbled about that before...

"Hey, boys. Thanks for coming today." Colleen smiles, walking to the front of the room holding a clipboard. "You're probably wondering why you're all here today. We wanted to do something fun for the holidays, so the latest segment we're doing for the channel is an escape room!" Colleen grins evilly as we all let out collective groans. "You're going to be split into four teams of five and the first team to escape the room in the fastest time, wins."

Elliot raises his hand like a pre-schooler. "But what do we get if we win?"

Several guys nod, muttering their agreement.

"Yeah, I wanna know the prize before I agree to do it. I don't wanna be locked in a fucking room with four of these dickheads for a shit prize," Petford grumbles under his breath.

I roll my eyes.

Can't the dude be fucking nice for once?

"The team that wins will get to choose the team mascot..."

There's a moment of silence, so quiet you could hear a pin drop, before a chorus of shocked gasps.

"We're getting a team dog?" Elliot asks.

Colleen laughs and nods. "Yes! So whoever wins will have the honor of choosing which dog from the rescue center will become the Thunder mascot."

"It's fucking on!" I rub my hands together excitedly, like a happy otter.

"I wanna choose the dog!" Mitch whines.

"I better fucking win!" Elliot grins over at me, bouncing on his toes.

We'd always wanted a dog growing up, but our mom constantly refused, saying she didn't want anything distracting us from hockey. Now, with my schedule being so hectic, it'd be cruel and unfair for me to get one, only to end up having to put it into doggy daycare every time I go on the road.

"Also, I must remind you that we will be filming everything, so please be mindful and use respectful language so we don't have an entire episode of beeps."

Oh, this is going to be so much fun.

We head downstairs and board a waiting bus that takes us forty minutes north of Chicago to an old, derelict school that's apparently been converted.

"Before we head inside, I'm going to draw names from an online generator to assign your teams," Colleen announces, retrieving her iPad from her bag. I get the dream team: Ethan, Mitch, Zach, and Elliot.

I high-five Zach and throw my arm around Elliot's shoulders. "We're gonna get the fucking dog!"

"I wanna call it Bruce!" Elliot slaps my stomach.

I let out an oof and rub my hand over the spot. "Bruce?"

"Yeah! Like Bruce Wayne, duh!" He rolls his eyes.

"But he hasn't got anything to do with Thunder. Surely we should call it something like…"

"Thor," Zach chimes in.

I point finger guns at the d-man. "Yeah!"

Ethan shakes his head. "Let's not get ahead of ourselves. We'll worry about naming the dog once we've won the damn thing."

"Okay, mister sensible," Elliot mimics.

We're directed to the room we'll be escaping from. It's done up like a prison cell, except much nicer than the ones you see on TV. There's carpet on the floors, several photos on the walls, a cabinet, desk, toilet, and sink, and a bed in the far corner of the room. It's dark, meaning it's hard to see, and given that there are five of us in here, the room suddenly feels very small.

"The previous inmate planned his escape but was moved to a high-security prison yesterday. It's now up to you to escape within sixty minutes using the clues he's left inside the cell. There are several padlocks to unlock, which will lead you to further clues," the instructor explains. "If you need to get out at any point, wave at the camera, and I'll come get you. But once you're out, you cannot re-enter."

We all nod when he asks if we're ready to start, and the second the door locks, the lights go out and we're in complete darkness.

"Oh shit, I don't think I like this," Elliot mumbles beside me. I can sense he's fidgeting, and ends up bumping into me. He lets out a loud shriek. "Fuck's sake, Blaine, are you trying to kill me?"

"I didn't do anything! I was just standing here!" I argue back.

"Fuck, I just swore," I hear him slap his forehead. "Fuck, shit! Colleen, I'm sorry!" he shouts then mutters under his breath that Colleen is going to kill him.

I roll my lips, trying to stop myself from bursting into laughter.

"Shut it, Olsen," Ethan grumbles as the TV flickers on in the corner.

Oh man, here we go.

It seems like a long time before we manage to get the keys we need to get out of here, only to find out we still need to go through a tunnel.

"You can go in first." Zach playfully shoves me. "You're smaller than me."

I peek my head into the tunnel. It's fucking narrow. I have no idea how we're going to fit.

"We're gonna have to go on our hands and knees and crawl." I nudge Mitch forward. "It's your time to shine, rookie."

He lets out a defeated sigh, dropping down to crawl through it, and comes back with a piece of paper with an L and an A written on it, with some lines underneath.

Ethan takes over. "There's a theory behind this."

He explains how the number of lines equals where the letters are in the alphabet, then points to where similar marks are etched into the wall. "So up there you have A, C, E, and R."

The three of us look at him, dumbfounded as Ethan crouches down to where Mitch is still sitting cross-legged in the tunnel. "Is it five letters?"

"Yeah."

"Try 'clear'."

We wait as Mitch disappears back inside the tunnel to try the lock, then we hear a cheer.

"We're out! We're out!" he shouts.

"Puppy dog time!" Elliot pumps his fist in the air.

After a quick clap of excitement, we make our way through the tunnel one by one, only to find we're not out.

We're in another fucking room.

"For fuck's sake! We're never gonna get out of here. If we don't get to choose the puppy, I'm gonna be really sad, guys." Elliot crosses his arms over his chest and pouts.

I head to the computer in the corner and read the clue on the screen while I notice the login screen photo is the Loch Ness monster.

A place you would go on vacation.

Easy. I type in Scotland, and *voila*, the computer unlocks to reveal another clue.

Zach's shocked voice comes from behind. "How the fuck did you know that?"

"Dude, the monster!"

He laughs, shaking his head in disbelief. "What's the next clue?"

"It says, 'Take the time on the clock in twenty-four-hour time format, divide by the cell number, and multiply it by three.'"

It's signed by Coach Harris, so we know this has to be the last one.

Right?

We enter the number and the last door unlocks. We all cheer in celebration.

"Fuck yeah!"

We run out of the room and back to the waiting lobby, and standing there waiting is Coach. He's wearing a shit-eating grin on his face.

"Well, holy shit. I should have thought it would have

been you boys to escape first, eh?" He chuckles, then looks at Elliot, his eyes widening in alarm. "I thought you were gonna cry at one point."

"I nearly did, Coach." Elliot sniffs dramatically. "I nearly did."

I can't stop smiling because we're finally getting a dog, but I'm even happier that I can finally go home and spend time losing myself in Alex in more ways than one before I have to leave him again.

Twenty-Nine

Blaine

"Tequila me, por favor!" Elliot holds his shot glass high in the air.

Coach has given us the green light to celebrate tonight after our spectacular win in North Carolina, which saw Elliot get his sixth career shutout and Mitch get his first NHL hat trick.

The rookie's been bouncing off the walls ever since, his energy levels rivaling those of a golden retriever puppy. I feel sorry for Peyton, who's rooming with him tonight.

Kendrick pours the amber liquid into Elliot's glass, then tops up the rest of our glasses, purposely skipping Mitch— the kid really can't handle his liquor.

Our road trip started in Nashville yesterday, and thankfully we have an off day tomorrow with our flight leaving for Tampa around lunchtime. We play in a matinee game in Tampa the following day, then head straight to Miami, meaning we should be landing back in Chicago just before midnight on New Year's Eve.

This is the first trip where I'm counting down the days until I'm home because I really didn't want to leave Alex.

The more time we spend together, the harder it is to leave him, and even though we have FaceTime calls, it's not the same as being able to take his lips in a kiss or to breathe in the sweet grapefruit scent of his hair.

Fuck.

Who knew I would ever feel this sappy over someone? I never imagined feeling like this—it's like I'm missing a limb when I'm away from him. I used to love away games, being able to lose myself in someone that I wouldn't likely see again. But now?

Now I just want Alex.

I take my tequila shot with a grimace.

"You always make the same face; I don't know why you drink it," Ethan chuckles beside me.

"El wouldn't let me hear the end of it if I refused tequila."

He shakes his head and watches Elliot wave his lime slice around as he stamps his feet, his face screwing up from the bitter taste.

"How's things going with Alex?"

"Good, really good, actually." I settle back into my seat, angling my body slightly toward Ethan. "I was wondering if you could help me with something…"

Ethan raises a brow, "Sure, what's up?"

Lowering my voice for only Ethan's ears, I give a very brief overview of Alex and Jacob's business struggles and mention I've offered to help, but Alex is adamant on not taking a penny from me.

"I understand his reasons, but I wish he'd let me help. I feel kinda powerless, you know?" I sigh. It's hard to see them struggle when I could relieve them of that burden. "So I was wondering if we could ask Colleen if there was something we could do for the team channel? You know, something fun, like us decorating cookies? We could pay to use the bakery facilities…" I shrug.

Ethan's lips twitch. "You really like this guy, eh?"

I nod, my hand gripping the back of my neck. "Yeah, I do."

Ethan's usually stern features turn soft for a moment. "I'm sure Colleen would be up for that. We could go and speak with her when we're back; I know she's always looking for new ideas."

"Thank you, it means a lot."

Ethan gives my shoulder a squeeze. "Anytime. I'm glad it's working out for you, and he seems to have a positive effect on you, too. Don't think I haven't noticed how well you're playing recently."

I duck my chin to my chest, suddenly feeling vulnerable.

Have I mentioned praise from Ethan is like catnip?

Plus, I wasn't kidding when I told Alex that Ethan was my idol when I came to the Thunder, because he still is. He's one of the greatest guys I've ever known, both on and off the ice.

"Coach has noticed, too, so keep it up. If you keep your head down and your stats up, I think you'll be okay." He doesn't need to say the words because I know he means when it comes to the trade deadline.

He gives me a reassuring smile before standing up. "I'm gonna hit the hay," he announces to the group. "Make this your last one, and I expect to see you all at breakfast bright and early." He then looks at Mitch. "You better go back as soon as you've finished that one. I'm trusting you," he says, giving Peyton a pointed look.

A chorus of *Yes, cap* echoes, followed by Elliot shouting, "*Aye, aye, captain!*" while saluting.

I use Ethan's exit as an excuse to leave as well. My phone's been burning a hole in my pocket all night, wanting to call Alex before he goes to sleep. I text him, letting him know I'll call him in five and head across the street to our hotel.

The elevator seems to take a decade to arrive, and when the doors open on my floor, I quickly close the distance to my room. The second I'm in my room, I'm dialing Alex's number.

There's no controlling the smile that takes over my face when the call connects and his face fills the screen.

"Hey, baby."

"Hey, great game tonight!" He grins.

"Thank you." I sit down on the bed, leaning back against the headboard. "I fucking miss you, though."

"I miss you, too. I can't wait for you to be home."

"It feels like it's going to be the longest five days ever." I groan dramatically. "And by home, do you mean you'll be waiting for me at my apartment?"

I note the surprise in his eyes. "Well, I meant Chicago, but… I will."

"How very domestic of us, Alex."

"Do you hate it?"

"No, I actually like that a lot." Knowing Alex will be inside my house when I come back feels more like *home* than anything else ever did. It feels right.

"Are you on your own?" he asks, after a couple of seconds.

"Why? Wanna take advantage of me?" I wink.

He drags his teeth over his top lip, and even with the low lighting of his bedside lamp, I can see his blue eyes glistening with mischief. "Maybe."

"What would you do to me if you were here?"

He raises an eyebrow, and his lips twitch, fighting off a smile.

"What?" I feign innocence.

"Did you really just pull that line on me?" He grins.

Sitting upright, I quickly shed my hoodie and shirt, throwing them down onto the floor, then kicking off my sweatpants. Once I lean back, I move the phone down to rest against my thigh, giving Alex the perfect view of my erection straining against my briefs and the expanse of my chest. I grin at the sound of his breath hitching.

"So?"

He licks his lips, his eyes wide as they gaze over my body.

"Alex?"

"Sorry, what did you just say?"

"What would you do to me if you were here?"

He swallows hard. "I'd take off your boxers first."

My dick gives an excited twitch as I hook my thumb under the waistband. "Do you want me to take them off, Alex?"

He gives a shaky nod.

I move to pull them off, then stop at the last minute, letting the elastic ping back against my skin.

Alex groans. "Why did you stop?"

"Because I want to hear you say the words, and you're still wearing a shirt."

I'm suddenly looking at his bedroom ceiling and hearing the sound of sheets ruffling. When he reappears, sans shirt, his hair is messy and his eyes are wild with heat.

"Much better," I say.

"Good, now get them off," he orders.

"Fuck, I love this bossy side of you." His demanding tone goes straight to my dick, and once I remove my boxers, I let out a sigh of relief when my dick is finally free. I take my hard length in my hand, lazily stroking up and down, circling over the weeping head.

Alex doesn't even blink; he just licks his lips and watches my hand as I give my dick a squeeze.

"Fuck, I want you so bad," Alex whispers.

I angle my dick to my phone. "Open up."

He opens his mouth and brings his phone closer, so his mouth is all I see. I laugh, then let out a groan when he moves his phone to rest on his bedside table.

I watch avidly as he smooths his palm down his lean torso. The lighting from his bedside lamp showcases the subtle outline of muscle, and his brown nipples beg for my mouth.

He stands up, his crotch perfectly in line with the camera, and he pushes down his boxers. His hard cock springs into view, a pearly drop of precome beading at the red, angry tip.

"Fuck, Alex. I wanna taste you." My words come out strained.

He lies back on the bed, camera positioned just perfectly so that I can see his gorgeous face and that equally gorgeous cock. "Stroke it for me, slowly."

He wraps his fist around his hard length, following my instructions. He slowly pumps through the tight grip, and strokes over the tip. His chest rises and falls in quick pants, and his lips part on a whimper. "Blaine…"

"Fuck, baby, does it feel good?" I grip my cock, squeezing the head. I'm so close to blowing my load already.

He jerks his head in a nod. "Y-yeah."

Our eyes lock through the screen, our hands pumping our erections in rhythm, and I come the second Alex moans my name, watching his release spill over his stomach and hand.

We clean ourselves up, and when Alex reappears on the screen, his smile is sleepy.

"I hate away games now." I frown.

"Me too, but at least we can FaceTime every night."

"I know, but it's not the same as being with you and being able to fall asleep with you."

Alex's eyes go soft. "I've been counting down the days and hours until you're home since you left your apartment."

Fucking away games—now I definitely hate them.

Thirty

Blaine

The sound of the TV filters down the hallway as I open the door to my apartment, wheeling my suitcase behind me. Our flight was delayed by an hour, and I was worried that I wouldn't be able to ring in the new year with Alex, but I made it home with six minutes to spare.

Leaving my luggage by the door, I take off my jacket and toss it onto the kitchen counter when I pass, then stop in my tracks when I see Alex asleep on the couch. His arm is flung above his head, the other resting on his stomach next to his phone. ESPN is playing highlights of tonight's game, and the light illuminates the soft features of his face.

Quietly taking off my shoes, I crouch down in front of him and run my fingers through his hair. His long blond eyelashes cast a shadow across the top of his cheekbones, and I gently stroke my thumb over his cheeks, pressing a tender kiss to the corner of his mouth.

He looks so peaceful. I don't want to wake him, but at the same time, I've missed him so much the past few days that all I want is to see those beautiful blue eyes and kiss him at the stroke of midnight.

Alex stirs as I sit back on my haunches and watch when he blinks a few times.

"Blaine?" He croaks, his voice all sleepy and tired.

"Hey, baby." I smile, leaning in and capturing his lips in a kiss. "I'm sorry I'm late, our flight was delayed."

"It's okay," he says with a yawn. "What time is it?"

I tap the screen of his phone. "It's eleven fifty-nine."

His eyes sparkle when he smiles. "Can we watch the fireworks?"

"Of course." I nod, taking his hand when I stand. Leading him down the hallway, we enter my bedroom just as the first firework lights up the sky over the lake. I pull him into my arms and cradle his face with my hand, sliding my lips over his.

"Happy New Year, baby," I murmur against his lips.

"Happy New Year!" He wraps his arms around my neck. "This is gonna be our year."

He's right, and I lose myself in him as we make love for the first time while the night sky turns technicolor.

Hours later, I wake up to the sound of my apartment door slamming, followed by the sound of my brother's voice. My eyes flicker open, quickly checking it didn't wake Alex up, but thankfully he's still sound asleep, and I watch the soft rise and fall of his chest and the slight parting of his lips.

Those dark blond lashes resting on the top of his cheek.

My heart swells in my chest at how fucking gorgeous he is.

The door swings open, and my brother appears holding a white paper bag from our favorite sandwich shop. "Good morning, twinny! We've bought bagels—whoa!" Elliot sighs dramatically. "Blaine, what have I told you about having your dick out? You know I bring bagels on non-game day Sunday's."

"Shush," I whisper.

I carefully slip out of bed, trying not to jostle Alex, and pull on my pajama pants before leading Elliot out into the hall, closing my bedroom door behind me.

Zach's in the kitchen sorting through different-flavored Nespresso pods, and raises his chin in greeting as I walk in.

"You guys need to be quiet; Alex is still sleeping."

"Sorry, bud, we didn't know he would be here," Elliot knocks my shoulder with his fist, then his eyes widen in alarm. "Shit, I don't have a bagel for him. What would he like, and I'll go grab one."

I smile at my brother. He's such a good guy.

"He'd probably like the same as us."

"You got it." He fires finger guns at me. "Reid, get that coffee brewing for when I come back."

Zach gives another grunt, finally choosing a pod and shoving it into the machine.

Elliot jogs out the door, and I take a seat at the breakfast bar. I watch the tightness in Zach's shoulders as he scoops the unused coffee pods back into the glass jar I keep them in and how his lip curls in discomfort whenever he moves his right shoulder. He took another nasty hit into the boards during our game last night against Miami.

"Is your shoulder still hurting?" I ask.

He turns to face me, and nods, raising his left hand to run through his shaggy, dark hair. "Yeah, I slept like shit, too, because no matter what position I tried, there was pain shooting through it."

"What did Joe say?" Referring to our trainer.

"I saw him again this morning and he said I've pulled a muscle. Joe's worked on it but I think he's a bit concerned."

As the coffee machine finishes one cup, he hands the mug over to me before putting another pod in and starting it again.

I lift my head to the sound of soft footsteps coming from the hall. Alex appears, looking all sleepy and disoriented, his hair disheveled and sticking all over the place, a clear sign of what we got up to last night. He's wearing a pair of my sweats and one of my t-shirts, which looks huge on him.

Fuck, I feel so overwhelmed with emotions.

Happiness because of the sight of him and the fact he was here when I got home so I could ring in the New Year with him. But there's also fear.

An all-encompassing fear because of how hard I'm falling for him and how I want him to be here permanently scares the shit out of me.

Is there an accurate timeline you have to follow when it feels right in your gut?

"Morning, gorgeous." I smile brightly.

His cheeks flush as he heads toward me. I spread my legs where I'm sitting on the stool, and he steps into them, pressing a gentle kiss against my lips. It takes him a few moments to notice Zach, and the second he does, his face turns a deeper shade of pink.

Zach chuckles. "Hey, man."

"Hey, Zach. Sorry, I didn't know you were there." Alex waves shyly.

My best friend simply shakes his head, a soft yet sad smile on his face. "Don't sweat it. Would you like a coffee?"

"Yes, please."

Zach turns around to empty the jar of coffee pods onto the counter again.

"How did you sleep?" I press a soft kiss to the underside of Alex's jaw.

"Amazingly, your bed's like a cloud."

I laugh, nodding. "It is."

"Plus, having you next to me is nice." He wraps his arms around my neck. His eyes are still small and tired. "I only woke up because I rolled over to cuddle you and you were gone."

"I had an alarm that I had forgotten about." And just as my twinny senses tingle, Elliot bursts through the door like he's being chased by a pack of rabid dogs.

"Holy shit, you're never gonna guess what I just saw." Elliot's eyes go wide with glee. "A man walking a rabbit on a leash. It had a fucking harness on like a dog, and it was just hopping down the street like—" He starts hopping through the kitchen, still holding the white bag that contains Alex's bagel.

We all burst into laughter at his ridiculous re-enactment.

"Hey, sleepy head! I got you a breakfast sandwich!" Elliot hands over the paper bag. "It's a toasted sesame seed bagel with sausage, bacon, egg, and cream cheese." He counts the ingredients on his fingers. "It's cheesy good."

Alex's eyes widen slightly in surprise as he takes the bag

from my brother. He looks down at it for a moment before looking back up at Elliot, his eyes filled with gratitude. "Thank you; that's really kind of you."

Elliot shrugs, completely unaware of how much his thoughtfulness means to my man.

My man?

I shake my head, at war with myself at how natural it feels while part of my subconscious screams that it's too soon. But then, seeing the wonderment on his face at what would usually be deemed a small gesture?

It makes me so happy to see Alex getting along so well with those important in my life and I know that this will mean a lot to him because it does to me.

Zach makes everyone a cup of coffee, and we sit at the breakfast bar to dig into our bagels. He tells me how Carter is feeling ahead of his game tonight, which we will be watching over at Ethan's apartment for boys' night, while Elliot discusses what snacks he's hoping people will bring.

"Would you like to come tonight?" I turn to Alex.

He looks up to face me, surprised. "Really?"

I nod.

"I… I'd like that, thank you."

I can't help but smile. That bubbling sensation in my chest heightens, making me feel like I'm walking on the fucking moon, and I completely let go of the timing issue.

It's not too soon at all.

"What the fuck are these?" Elliot shrieks from the kitchen.

I glance over my shoulder to see him holding up a bag

of chips between his thumb and forefinger like it's a dirty jockstrap, his nose scrunched up in disgust. "Oyster mushroom chips? Who the heck bought oyster mushroom chips? Why would you even have mushrooms as chips?"

"Hey, don't knock 'em 'til you've tried them. Maria got them for me; they're like super food in the shape of potato chips." Kendrick gets up from the couch and walks toward the kitchen where Elliot's still standing with the bag in his hand as if it's some kind of deadly fungus.

Elliot quickly throws the bag of chips at Kendrick, then continues his pursuit of the selection of snacks. Ethan makes a kickass spread when he hosts boys' night: pizza, wings, a wide selection of meats, cheeses and olives on a charcuterie board, fresh fruit, potato chips. You name it, it'll be on the counter.

Elliot's eyes widen when he spots the box of cupcakes Alex made earlier.

"As the great Obi-Wan once said, *Hello there*." He opens the lid and takes a deep inhale. "Mmm, I can already smell the tears from an extra workout, and it smells divine."

He takes one out, and then, just as he's about to take a bite, Zach jumps up from his spot on the couch and practically runs to the counter. He's already had two since we got here just thirty minutes ago.

Elliot slaps his hand away from the box and points his finger. "Hey now, big guy, you've already had two, and while I know you're a growing boy, didn't ya mama teach you about sharing?"

I can sense Zach's pout from here, even with his back turned to me. The man's such a weakling for cupcakes or donuts.

"Aw, man. Don't pout; don't do the pout! You know I have no willpower when you pout." Elliot holds his uneaten cupcake out for Zach to take a bite. "Fine, have half of mine." Zach wastes no time taking a huge bite out of the cupcake, way more than half.

Alex chuckles beside me.

"What?"

He shakes his head, humor dancing in his eyes. "Nothing… I just… I guess I didn't expect you guys to be like this."

"Fun?" I smirk.

"Yeah." He laughs. "You don't really get to show much of your personality in interviews, I guess."

"And we're not really allowed to show ourselves completely," I add.

Elliot flops down next to me and points his thumb at me. "Mainly because he'd probably say something rude."

"No, I wouldn't."

"Uh, yes, you would," Elliot argues while eating what's left of his cupcake.

Ethan rolls his eyes, then leans into Alex. "I swear it's like I'm a dad to some overgrown toddlers."

Elliot's eyes light up. "Can I call you Daddy?"

Ethan throws his head back with a groan, covering his face with his hands, and when my eyes land on Alex, we burst into laughter.

We get comfortable as the game kicks off, and Zach goes silent as usual, chewing on the side of his nail as he watches his buddy out on the field.

Alex's phone vibrates in his pocket, and when he takes it

out and reads whatever is on the screen, I feel his body go rigid.

Another beat goes by until he quietly says, "Excuse me for a minute."

There's an uneasy feeling in the pit of my stomach when he gets up and heads down the hallway.

I let a few minutes pass by before I get up to follow him, finding him sitting at the far end of the hall in front of a huge window, his head looking down at his phone.

"Alex? You okay?" I ask.

He looks up, and when I see the expression on his face, it's like I've been sucker punched in the balls. There's sadness in his eyes, and his forehead creased with a frown. I crouch down in front of him, placing my hands on his hips.

"What happened?"

He takes in a shaky breath and closes his eyes for a beat before he speaks. "Since Christmas, I've been receiving some … uh … not so nice messages on Instagram…"

"Messages?"

"Yeah… I thought it was going to stop, but it didn't…" He hands over his phone. "They've been saying some pretty horrible things, and they're supposedly fans of yours…"

I take the phone from him, and that uneasy feeling is replaced with dread, then anger, as I begin to scroll through a few of the endless messages.

*Don't get too comfy. He's only with u to clean up his image. He'll soon get bored of u and come crawling back to my *kitten emoji* soon enough.*

Do u realize he's only with u because ur shiny and new? He will soon get bored of u

I don't understand why he's with u. He's a ten and ur a two at best.

U do realize he's using u, right? Who am I kidding, ur probs too stupid to know that ur not enough for him.

Tell Blaine I said hi, I'll be here waiting when he gets tired of u.

LOL imagine being the reason Blaine's career is going downhill. He's been underperforming these last few games because of u. If u actually cared about him, u would leave him because he's a better player when he's not dating u.

How does it feel to be a prop in his image clean-up so he doesn't get traded? As soon as the trade deadline has passed, he'll dump ur ass quicker than u can ask him to stay.

I feel sick to my stomach.

"You know none of this is true, right?" I look at Alex, pleading that he believes me and not this bullshit. My voice shakes with panic. "Yeah, when we met, I was in the shit and was told I had to clean up my image, but I'm not using you, I promise. You've made me wanna be a better person, you mean everything to me."

"I do." He nods, and my heart cracks when tears begin to fill his eyes. "I do believe you, it's just… it's horrible. It's constant, too. They send something almost every day and it's getting to the point where I don't know what to do. I block them, but they make another account… I don't know what they're expecting to achieve apart from breaking us up. I just don't understand how people can be so cruel."

Anger riles up inside of me, bubbling like a volcano ready to erupt. How fucking dare these people—so called *fans*—think they can try to interfere with my private life?

And coming after Alex? Completely un-fucking-acceptable. Part of me wants to message these people and give them a piece of my mind, but I know I'd have Hayden and Colleen on my ass quicker than I could retract my messages. How can I just sit by and let it happen, though?

"Is everything okay?"

I glance over my shoulder to see Ethan, worry laced in his eyes.

If there's one person who might be able to help, it'll be Ethan.

"You know that photo I posted at Christmas? Well, Alex has been receiving some pretty shitty messages."

He frowns. "What do you mean by shitty messages?"

I turn back to Alex, asking without words whether Ethan can read them. He gives a small nod and hands over his phone. Ethan's silent as he reads, the crease on his forehead deepening.

"Fucking assholes," he mutters as he hands the phone back to Alex.

"Any idea what we could do?" I ask.

Ethan rubs a hand over his face. "We could ask Kendrick if Maria still receives anything like it. I know she used to as it's not unusual for this shit to happen out of jealousy over someone else getting what they want."

Shit, I didn't even think about asking Kendrick.

Ethan spins on his heels and heads back down the

hallway to where Kendrick is sitting watching the game. We follow closely behind, and I take Alex's hand in mine, lacing our fingers together and giving it a gentle squeeze.

"I don't want this to carry on, I just gotta find the right way of dealing with it… If I do what I want to do, I'll end up in big trouble." I stop and take his face into my hands, pressing a gentle kiss to his lips. "Please don't let anything they've said get to you. I know it's easier said than done, but I fucking adore you, okay? I promise you, I'm not using you. I'd rather take out my eye with a broken stick than use you, even for a second."

He smiles, but it's still tinged with sadness. "I know, thank you."

We take a seat back on the couch and I open my arm up so he can curl into me. Ethan talks quietly to Kendrick, trying not to interrupt Zach's zone as the defense are out on the field.

Kendrick leans over and says, "Come over one night this week for dinner, 'kay? Maria will help you out." He gives Alex's shoulder a reassuring squeeze.

"Thank you." Alex smiles.

I kiss the top of his head, holding him protectively to my body.

I want to climb onto the roof and roar in anger over those who have upset him. Those who are supposed to be my fans, and don't appreciate that Alex actually makes me *better*.

And if I have my way, he'll be with me until I'm old and gray.

Thirty-One

Alex

The headlights of Blaine's Range Rover light up the street as he pulls up in front of my house.

We're going to Kendrick's tonight for dinner, so I can meet his wife. After the night at Ethan's, Kendrick kept to his word about the two of us going over to see if she has any advice for me.

"He's here; I'll see you in the morning," I call out to my brother.

"Have a nice night," Jacob shouts back from where he's curled up on the couch.

I pick up my duffel bag from the floor and hightail it out of the house and down the steps to the sidewalk. Snow crunches beneath my feet, and a cold shiver takes over my body when I slip into the passenger seat of Blaine's car.

He leans over the center console, pressing his lips to mine in a warm kiss. "Hey, baby."

I melt like butter.

"Hey," comes out all breathy.

He pulls away from the sidewalk and heads to Lakeview. "Maria's cooking her famous paella tonight; it's so fucking good."

He tells me about Maria—how Kendrick met her in college ten years ago and they've been married for six—but all the while, anxiety builds up inside of me.

I'd suggested to Nate that maybe I should delete all forms of social media, but his answer was that I shouldn't remove myself from social media just because some people can't handle the fact that I'm with Blaine. But I can't see any other option.

I care so much for him; hell, I'm falling in love with him. I just need to make sure I'm mentally strong enough to deal with what comes with being with someone like Blaine.

Thankfully, he doesn't notice my internal war, and we pull up in front of a three-story red brick home, surrounded by wrought iron gates. There's a warm, homely glow seeping from the windows, and my anxiety eases slightly at the sight. Blaine parks his car and takes my hand as we walk up the steps to the front door. He knocks on the black door twice, and moments later the door swings open to reveal a pint-sized woman with bright pink hair.

"Hey! I'm glad you could make it; come in." She steps aside to let us in.

I wipe my feet on the doormat and toe off my sneakers. She takes our coats and hangs them on a hook.

"You must be Alex." She opens her arms, and I have to crouch down to hug her. "It's so lovely to meet you. Adam's told me all about you."

I grimace, and she laughs.

"Nothing bad, silly." She pulls away and leads us through into the kitchen, where Kendrick's lurking near a pie. "You better not be touching that apple pie, mister."

Kendrick's head whips up, guilt written across his features. "I wasn't doing anything."

She wags her finger. "It's meant to be shared. You can't eat it all."

Blaine steps behind me and wraps his arms around my waist, resting his chin on my shoulder. Kendrick gets us drinks, and we watch in fascination as the pink-haired pixie whizzes around the kitchen.

As Blaine promised, her chicken and chorizo paella is divine. We talk about the upcoming games and playoff contention, and when we move onto the topic of the trade deadline rumors, Blaine goes tense, but Kendrick waves him off.

"You have nothing to worry about. Coach wouldn't trade his star forward. I have a feeling it'll be Petford, or someone like Tait. They're not really bringing in the points or adding value to the team. Tait is raking up the penalty minutes, and Petford is just an ass."

But I know Kendrick's reassuring words won't ease the underlying anxiety Blaine is feeling.

Maria dishes out another one of her staple dishes. "Tarta de manzana," she announces. "Basically apple pie. My Abuela used to make this every Sunday or for a special event."

"And it's my favorite." Kendrick grins.

Maria rolls her eyes lovingly.

We dig into the delicious pie dish, and Blaine's hand

remains fixed on my thigh as he demolishes the dessert within a few mouthfuls.

"Every time." He shakes his head with a satisfied groan. "You, Maria, are a saint to the food gods."

She flicks her pink bob with her hand. "And with compliments like that, you are welcome anytime, sweetie."

Kendrick stands and takes all our plates, rinsing them off in the sink before stacking them into the dishwasher. Blaine leans in, pressing a soft kiss under my ear.

"They're good people," he whispers.

Maria pats Kendrick on the ass as he bends over to fill one of the racks. "You always look so hot doing the dishes."

"I know." He stands to his full height, then leans down to press a kiss to her lips. "Thanks for cooking dinner, baby."

"They're wonderful," I reply to Blaine. "And she's really happy."

He nods. "She is, but she still deals with the same shit as you."

As if she's aware we're talking about her, she whirls around to face both of us, a large glass of white wine in her hand. "You." She points to me. "You come with me and Blaine," she says, facing my man. "You can go with Adam to the man cave for a while."

I turn to Blaine. His eyebrows crease in concern.

"Oh, sweetie. I'm not going to hurt him." She walks over and ruffles Blaine's hair. "You can have him back; I just wanna talk to him, spouse to spouse."

He opens his mouth to argue, but I interrupt. "It's okay."

When he looks at me, his eyes ask, *are you sure?*

I nod and press a kiss to his lips. I follow Maria through

the house to an impressive living room. The fire in the hearth crackles in front of a sectional couch, and when I sit down, I sink into the softest cushions.

"Adam mentioned you've been receiving some rather alarming messages recently," Maria begins, tucking her feet beneath her. "You don't have to tell me what they said, because I can imagine."

I sigh, running a hand through my hair.

"It's not that I don't trust Blaine, because I do, but it makes me question whether I'm good enough for him. Whether I'm strong enough *for him*."

I've spoken about these worries with Jacob and Nate, but they haven't been able to fully understand. Sometimes at night, I find myself scrolling through the bunny blogs. Reading through their theories of how Blaine is using me to avoid being traded. How his agent and Coach demanded he clean up his act or else he'd be traded, and how that conversation happened the day he met me.

It's hard not to begin allowing those negative thoughts to seep in. And while I trust Blaine…

What if he gets traded and he doesn't want to do long distance?

Her face turns sad.

"You know, I get it, literally. I've been with Adam since we were in college, about ten years now, and I still get messages from people trying to insinuate that he cheats. Every away game, I'll get some photoshopped image that's supposed to be him DMing them and asking to meet up. Little do they know that Adam tells me and shows me the shit they send him. I trust him wholly, but it still hurts. That someone is so jealous of your life that they want to hurt you because of who you love, and still call themselves fans." She shakes her head. "It baffles me, so I understand what you're going through, and I hate to say this won't be the end of it. If anything, it will probably become more frequent."

"Can I ask what kind of things they say to you?"

She takes a sip of her wine, then takes a deep, shaky breath. "Some are really awful messages, targeting me as a person. They'll send degrading comments about my appearance and my body, or they'll send stuff pretending that he's sent them explicit messages."

"I'm so sorry," I whisper.

How can people be so fucking cruel?

"I've got a fairly thick skin now, but every one of us knows what you're going through. It makes you feel like you shouldn't be on social media, that you need to distance yourself from the online world to stop the negativity, but it won't stop it. You shouldn't have to hide yourself because some idiotic people are jealous."

"How do you deal with it?"

"It's easier said than done, but I ignore it. I trust Adam with my life. I'm honest with him when I need reassurance because sometimes the negative gremlins in my brain get too loud, but even then, it's not because I'm doubting him as a person or as my partner. We're still human at the end of the day, but knowing that Adam's in my corner? Knowing he loves me no matter what the trolls say, and is always faithful to me?" She smiles, and it's filled with love. "It's what keeps me strong."

"Some of the things they've said…" I trail off, shaking my head. I rub my chest, trying to ease the ache that's been present since I saw the worry fill Blaine's eyes at Ethan's apartment. "It's been awful. I thought it'd stop. I thought that these people would get bored of harassing me, but little did I know it was only the beginning."

"People can be assholes. They can say the cruelest things, but most of the time it's coming from a place of bitter jealousy." Maria leans in and places a warm hand on top of mine. "What you should be feeling is empathy, because that person's life must be so freakin' dull that they feel the need to rain on someone else's parade. Blaine adores you. I've never seen him so in awe of someone before, and I can tell that he's falling pretty hard for you."

I roll my lips, squeezing my eyes closed to stop them from filling up. I'm falling hard for him too, and what worries me is that I'm going to do exactly what they are saying and hinder his career.

"Do you trust him?"

"Yeah, I do." I nod.

"Do you believe him when he says he's not using you for his image?"

I nod again.

"Do you love him?"

"Yeah, I love him so fucking much."

She smiles wide, and her dark brown eyes begin to glisten with her own unshed tears. "I'm here for you, for when you struggle with the trolls, but Blaine? Blaine would set the world on fire for you. He loves you more than hockey. Heck, he was ready to fight those trolls himself because he was so angry that they tried to take you away from him."

I let out a croaked laugh.

Pulling the sleeves of my hoodie over my hands, I wipe my eyes and sniff. "Sorry."

She shakes her head, patting her palm against my arm. "Don't apologize, sweetie, and don't worry about Blaine. These boys get so amped up on their emotions sometimes that the best outlet for them is on the ice." She leans in again, lowering her voice, "I think it's good for him, to be honest. It's about time he finally fell head over heels for someone." She winks.

"Thank you."

"You're welcome, honey. Us better-half hockey partners have to stick together because it can get really lonely. People think being with a professional athlete is this incredible lifestyle where you can have everything you could ever want, but what they don't see is the time you spend on your own because they're traveling. How you have to pack up your life and move when they get traded or sign with another team, leaving behind friends and connections you've made. But you know what makes it all worthwhile?"

"What's that?" I ask.

She smiles wistfully, like she's remembering a happy memory. "Seeing their faces when they win games, when they win their division or conference, or when they lift the Stanley Cup. Watching them achieve their hopes and dreams from when they first picked up a hockey stick. They share all of that with you. Their love is unconditional, and they make up for that lost time by loving you, every fiber of you, so wholly and fervently."

"Thank you," I croak, "for welcoming me into your home and for helping me shut down those nuggets of doubt."

She leans over, bringing me in for a warm hug. "Anytime, honey. I can tell Blaine worships the ground you walk on. He looks at you like you've hung the moon and every star in the sky, and I know that he'll love you in such a way that you'll never have an inkling of doubt."

The ache in my chest eases.

Maybe I can do this.

Maybe I can be the man Blaine loves and needs without allowing the trolls to beat me down.

Thirty-Two

Blaine

"Please remember we will be filming, so use respectful language at all times." Colleen gives us a pointed stare.

I hold up my hand in a Vulcan salute. "I promise."

"I don't think that means that," Zach chuckles.

"I dunno, dude. I've never watched Star Trek."

Ethan gives me a disgusted look. "What planet have you been living on that you've never seen Star Trek?"

"What?" I shrug. "I was a Star Wars prequel kid, not Star Trek. Plus, I only cared about hockey and making sure I beat my brother to calling shotgun in the car."

"That's true." Elliot nods in agreement. "He used to win every time as well."

"Probably because you were too distracted raiding the fridge for snacks."

"Also a valid point." Elliot lifts a shoulder in a shrug.

We're en route to the dog shelter to pick our new team mascot—the best thing about winning the escape room challenge aside from bragging rights—and I'm so fucking excited. I've wanted a dog my entire life, and the day I retire from hockey, I'm going to adopt as many dogs as Alex will let me.

Wow, look at me, planning the future.

"Are we allowed to name the dog?" Mitch asks Colleen from the back of the minivan.

Colleen turns in her seat. "If the dog doesn't already have a name or is young enough that we can change their name without them getting confused, then I'll take name suggestions. But I can't make any promises since they're going to be put on a poll on social media pages for fans to choose..."

Elliot huffs. "But I wanted Bruce."

Colleen scrunches up her nose. "I don't think it'll be Bruce, sweetie."

Elliot's head hits the headrest of his seat dramatically, and when we pull up in front of Paw-Loved Adoption Center, he stomps inside, mumbling how he'll create multiple accounts to vote for Bruce in the poll.

"Hey!" A guy with a bright smile steps around the counter to shake our hands. "Welcome to Paw-loved Adoption Center. I'm Brent, and I'll be helping you find your furry companion today."

We exchange handshakes, then he leads us through into the kennel area. The sound of dogs crying, barking, and howling makes my heart heavy because who the fuck abandons their dogs?

But this place is really nice. The kennels are clean with plenty of room for the dogs to move around, and there's a dog flap at the far end for them to go outside whenever they need.

I really hope they all find their forever home. I wish I could take them all myself.

I lean into one of the kennels and stroke the soft fur of a gorgeous husky puppy. His two different-colored eyes gaze up at me happily as I scratch behind his ears.

"You see a lot of puppies here now because, after Christmas, most people realize they don't have the means to take care of a dog. Also January is the month when most couples separate, and usually that leads to putting their dog up for adoption," Brent says.

Well, fuck. "That must be so hard on them." I frown.

He nods solemnly. "It is. There's a lot of confusion, especially when they've been in the same home for quite some time, but we have a great team here that ensures the dogs don't feel abandoned. If a particular dog is finding it harder than normal, we'll take them home with us."

"I'm glad they have some good people in their corner." I smile.

The rest of the guys are petting various dogs; Ethan's crouching in front of a Great Dane, Zach's giving smooches to the husky I spotted earlier, and I stop in front of a golden retriever.

The name on the whiteboard says, "Boomer, fourteen weeks old," and I can't help but grin. He's jumping up at the gate, his tail wagging like crazy.

"Hey there, little guy." I crouch down, putting my hand

through so he can sniff it. He licks it, then starts to chew excitedly on my fingers.

"Would you like to meet Boomer properly?" Brent asks.

"Hell yeah." I stand up so Brent can open the gate, and I step inside the kennel, kneeling down. Boomer climbs into my lap instantly, his paws resting on my shoulders as he licks my neck and under my chin. My fingers sink into his super-soft golden fur, and I stroke his body as his tail wags excitedly.

"You are so freakin' cute," I say in that baby voice everyone makes when talking to a dog.

His tiny teeth feel like needles as he nibbles my chin, and I burst out laughing. Taking my phone out of my pocket, I take several selfies before filming Boomer trying to eat my chin and tugging on my t-shirt collar with his tiny teeth.

"Alex, if I survive the puppy onslaught, I've decided we're going to have a house full of dogs when I retire," I say to the camera, and when I blow Alex a kiss, Boomer shoves his wet nose into my mouth.

"Omigod!" I hear my brother shriek, then erupt into a fit of giggles.

Picking Boomer up in my arms, I stand up and carry him out of his kennel to find Elliot two kennels down. He's on the floor, currently being tongue-attacked by five Dalmatian puppies, climbing all over his chest and licking his face. Mitch laughs, filming the entire thing on his phone as he stands to the side.

"This," he giggles, "is the best," another shriek, "day of," another burst of giggles, "my life!" Elliot says.

I take my phone out again and take a video to send to my parents, and when Elliot's finally able to sit up, all five puppies climb into his lap and bounce to keep kissing his face.

"Colleen, I want all of them! Every single one!" he demands, taking turns to kiss each puppy on the nose.

"I'm afraid we can't have them all; we can only have one team mascot," she chuckles from behind the phone she's holding up.

Yep, this is going to be a big hit on socials.

Elliot pouts. "Damnit, I need to find a way to have all of them."

I feel that right in my soul. I look down at Boomer, his wide brown eyes looking up at me with so much love that my heart squeezes.

"Colleen," I say, shifting Boomer in my arms so he's facing her. "Can we keep him?"

She walks over to me, stroking his soft fur and smiling as he wraps his front paws around her arm. "He would be the perfect mascot; Boomer kinda goes with Thunder too."

I grin. "Boys, what do you think? Boomer for Thunder's mascot?"

I hold him up in the air, Simba-style.

Ethan walks over, taking the puppy out of my arms and cradling him close to his chest. "I think he'd fit in great."

As the guys take turns with the golden floof and agree, my heart expands in my chest.

Colleen fills in all the paperwork while we're left in a room with Boomer, sitting on the floor, passing a ball between us for him to chase, and when we're back at the practice facility, Coach Harris greets us holding a mini jersey with "Boomer" on the back.

"Wow, you work fast." Ethan shares a rare grin.

Coach chuckles. "As soon as Colleen gave me the heads up that a decision was made, I got the team on it." He kneels down in front of a bouncing Boomer and puts the miniature Thunder jersey on the puppy. "Welcome to the team, Boomer; I'm sure you're going to cause less trouble than these knuckleheads."

Boomer responds by smothering Coach's face with excited kisses.

✕

BLAINE

<sends photos and videos from the adoption center>

BLAINE

I want them all so bad.

BLAINE

I wish I could bring them all home and love them so hard.

ALEX

That's so fucking adorable!

ALEX

LOL at Elliot!

BLAINE

He was living his best life :D

ALEX

It sucks your schedule is so grueling.

BLAINE

Would you like to adopt them all with me when I retire?

ALEX

That sounds like an amazing plan <3

"Hey, bud. You got a sec?" Ethan's voice startles me.

I look up from my phone and nod. "Yeah, what's up?"

We introduced Boomer to the rest of the team, and now he's flat out asleep on the couch in Coach's office, worn out from all the excitement, and I'm lazing on the couch in the team lounge after finishing up a session with Joe.

"I thought we could have a chat with Colleen about your idea for the bakery."

"Oh, okay, sounds good," I say, following Ethan up the stairs to where the offices are located.

"Hey Colleen, are you free for a quick chat?" he asks.

"Of course, come on in!" she says cheerfully.

Following Ethan into her office, I take a seat in one of the black leather chairs in front of her desk and twist my hands in my lap.

Why am I nervous?

"To what do I owe this pleasure?" She smiles.

Ethan gets straight down to business. "I'm not sure if you're aware, but Blaine has been dating Alex for some time now, and unfortunately, he's having a rough time... financially. You know how it sometimes goes for new start-up businesses..."

Colleen goes to open her mouth, but Ethan holds his hand up to stop her. "And before you ask, no, I don't believe Alex is only dating Blaine for his money, because he's declined Blaine's offer to help multiple times."

Colleen looks over to me, her smile laced with sadness.

"So, Blaine came to me, asking whether there was something we could do to help. I know you're always trying to come up with new, fun video ideas and thought maybe this could be a good opportunity to inadvertently help Alex and his brother out while making content for the team."

"They have a bakery in Lincoln Park. I thought maybe we could do something involving baking for the team's channel?" I suggest.

Ethan reaches into his pocket and retrieves his phone, tapping away on the screen before handing it over to Colleen. "This is it. It's pretty small, so it would probably only hold maybe six of us, seven at most, but it's possible."

Her eyes light up as she takes his phone for a closer look, and then, after a beat, she claps her hands with an excitable squeal. She finds a pen and begins writing frantically in her notebook.

"We could do a Thunder bake off." She taps her pen on her pad, gnawing on the side of her nail. "You know, this is kinda spooky, as I've been binge watching The Great British Baking Show and wondered if we could do something similar."

I laugh. "I wouldn't have the first clue on where to start."

"That's the whole point!" Colleen throws her hands out. "But no actual baking. I think that might just be asking for disaster to happen, but decorating is safe. I can't imagine you being delicate with those big mits, so it'd still provide endless entertainment."

"Great. Will you see this through?" Ethan asks.

Colleen nods. "Of course, leave it with me. I'll pay them

a visit, but don't mention it to Alex or his brother until I've gotten the green light from the powers above. I'd hate to get his hopes up for nothing."

I nod, unable to stop the wide grin from appearing on my face. "No worries; thanks for your help, both of you." I look at Ethan. "It really means a lot."

Thirty-Three

Blaine

Since we adopted Boomer a week ago, it's been a whirlwind of practice, home games, puppy cuddles and away games. We landed back in Chicago in the early hours of the morning after a three-day, two-game away stretch.

It's also been two weeks since dinner with the Kendricks, and while Alex is feeling a lot better since his talk with Maria, the messages haven't stopped. He's shown me a few of the recent ones, and no matter how many accounts he blocks, they just keep coming. Alex has said he isn't paying them any attention, just blocking and deleting, but I know they are getting to him.

When he thinks I'm not looking, his shoulders go rigid, and I can sense the inkling of doubt seeping through.

I'm not sure what I can do to prove to him that they are lies, and I don't understand how these people think they're entitled to interfere in my personal life.

They don't know me. They only know the person they see on the ice, or the professional front in interviews. They don't see the better person I am because of him or how fucking in love I am with him.

But I push those frustrating thoughts out of my mind because I have more important things to do.

Like seeing Alex for the first time in three days.

Shoving a team beanie on my head to hide my messy hair, I pick up my keys and head out the door.

The traffic heading up toward Lincoln Park is a sea of brake lights, meaning my usual twenty-minute journey takes fifty, and by the time I reach the bakery, he's already outside.

He's huddled in a thick coat, with a scarf wrapped around his neck multiple times and a hat pulled low on his head. I find somewhere to pull over, flashing my headlights at him to alert him of my arrival. The interior light comes on when he opens the door, highlighting his cold, pink nose. I take a fistful of his coat as soon as he closes the door and pull him toward me, pressing a hot, needy kiss against his lips. They're cold against mine, and a small, satisfied noise escapes him.

Fuck. I've missed him.

I didn't realize how much I'd miss someone when I went on away games, but these last three days have felt like three months. Even with texting and nightly FaceTime calls, nothing beats the feel of his soft lips against mine, and the smell of his grapefruit shampoo.

"Hi," he whispers as he pulls away.

His cheeks are rosy and pink, and his lips quickly get puffy and swollen from the scruff of my beard.

"Hey!" I grin, rubbing my thumb against his bottom lip.

I'm about to lean in to kiss him again, but a car honks, reminding me where I am.

"Why do they always fucking honk their horns at me?"

Alex laughs.

I flip my middle finger at the impatient driver and head back downtown toward my apartment. "How's your day been?"

Alex rests his head back against the seat and closes his eyes. "Long. I swear the last two weeks of January are insane for birthdays, then it's the run up to Valentine's, which always gets crazy because people want to order last-minute stuff…" He opens his eyes and turns to face me. "We've had to turn away quite a few people, and Jacob isn't taking it well."

I frown. "But there's only two of you; there's only so much you can do."

"I know," he sighs. "It's a perk of getting busier, but also a disadvantage when we're short-staffed. We're going to look at finances and see if we can hire someone."

"I get that."

And I feel kinda bad that a lot of it is because of me, but at the same time, I feel proud of Alex and his brother.

"How does a chill night sound? We'll get some food delivered and watch a movie?"

"That sounds good to me."

His smile is tired but still beautiful, and when I stop at a red light, I lean over and steal another kiss. I've been desperate to taste him again.

"How was your game in Dallas?" he asks.

"It wasn't our best. We struggled; it was like we were asleep at the start of the game."

"I'm sorry. Does losing a game impact team morale a lot?"

"Every now and again it does, but we gotta keep in mind the game is going to test your character sometimes, and it'll test your pride. You can't go into the next feeling embarrassed or pissed that you lost one before you just gotta put it behind you and focus on winning it."

"That's very sensible." He smiles.

"Did you watch it?"

"Yeah, I did. I had it on my laptop while I was finishing up an order. I just like hearing your side of it."

"I dedicated my goal to you." I give him a quick glance, waiting for that blush to hit his cheeks, and I'm rewarded a second later when he dips his head, hiding his smile behind his scarf.

The light changes to green, and I hit the gas, eager to get home and help my man unwind.

Inside my apartment, he takes his duffel bag to my room, and when he reappears, he's wearing a pair of my sweatpants and a hoodie.

I grin. I fucking love seeing him in my clothes.

He walks over to where I'm sitting on the couch, browsing through the takeout selection on my phone, and sits down beside me.

"Made yourself comfy, I see," I tease.

He smirks, putting his legs over my lap and curling into my side, resting his head on my shoulder. I wrap my arm around him, pulling him in close, and take a deep inhale of his hair, feeling all the tension disappear.

I'm addicted to him.

To his taste.

His smell.

His smile.

Everything that makes him, him.

Tilting his head up, I cup his jaw in my hand, and our lips connect in the sweetest kiss.

His hand rests on my thigh, his fingertips curling into the hard muscle as our tongues become reacquainted. His low mewls and gasps between kisses cause my cock to become a steel rod in my pants.

I can't get enough, and soon kissing isn't enough anymore.

His knees land on either side of my hips as I tug him onto my lap, and I cup the peachy globes of his ass, massaging and kneading the firm cheeks.

We're a mix of tongues colliding with frenzied strokes and heavy breaths.

He rolls his hips, and the friction of his cock brushing against mine makes me lose my mind.

"Fuck," I murmur against his lips. "Food can wait; I can't."

Alex sits upright in my lap, pulling my shirt over my head and tossing it on the floor before doing the same with his own. He then stands and pulls his—my—sweatpants down, revealing his hard, leaking cock.

I lean forward to take him into my mouth, but his hand goes to my shoulder, halting me.

"Take off your pants," he demands.

I smirk, loving this bossy tone of his.

When I don't move, he raises a brow. "I'm waiting. Lose the pants, Blaine."

I quickly peel myself out of my jeans, taking my boxer

briefs with them, and then take my cock in my hand. Keeping my eyes on Alex, I twist my fist against the sensitive head as he drops to his knees between my legs.

"You're so fucking hot," he states. His hands roam up the front of my thighs, watching my abs ripple from my shaky exhale with fascinated eyes.

"You're the hot one," I argue. "Look at you." I lean forward, taking his chin in my hand. "Your bluer than blue eyes, that sexy as sin mouth, your body…" I take his lips in a heated kiss, our tongues colliding in needy strokes. "Your delicious dick, and don't get me started on that sweet ass."

He smirks against my mouth. "It's all yours, baby."

"Damn fucking right it is."

Alex presses a hand against the center of my chest and pushes me back into the couch, then curls his fingers around my throbbing erection. His strokes are teasing, and I spread my legs wider, pushing my hips up into his fist impatiently.

Alex halts his movements at the base of my cock, and then, the little fucking tease that he is, licks my balls with the tip of his tongue.

I hiss through my teeth. "You're cruel sometimes."

Another tantalizing lick before he sucks my sac.

"Fuck, just suck it already," I groan, clenching my hands at my sides.

Alex gives me a pointed look, and I'm about to argue that he's killing me when he takes me to the back of his throat, swallowing around me.

An animalistic noise escapes the depths of my chest as my balls draw up tight.

"Your mouth," I say between heavy breaths, "is fucking incredible."

He hums around my cock as he bobs his head, his tongue swirling around the sensitive head before taking me to the back of his throat again.

Every time he has me in his mouth, it's like I'm on another planet. I could be on Jupiter or fucking Neptune for all I know, because the only thing on my mind is how good his mouth is and how much I fucking love this man.

Yep. I said it.

I *love* him.

Lacing my fingers into his hair, I give the strands a tug to make him stop. "I'm so close, and I wanna be inside you."

His oceanic eyes sparkle as his tongue licks over his lips.

"I need to get some lube and a condom." I go to stand, but my legs are weak, so I fall back onto the couch, my quads shaking.

"I'll get it." Alex stands up, and I watch his peachy ass moves as he disappears down the hall, returning seconds later with the…

"Condoms are in my bedside drawer," I say when he returns with only a bottle of lube.

"I'm negative…" he begins, biting down on his bottom lip. "And I'm on PrEP…"

It takes a few moments for my brain to catch up.

"You wanna go bare?"

He nods. "I wanna feel you inside me with nothing between us."

Grabbing hold of his hips, I pull him down on top of me to straddle my lap once again.

"You mean it?"

He nods again, pressing a kiss to my lips.

"I've never gone bare with anyone before," I confess.

"And I get tested every month with the team. I'm on PrEP, too."

Alex kisses me once more, then takes both of my hands from his hips, pulling them back to rest behind my head.

"Don't move," he demands, then picks up the lube and begins to work himself open.

Every time I go to move my hands on instinct, wanting to touch him or help him, he glares at me.

"No touching," he says sternly. "I'll tell you when you can touch."

A devilish grin spreads across my face. "Fuck, you could make me come with just this bossy bottom attitude of yours."

He winks, then his head tilts back as pleasure takes over.

"That's it, baby, open yourself up so I can fill you with my cock."

Alex lifts himself on his knees and takes my shaft in his hand, lining himself up before sinking down on me, taking me to the hilt.

When I'm fully inside him, he whispers against my lips, "Now you can touch."

And there's no need to tell me twice.

I grip his hips and thrust up into him, swallowing his moans with my mouth. The silence of the room is filled with heavy breaths, soft moans and the sound of him riding my dick. My mind travels back to our first date, when I teasingly asked what his favorite sex position was.

"I want you to cover my abs with your come," I demand, "and I'm gonna fill you with mine."

Alex looks down at me, his eyes heavy with need, his cheeks flush with desire as he nods.

His movements start to falter when I angle my hips. I know I hit the spot when I see his cock leave a trail of precome against my abs.

"Blaine." Alex's head lolls back between his shoulders.

His fingers dig into my pecs as his release hits. Spurt after spurt of come hits my abs, my chest, even my neck. My name is an erotic moan, and the sight of his blissed-out state is all I need to give in to the ache in my tight balls and the tingling at the base of my spine.

I let go with his name on my lips, and I come inside of my man, marking him as mine, falling into a vortex of pleasure as my body shakes.

"Fuck," I pant as Alex collapses against me, hiding his head in the crook of my neck.

My cock softens inside of him, and I wrap my arms tightly around him as he gets post-release shakes.

"I love you," I say into his soft hair.

He lifts his head, and those eyes lock with mine. "I love you, too."

I feel like I'm king of the fucking world when I'm gifted one of his beautiful smiles, and when he kisses me, my heart feels complete.

Thirty-Four

Alex

The bell jingles above the door as it opens, bringing in a draft of frigid cold air and a blond lady wrapped up in a bright pink coat.

"Gosh, it's cold out there," she says with a small chuckle, rubbing her hands together.

When she turns around, I recognize her from the Thunder games—their PR manager, Colleen.

As she stands in front of the counter, her bright eyes sparkle along with her smile. She holds out her hand. "I'm Colleen Chambers; I work for the Chicago Thunder hockey team. I know we've met before, but I don't think I properly introduced myself."

I shake her hand but struggle to refrain from frowning.

Is Blaine in trouble? Is she here to tell me to stay away from him? She must notice my brain going into overdrive and pulls me out of my misery spiral.

"Don't worry, I'm not here for Blaine or anything negative."

A relieved breath escapes me. Well, thank goodness for that.

She glances around the shop then asks, "Is your brother here?"

My brother? What could she need from Jacob?

I nod, then clear my throat to find my words. "Yeah, he is; let me get him for you."

Wiping my sweaty hands down the front of my apron, I head into the kitchen, where Jacob is working on a custom order. "Hey, there's someone here who'd like to speak with you."

His forehead creases with a frown when he looks up.

I lower my voice so Colleen won't hear me. "She's from the Chicago Thunder. She asked to see you."

Jacob puts down the piping bag and washes his hands before following me out into the main shop. Colleen's crouching down, admiring the cakes in the display cabinet, but straightens to her full height when we appear.

"Hello, I'm Colleen Chambers. I'm the PR Manager for the Chicago Thunder hockey. You must be Jacob." She holds her hand out.

Jacob shakes her hand, casting a confused glance at me, but I'm as clueless as he is right now.

"Yeah, that's me. It's nice to meet you. How can I help?"

"I'm here with a proposition for you, actually."

A proposition? That sounds… ominous.

"Can I get you a drink, and we'll take a seat?" Jacob asks.

"That would be lovely." She glances up at the chalkboard we fitted onto the wall this morning. "I'll have a mint hot chocolate, please."

"I'll make these; you get started," I say to Jacob with a smile.

He mouths his thanks as he removes his apron, hanging it on the wall before leading Colleen to one of the booths. I make her hot chocolate, along with a coffee for Jacob, and take them over, taking a seat next to him as Colleen explains something.

"So, in exchange for us using your premises for the day, we'll reimburse you for the cost of closing the shop during the morning, and when we open up to the public, the guys will act as your servers to sell their creations. We'll also pay for all the ingredients used and preparation time, plus an additional sum as a thank you. On top, we'd promote your bakery in the video and on our socials."

She writes a figure down on her notepad, then slides it across the table to us. My eyes pop out of my head when I see the number because *Holy. Shit!* This is an insane amount of money. This would pay off nearly half the money we owe.

"We'd also like to invite you to the Thunder HQ to discuss the opportunity to be the main dessert supplier for our VIP boxes at every home game and special event."

"Why us?" my brother asks, then shakes his head. "I'm sorry, I don't mean to be rude, I'm just… I'm puzzled as to why you chose us over the bigger, more popular bakeries in Chicago."

Colleen doesn't seem phased by Jacob's question, chuckling to herself before looking over to me.

"Blaine," she says simply, then takes a sip of her drink,

cupping the mug between her hands. "He came to me wondering how he could help you."

Blaine did this?

My heart fills, and tears prick the back of my eyes. He wanted to do this for me. There was no way I was going to accept money from him, so he's gone above and beyond to find other ways to help us. It means more than I could ever put into words.

I bite down on my bottom lip, willing my eyes to stop filling. Jacob leans across and puts his arm around me, giving me a gentle squeeze.

"I had my doubts about him, but he's a good guy."

I nod my head, unable to speak. I pull my sleeves over my hands and wipe my eyes.

"Blaine's been aware of how I've been trying to think of fun ways to bring fresh content to our social media channels. We have a segment on our YouTube called 'Off the Ice' where we show interactions with the team and they participate in fun activities. Also, it'll be entertaining to try and see these big guys attempt intricate cake decoration."

We laugh at that. It will be entertaining, and I guarantee there will be some disasters. But most of all, I still can believe how thoughtful Blaine can be.

I mean, I *can* believe it.

He's been surprising me constantly. He shows his love through selfless actions, heartfelt gestures and sweet words. He makes me take back my words that hockey players don't equal Prince Charming, because I think my Prince Charming may just be a hockey player.

"So, what do you say? Want to host some hockey players

trying to decorate some cakes?" Colleen asks with a wicked gleam in her eyes.

"Count us in; where do we sign?" my brother asks, smiling.

And I instantly feel some of the stress and worry easing off his shoulders.

X

Later that evening, Jacob and I are making lists of everything for the team event. We agreed to host it in three days, as the team has a game tomorrow night, and it'll give us time to complete the custom orders and notify customers we'll be closed for the day.

"Do you think this will be enough?" I ask, holding up the list of ingredients we'll need to pick up from the wholesaler.

"We could add a little extra because we'll always use it anyway…" Jacob taps the end of his pen against his chin. "Let's add one more of everything."

I nod, tweaking the quantities on the notepad.

"This was really kind of him," Jacob announces.

I look over to where he's sitting on the couch, curled up under a blanket.

"Blaine," he clarifies. "I'll admit I doubted him in the beginning. I questioned his motives, whether he was genuine or just saw you as a conquest, but he's proved me wrong."

Even though he's never said that out loud, I often wondered what Jacob really thought of Blaine. So it pleases me to no end that he's finally seeing Blaine for who he is, not just the hockey player who found himself on the gossip blogs too often.

They're the two most important people in my life, and it means the world to me that Jacob likes him.

I smile. "He's an amazing guy."

Jacob nods in agreement. "He is. He didn't have to do this, but it's another way of showing you he cares. Sometimes when there's a money difference, the richer of the two can be inconsiderate of the other, but Blaine isn't like that."

I think back to our first date, and he's right. Blaine could've easily brushed me aside after my momentary freak out, but he didn't. He ensured I was comfortable, reassured me, and apologized for not thinking about my circumstances.

It takes a lot for someone to hold their hand up like that, and he's been incredible since. I've never felt inadequate.

"I'm glad you've found someone who is worthy of you, Alex." My brother smiles, then hides a yawn behind his hand. "I'm gonna get into bed, I'm exhausted."

I say goodnight, then tidy up the living room and kitchen before heading to my own room.

Blaine had a game tonight against Calgary, but I had to pass on the tickets so we could get ahead on custom orders. Whenever I can't make it to games, he'll FaceTime me when he gets back to his apartment, so knowing he'll call any minute now, I head to my room and change out of my clothes. I pull on a pair of plaid pajama pants and slip under the covers.

Idly tossing the warm-up puck from that first game in the air, I scroll through social media, avoiding the "Requests" on my Instagram, and stop when I come across a post from the Chicago Thunder. The graphic shows Thomas Tait has been traded to Ottawa.

TRADE NEWS: Chicago Thunder acquires Caleb Blomqvist from Ottawa for Thomas Tait. #ThunderHockey

I feel awful for feeling relieved it's not Blaine, but reality settles in. It could be Blaine, given that he doesn't currently have a no-trade clause in his contract. The team might be presented with an offer they can't refuse, and Blaine will have to pack up his life within hours and move on to another team.

Will he want me to follow him if he's traded?

There's an ache in my chest at the thought of going with him and leaving my brother. I can't leave him; we're the only family we have.

But Blaine…

I love him, and the thought of not being with him makes me nauseous.

There's no point in getting worried over something that may not happen. Blaine's still in Chicago, and he's playing the best hockey of his life, so I can only hope it's enough for the Thunder management.

My phone vibrates in my hand, pulling me out of my spiraling thoughts. Placing the puck back on my bedside table, I smile at Blaine's name lighting up the screen.

"Hey, baby." I smile when his tired face fills the screen.

His eyes soften when he sees me. "Hey baby, I missed you tonight."

"I missed you too, sorry I couldn't be there. You'll never guess who came to the bakery tonight."

I tell Blaine all about Colleen's offer and our plan to get everything prepared to do it in a couple of days.

"Thank you," I say, bringing the phone closer. "You have no idea how much this means to me, that you'd try and find a way to help us."

Blaine gives me a shy grin. "I couldn't just sit back and do nothing. I understand why you don't wanna take my money, so I wanted to find another way to help."

"I really appreciate it, more than you'll ever realize." My eyes begin to fill with unshed tears as gratitude bubbles in my chest.

"Will it help? I don't know what Colleen offered, and I don't want you to tell me, but will it help?"

I nod. "It's not going to clear it all, but it's a considerably large amount that's definitely going to take a good portion of the burden away."

"Good." His eyes crinkle at the sides as he smiles. "Does this mean you'll give me some tips so I can have the best-looking ones?" He grins.

I tip my head back and laugh. "No, that would be an unfair advantage. I'll be there to make sure nothing bad happens, but we're not allowed to actually help."

"Fuck's sake."

I chuckle. "I'm sure there's other advantages to dating me that doesn't involve decorating cakes."

"I know, there are a million things I love about you, I just wanna win, too."

"You'll be great. Just do your best. You've seen me decorate before; try to remember that and take your time. The fans will love it no matter how it looks."

I know he'll try to get me to help him out, but I won't give in.

"I guess," he sighs. "Did you hear about the trade?"

"Yeah, I did. How did that go down? Was it after the game?"

He nods. "Yeah, they didn't play him tonight due to 'roster management'", he air quotes. "So we had an inkling it was because of a trade."

"That sucks."

"Yeah, it does," he sighs. "Caleb is a decent guy, though."

I've seen Caleb Blomqvist play a couple of times, and he's a pretty good player.

"I just feel on edge a lot, you know? I'm just waiting for that phone call to tell me to pack my bags and go."

"Has Hayden said anything?" I ask.

Blaine shakes his head. It's evident that it's wearing him down. I can't even imagine what it must be like to wonder if this city will still be home the following day.

The phone jolts as he slumps on his bed. "He's told me not to worry but hasn't really elaborated on it. I know he's working on getting a new contract, but he's so vague about it."

"Maybe he doesn't want you to get your hopes up until everything is finalized?"

He shrugs. "Probably. I just want the whole trade deadline cloud to pass, so I know I'm safe."

I open my mouth to reassure him, but he yawns. He looks exhausted.

"Why don't you get some sleep, and I'll speak to you tomorrow?"

He mumbles something incoherent.

"What's that?" I ask.

"I wish you were here; I don't like going to sleep without you, even though I know you're only twenty minutes away. If I wasn't so tired, I'd come to you."

My heart squeezes. "I know, but I'll see you soon, 'kay?"

He nods sleepily, his face sinking into his plush pillows. "Goodnight, baby, I love you."

"I love you too, goodnight."

My breath gets stuck in my throat as we end the call.

I really hope Blaine doesn't get traded, because I don't know what I'll do without him.

Thirty-Five

Blaine

"Do you think I'm going to need to wear a hairnet?" Zach asks, nervously picking at a hole in his jeans.

I take a quick glance over at him before focusing back on the road. I'm driving Zach and Elliot to the bakery, meeting Ethan, Mitch, and the new guy, Caleb Blomqvist, there.

I can't explain the feeling that overcame me when Alex called me the other night, thanking me for being so kind and helping get this set up.

I'm really grateful the team has been able to pull it off, though, as I know how much this means to Alex and Jacob, plus the publicity it'll bring to the shop will be immense.

Alex told me how much the team is paying for this to happen. It's going to really help, especially with the publicity it'll bring, and I'm so freaking pleased because Alex and Jacob truly deserve it.

"Possibly." I shrug. "It is a kitchen, after all."

Elliot cackles behind me, sticking his head through the two front seats.

"You'll look like a cabbage." He leans over and ruffles Zach's hair.

We pull up outside the shop and I send a silent thank you to the parking gods for having a space open out front. We quickly make our way inside to see the other guys have already arrived.

"Hey!" Colleen greets us, then flicks the lock on the door, locking us in. "Jacob and Alex are just in the kitchen getting everything ready. Take a seat; we won't be long."

We join the boys in the booths, where there are some cupcakes and donuts stacked on a plate, along with bottles of water. I twist the cap off a bottle and gulp down half before picking up a confetti donut and taking a large bite. Zach's halfway through his second by the time I've finished mine.

"It still amazes me how many sweets you can eat, dude." Mitch laughs, nudging Zach's bicep with his elbow.

He shrugs, then pats his solid abs. "It's called good genes and going hardcore in the gym."

"Do you know what they're going to have us do today?" Caleb asks, throwing a piece of cake into his mouth.

He arrived two days ago from Ottawa and he's fit in really well. We're gelling on the ice, and the guy has good banter.

I think he'll get along great here.

"Alex mentioned something about decorating, and then we'll be selling them to fans. He said he wasn't going to help me either 'cause he doesn't want to give me an unfair advantage." I roll my eyes dramatically.

No matter how many times I begged and pleaded for him to give me tips, he wasn't letting up. Even when I swallowed his cock to the back of my throat and made him see stars last night, he still didn't budge.

My blow job skills must be rusty. I'll have to rectify that by getting his dick in my mouth as often as I can.

When we're finally called into the kitchen, Colleen's team has set up several cameras on tripods in various corners of the room, with two of them holding handheld cameras so they can get up close and personal. Their kitchen is always pristine; it looks like something out of a magazine. The silver countertops are so shiny, you can see your reflection in them. A large fridge takes up one corner of the room, and metal racking stands at nearly six feet. There are free-standing mixers, and more bowls, pots, and pans stacked neatly than I've ever seen.

Colleen lets us know when we're rolling, reminding us not to curse.

"So this morning you will be tasked with decorating today's selection of baked goodies. Each of you will be responsible for creating some Thunder-themed treats, which fans will be able to purchase this afternoon before voting for their favorite online," she explains. "Everything has been baked; all you have to do is create the design."

We're all handed a white apron with *Chicago Thunder* embroidered on the front with the iconic logo, and once we put them on, Zach cautiously raises his hand.

"Do I need to wear a hairnet?" He points to his man bun tied high on the back of his head, and raucous laughter bounces off the kitchen walls.

Jacob shakes his head, a soft smile on his face. "No, it's fine as it is."

Colleen places us at our designated counters and clearly states that we can't ask Alex or Jacob for help.

We'll see about that.

I glance up, flashing a wicked smirk at Alex.

He blushes, dropping his chin to his chest, so I blow him a few kisses and give him a couple of exaggerated winks.

"Blaine, stop trying to get your boyfriend to help you." Elliot smacks the back of my head with his hand.

I rub the tender spot and flip him the bird.

"Alex, as your favorite brother-in-law, I think you could help me, though." Elliot grins.

Huh. Why am I not horrified by that idea?

"I'm sorry, it's only fair that I don't get involved. I'm just here to prevent any disasters from happening." Alex laughs, shaking his head.

Colleen claps her hands to get our attention. "Okay, we'll be starting in three… two… one… and decorate!"

On the station in front of me, there's various piping bags filled with different colored frosting and twenty-four plain cupcakes. I pick up the red one first and start to write "Thunder", but it starts blending together.

I end up with more frosting on my hands than on the cake, as was to be expected.

"I'm like a freakin' child," I mumble before wiping my hands down my apron. Red smears down the front of the white apron, making it look like something out of a horror movie.

"Ugh!" I groan.

Elliot starts to sing "Cake by the Ocean" as he decorates

his own cupcakes, and instantly Colleen waves her hands for him to stop.

"Elliot, stop it! We'll need to cut that out."

He looks up, his hair flopping into his eyes, and grins mischievously.

Ethan and Zach are decorating donuts—what a surprise —in the colors of our jerseys, and Caleb and Mitch are decorating sugar cookies.

An hour later, Colleen claps again. "You've got ten minutes left, boys, then we've gotta get ready to open the doors."

I look down at what can only be described as catastrophic. The writing has blended into an unreadable mess, and the hockey stick and puck I attempted look nothing like a stick and puck. I peek over at Zach's, and he's put big smiley faces on every donut.

"Nice job, dude!" I laugh.

He grins. "Nothing says happy donut day like a smiley face."

Alex looks over my shoulder.

"What do you think? I think I'm a cake decorating master."

He rolls his lips together, suppressing his laughter. "Wow, you're definitely something. A solid B for effort"

"A B?! What the heck! I deserve more than that. This is a lot harder than it looks."

He mock-gasps, "No way, seriously? We've found something else you're not good at?"

The boys burst into laughter around me.

I flip them the double bird. They can censor it or cut it out; that's what editing is for.

He pats my bicep and smiles. "You did good, baby."

"But what about mine?" Elliot whines, tugging on Alex's arm like a child. "Alex, come look at mine."

Alex goes with Elliot, and as soon as his eyebrows raise in surprise, I go over to inspect my brother's work. He's lined up all his cupcakes together, and when you look at them, they make up a rink. There's lines of red and blue icing, then he's done the blue crease and red posts of a net, then on one cake is a stick man with a speech bubble saying "Again!"

"Holy shit, El, this is amazing."

Elliot puffs his chest out, pretending to flick his hair over his shoulder. "I know," he says with a cocky grin.

When Coach Harris walks in, his eyes widen slightly in alarm at the state we're in. I have red icing on my apron, but Elliot has icing everywhere—quite literally. Zach's squirting the remnants of his icing directly into his mouth. Mitch is wearing some black frosting on his face like a football player, which makes Ethan and Caleb the only two who look presentable.

Sensible adults, ugh.

Coach walks around to admire our handiwork, and when he gets to Elliot, he's visibly shocked.

"Wow, 'tendy Olsen, I never knew you had it in you. This is pretty sweet."

"Fuck yeah!" Elliot pumps his fists in the air, then realizes his mistake. He casts Colleen a guilty look. "Sorry, let me do that again."

She rolls her eyes and nods, a small smile twitching on her lips.

"Oh yeah, I'm awesome!" Elliot tries again, pumping his fists in the air again.

We wash up while Colleen and her team move the filming equipment into the main shop area. "Let's get some photos before we open the doors," Colleen announces before we pose for photos in our aprons in front of the illuminated *"Jacob's Delicious Desserts"* sign.

For today's event, everything's priced the same to make it easier to take payments, which is Ethan's responsibility. Zach, Caleb, and I are assigned as servers to box up the chosen goodies, and Mitch and Elliot are taking orders.

When the doors open, it's chaotic. The police are helping control the crowds who are eager to get inside and take photos, and I can sense the anxiety radiating from Zach from the sheer number of people in the shop, making it feel like the walls are closing in. The six of us get into a smooth routine, smiling for photos and thanking fans for coming out.

"Can I get a Zach donut, a Mitch cookie, and the greatest Olsen cupcake?" Elliot shouts like he's impersonating a well-known chef. "And that means *ME*!"

I glance up at my brother and raise a brow. "Why are you shouting at me like you're Gordon Ramsay?"

"Because I'm the one in charge today, broski. Now get me a Zach donut, a Mitch cookie, and a *me* cupcake!" He counts on his fingers then snaps them for me to hurry, while sporting a wicked grin. "Chop chop! Don't keep the good people waiting!"

We sell out within thirty minutes, and there's still hundreds of people outside.

"Wow, who knew it would be such a hit…" Caleb says.

"I don't think I could cope doing that again," Zach admits, running a hand through his hair that ended up falling out of his man bun during all the manic serving. He looks frazzled.

"Thank you, guys, for such a fun day." Colleen smiles, then turns to Alex and Jacob standing in the entrance to the kitchen, both of them looking startled. "Thank you for allowing us to use your premises; we'll make sure the area is safe for you as well." She refers to the one man who's pressed up against the window with a sign saying, *"I WANT A ETHAN PARKES DONUT."*

The team begins to pack away all the equipment, and once we say goodbye to Coach, Ethan, Caleb, Mitch, and the rest of the PR team, it's just me, Zach, and Elliot left. We head into the kitchen, where Alex and Jacob are cleaning up.

"Here, let us help; we're the ones who made the mess," I say as I fold my frosting-covered apron.

The second I place the apron down, Alex leaps into my arms. I manage to catch him, and he wraps his legs around my waist, his hands cup my face, and he presses a kiss to my lips.

"Thank you," he whispers as he pulls away.

He rests his forehead on mine. His eyes are full of gratitude and love, glistening with unshed tears.

"Thank you," he whispers again.

"You're welcome, baby." I smile. "I'd do anything for you, you know that. If you asked me to find you a leopard-printed dinosaur with a unicorn horn, I'd go to the ends of the earth to find you one. Whatever you ask me, I'll give it to you in a heartbeat."

And I mean every fucking word.

He might not let me help him with money, but I can show him I'm there to support him in other ways.

Need help to run the shop? I'm there.

Need me to hold him all night and whisper sweet nothings in his ear? I'll be there in a nanosecond.

I want to make him laugh and smile every day, for all the days I'm on this earth. I want to be the one who makes him smile all the fucking time, and I will do anything to make sure that happens.

Thirty-Six

Alex

I let out a low whine into my pillow when the soft beep of my alarm echoes through the silent room. I quickly switch it off so it doesn't wake up Blaine.

Waking up at 4 a.m. isn't something I've gotten used to yet, despite doing it for so long. I gently pry myself out of Blaine's hold and tiptoe into the en-suite bathroom, quietly closing the door behind me so the shower doesn't wake him up.

He has a week off from games with it being All Star weekend; for some reason, he declined his invite. When I asked him why, he simply shrugged and said he had better things to do. With how sore I am, I'm starting to realize what he meant.

Standing under the hot spray of the shower, I close my eyes and relish in the warm sensation seeping into my bones.

It's been snowing for over a month now, and Blaine has been non-stop complaining about the cold.

I'm about to pour some shower gel into my hands when the shower door opens, and Blaine appears through the steam. His eyes are small and sleepy, and his face has sleep lines from the pillow.

"Morning, baby." His voice is thick and raspy, and the sultry sound goes straight to my cock.

He steps under the spray with me, wrapping his arms around my waist and pressing his face into the crook of my neck. The heat of his morning erection warms the crease of my ass as he pulls me flush to his chest.

"I'm sorry, did I wake you?" I ask, tilting my head back slightly to lean against his shoulder.

He shakes his head, pressing a kiss just below my ear.

"No, I'm gonna come in with you today and help you out."

Surprised by his admission, I turn around in his arms and wrap my hands around his neck.

"But… It's your week off. Don't you want to relax and have some downtime?"

He shakes his head again, his eyes blink slowly, still heavy with sleep, and takes my lips in a gentle kiss.

"No, the only thing I want to do is be with you, and I don't think kidnapping you will gain me any points with your brother."

We laugh.

While Jacob's definitely warmed up to him, Blaine continues to make an effort, showing my brother that he isn't like the jerks he knew in high school or the idiots I dated back in college.

"I figured I'd come and help out. I was an awesome cake server person last time. It'll be fun," he says.

I'm at a loss of words. There's so much emotion bubbling in my chest: gratitude, adoration, love.

I whisper "thank you" before kissing him again. His hands glide over my body, moving down my lower back and squeezing the globes of my ass.

"We don't have time for that," I murmur against his lips. "Jacob will kill us both if we're not there at five."

He takes a step back and grabs the loofah, squirting some shower gel on it before handing it to me.

We manage to keep our hands to ourselves in the shower and then get dressed in contented silence. Blaine makes us some coffee to go, and when we're just parking outside of the shop, we see the light flicker on.

The bell chimes above the door as we step inside, and I walk over to greet my brother with a hug.

"Good morning… I wasn't expecting to see you here," he says to Blaine.

"Mornin'," Blaine returns the smile, shoving his hands into the pockets of his sweatpants. "I've come to help out; hope that's okay."

Jacob's eyebrows rise slightly in surprise. "Oh, thank you, you didn't have to."

Blaine shrugs. "Nowhere else I'd rather be than spending time with Alex and maybe getting some of those delicious raspberry ripple cupcakes."

Jacob chuckles with a shake of his head. "I'm sure we can sort something out."

I laugh when Blaine fist bumps the air. "Let's go get you an apron."

Jacob heads into the kitchen while I find a clean apron for Blaine, and once he's tied the strings behind his back, he twists his baseball cap backward and whispers gleefully, "Did you see that? I think he likes me."

I laugh, pinching his ass. "Keep up the good work, big boy. You'll win him over soon enough."

Fetching my own apron, I lead Blaine into the kitchen, where Jacob's already starting on the cake mixture.

"What do you need me to do?"

"How good are you at measuring? Want to help me get started on the cookies?" I ask.

Blaine looks a little apprehensive but nods. "Can't be hard, right?"

Jacob scoffs.

"I'll show you," I say.

He follows me to the sink to wash our hands, then I retrieve a bowl from the shelf, along with the ingredients we need.

"I tend to mix a batch of cookie dough, then split it into portions before adding the different mix-ins, so we use the same cookie dough base, but I'll add milk chocolate chips to one, white chocolate to another, M&Ms to another, peanut butter, etc."

He nods. "I think I follow…"

Placing the digital scales in front of him, I write down how much of each ingredient I need. Once the cookie dough base is done, I split it into different bowls and add the ingredients Blaine's weighed out.

"Okay, onto the M&M's…" I look up just as he's throwing some of the chocolate into his mouth.

"You're not supposed to eat it all!" I laugh.

He flashes a toothy grin, colorful pieces of M&M shell still stuck in his teeth.

I pry the bowl of chopped-up chocolate from his hands and mix it into the cookie dough.

"Can you help me carry these to the fridge, please? We let them chill for a while before baking."

Blaine helps carry the mixing bowls over to the fridge before getting started on the donuts. I'm in awe of Blaine's excitement and enthusiasm as he drops the rings into the oil, and a few hours later, we're sliding the tray of finished donuts and cookies onto the glass counter.

Blaine takes to serving customers with ease, and when the door opens and Nate waltzes in, he gives my best friend a bright smile. "Hey there, Nate, what can I get for you?"

Nate stops dead in his tracks, his eyes wide in alarm. "What are you doing here, hot hockey player?"

Blaine laughs. "I'm helping Alex out."

I walk around the counter and give Nate a hug. "It's All-Star week, but he's gracing us with his presence here."

Nate returns my hug, then turns to lean against the counter. "Where's that hot twin brother of yours?"

"Elliot?" Blaine's eyebrows go up slightly.

"Well, duh!" Nate rolls his eyes. "Unless you've got another twin brother you're hiding from us?"

Blaine casts me a confused look, and I shrug. Nate has no filter, and whatever wild crush he's got on Elliot isn't something I'm going to get involved in.

"He's in Cali with my parents for the week."

Nate sighs. "Damn, that's a real shame."

Blaine's forehead furrows; I can practically hear the cogs in his brain turning. "Yeah?"

"Anyway…" Nate looks at me with a wide smile on his face, blissfully unaware of the confused state he's left Blaine in. "You haven't been in the gym this week. I expect you to be there tomorrow or there's going to be trouble!"

"Sorry, it's been a little crazy recently."

I'm not going to mention the exercise I've been doing with Blaine—the bedroom kind.

"I'll take partial blame." Blaine puts his arm around my shoulder, tucking me into his body. "I've been holding this one hostage whenever I can, and we've been… busy."

Nate smirks and wiggles his brows, his mind clearly going to the gutter.

But I'm not going to correct him.

Because he's exactly on the mark.

Over the next few days, Blaine becomes a permanent fixture in the shop. He either comes in with me in the morning and leaves just after lunch to head to the gym or comes after he's been there already.

But today he's spending the day with Boomer, as Colleen allowed him to take the puppy home for the day. He's been blowing up my phone with endless photos, videos, and texts wishing he could have a dog of his own.

Not having him here today has been a blessing in disguise since one of our ovens has stopped working and we've just found out it's out of warranty. It's just another thing we'll have to find the money for.

Trying to distract myself from it, I wipe down one of the tables and glance up at the sound of the bell jingling above the door, freezing when the last person I expected to see walks through the door.

"Ethan, hey."

He gives me a small smile, his eyes searching the store. "Hey, Alex. How's things?"

"Uh, good, thanks?" It comes out as a question. "Blaine's not here today; he's got Boomer for the day."

"I'm not here to see Blaine, I'm here to see—" He doesn't get to finish his sentence as my brother appears from the kitchen, and a boyish smile appears on Ethan's face.

Jacob's eyes widen when he spots him, and then his cheeks flush slightly.

"Hello, Ethan," he says shyly.

What the heck?

I'm so confused right now. How does Ethan even know Jacob? I'm pretty sure they've only met once when Ethan came for the team event, as Jacob doesn't come to any of the games, and I don't recall Ethan coming in here.

Ethan closes the distance to Jacob, cupping his elbow with his hand, and says something I can't decipher.

"Is... everything okay?"

Because what the fuck is going on right now?

Jacob looks around Ethan's large body and sighs. "Alex, let's take a seat."

He goes to the door, flipping the "closed" sign before sliding into the booth next to Ethan, folding his hands in his lap.

"Jacob..." I prompt when my brother doesn't speak.

Jacob goes to open his mouth, but Ethan raises his hand to stop him.

"Alex, a couple of weeks ago Blaine came to me wanting to know how he could help you out, given the financial difficulty both you and your brother are dealing with. I know the team activity helped somewhat, but it hasn't cleared it all..." He turns to Jacob and gives him a small smile. "I could see how much it meant to you; this bakery, everything you've built, and I wanted to help… Blaine's too close, I get it but I'm like an outsider, in a way."

"What do you mean, help?"

And finally, my brother speaks up.

"Ethan has kindly offered to pay off our debts, and we'll repay him monthly—"

"Without interest," Ethan interrupts.

"Without interest," Jacob echoes. "It's an amount that allows us to live and breathe a little easier and also means we don't have to worry about how we're going to pay for the oven to be fixed."

My mind races. Not having the huge monthly outgoings will help significantly, and we'll be able to hire some more staff to help, but there's something in my gut that is wondering—*why?*

I know Ethan's a good guy, but it's a lot of money to give to your teammate's boyfriend.

"What do you get out of it?" I ask him.

Ethan leans forward, resting his forearms on the table. "Honestly? Being able to give back and help someone in need means more to me than the money sitting in my bank account. I know what it's like to struggle."

Well, color me speechless.

"And with the repayment plan we've agreed on, we'll be able to look into hiring more staff…" Jacob gives me a reassuring smile.

I search my brother's eyes, because while this is an incredibly generous thing Ethan is offering to do, I want to ensure Jacob is happy. Financial issues are secondary; my brother's mental health and happiness are what's important to me. He was bullied profusely in college by jocks, and I know it still comes back to haunt him, even now in his late twenties.

"As long as you are happy with all of this," I say, looking him in the eye so he knows what I mean.

The smile he gives me is genuine, and he nods. "I promise you, I wouldn't have accepted Ethan's offer if I wasn't comfortable."

I nod, understanding, then look at Ethan. "Thank you for your kindness; I really appreciate it."

Ethan flashes me a bright smile, one that would have knocked me off my feet if I wasn't already sitting down. "No problem; I'm happy to help. Anyway, I gotta go…" He looks at my brother as he stands. "Let me know if you need anything, okay?"

Jacob nods with a smile. "Thank you."

Ethan says goodbye, but the heated look he gives Jacob makes me question what his intentions really are.

When the door closes, I lean forward on the table. "Are you sure about this?"

"I think we'd be stupid to turn down an offer like that." Jacob sighs, running a hand through his perfectly styled hair. "I can tell he's different, that he's got a good heart. It's not my story to tell, but he understands our situation more than you realize."

"Is there something in writing to protect you? Not because I think Ethan will screw us over, but there's a lot of money involved."

He nods. "Yeah, there is. Even though this is a business agreement, he is a good guy, Alex."

"I know that," I grumble.

I chew on my bottom lip, not sure how to put into words how I'm feeling. I'm nervous because I care. I'm protective because I want him to be safe. On the other hand, I'm so relieved that this burden is going to be lifted.

"Plus, seeing you and Blaine together… This is going to give me the chance to have that for myself. I've put dating to the back of my mind, throwing myself into work, but I wanna meet someone. I wanna have what you and Blaine have." His smile is sad. "I know it took me a while to warm up to him, but I'm so happy you've found someone who worships the ground you walk on. Those guys from college weren't worthy of you, they didn't appreciate what an incredible person you are, but Blaine… I think he'd walk through fire just to tell you he loved you."

I look down at my feet, trying to hide my heated cheeks because he's right about Blaine, but he can't just distract me from the bombshell he's just dropped on me.

"So, you and Ethan, huh? Since when did you start talking?"

Jacob picks up a napkin and begins to fold it over several times, his teeth buried into his bottom lip. "He came in after the event and we've been texting a little here and there."

My eyes widen. "What?"

"Don't make a big deal out of it." He glares. "We're just friends."

"Sure." I smirk. "And suddenly it coincides with you being ready to date again?"

He hides his face in his hands, but not before I catch his grin.

Thirty-Seven

Blaine

Alex's soft snores are soothing compared to the chaotic mess running through my mind. A whirlwind of emotions rattle in my chest as I scroll through the pits of social media. Endless gossip and people talking nonsense, but there's something in my gut telling me to keep going.

Scroll.

Refresh.

Scroll.

Refresh.

I don't usually give social media the time of day, aside from the occasional post on Instagram when Colleen reminds me to be more active, and don't get me wrong, social media can be incredible, but damn, people can be assholes. They'll happily tear into you without a single thought.

They don't care that you might be having an off day, or what struggles you might be facing mentally that can affect your game.

They don't care that you worked on those drills for seventeen hundred hours—you bounce the puck off the post once and suddenly you're a shit player.

They're just sitting in their armchairs, berating hockey players, and most of the time they've never picked up a stick and stepped foot on the ice themselves.

So I stay away from it.

But today, there's something in the force telling me that I need to keep scrolling.

Alex rolls onto his side. His lips part, and I can feel his warm puffs of breath against my bicep. He looks so peaceful—the complete opposite of what I'm feeling inside.

Just put the damn phone down.

I curse at my internal thoughts. I want to, I really do, but as I argue with myself, I refresh my feed again, and my heart plummets into my stomach when a tweet catches my eye.

Posted three minutes ago.

@TheWarrenPost: BREAKING NEWS just in from Chicago Thunder!! Blaine Olsen has been traded to Buffalo, and Chicago receives Jackson Wilde #ByeByeOlsen

I feel sick to my stomach. I drop my phone into my lap, closing my eyes, and hit my head back against the headboard. Sweat beads at my temples, my hands tremble, and my heart is beating so hard it could crack a rib.

Shit.

This can't be happening.

I thought I'd done everything right; I cleaned up my act and kept my name off the blogs. I've been fucking stellar on the ice, and even done something I never in a million years would have ever expected to happen. I fell in fucking *love*.

I've achieved my dreams of playing in the NHL on the same team as my brother, and just like that, it's all gonna be taken away from me.

Alex won't leave his brother to follow me to Buffalo.

Elliot's tied to a four-year contract.

I've been on such a high these last couple of months that the impact of hitting the bottom is going to be catastrophic.

"Hey, what's wrong?" Alex's sleepy voice breaks me from my spiraling thoughts.

He sits up and rests his hand on the side of my face, his thumb wiping away a tear I didn't realize had fallen.

"Blaine, talk to me, what happened?"

My words get stuck in my throat. I feel like a hollow shell. Trades are inevitable; they happen to almost every hockey player. You're always at risk of being traded unless you have a clause in your contract.

And while I see this team as my family, it's still a business at the end of the day. The head honchos don't care that I have found family here. They don't care that I've fallen in love and met my soulmate.

I'm just a chess piece that's no longer needed on their board.

Alex moves to kneel in front of me between my legs. His soft, warm hands cup my face, tilting my head up.

I open my mouth, but the words get stuck in my throat. I squeeze my eyes closed, trying to find the strength to say what I know will break his heart.

"It's happened… I've been traded," I croak.

My heart cracks in two as his eyes fill with tears.

He takes a shaky breath and asks, "Where?"

"Buffalo," I manage.

"Buffalo…" He repeats, confusion lining his forehead. "New York?"

I nod.

He frowns, dropping his hands from my face to pick up my phone that's still lit up with that fucking tweet. He reads it, and when he looks up, his expression is full of determination.

"We can make this work."

I shake my head, letting out a small laugh. "I couldn't expect you to move for me, and it's over five hundred miles…"

"Yeah, I might not be able to move right away, but now that Jacob and I are able to hire some staff, I'll be able to visit." He types away on my phone, then holds up a list of flights. "It's not even a two-hour flight… and why wouldn't I move to be with you? You're not alone in this, Blaine. I love you, and if this is what I need to do to be with you, then I'll follow you wherever you go, every single time."

A choked sob gets lodged in my throat. How did I get so lucky to find the most incredible man, willing to up his life and follow me to another state? I'm about to open my mouth when my phone begins to ring in his hands. He holds it up, and Hayden's name flashes on the screen. With a shaky finger, I swipe to accept and put the phone on loudspeaker.

"Hey." I clear my throat.

"I'm so sorry, Blaine," he begins, causing my heart to plummet once again. "I have no idea where that person got their information from, but it's incorrect. You're not being traded; you're staying exactly where you are."

"What?"

"It's Petford who's been traded, not you."

I feel like a prized asshole for thinking this, but thank fuck it's Petford.

"Between you and me, Petford's been a naughty boy. It was a very last-minute trade that's come about within the last couple of hours, and nobody knows yet, but I'm guessing it's someone in Petford's inner circle that's shared the info to try to give him some time."

"So I'm staying in Chicago?"

I know he's just said it, but I need the reassurance that I'm not imagining things.

"Yeah, you're staying in Chicago, probably for a long time too. I was gonna tell you tomorrow and surprise you with the news, but given the shitstorm, I'm telling you now. If you want it, the Thunder have offered another eight years, including a no-trade clause."

I look up at Alex.

Those beautiful blue eyes are still glistening with tears, but now they're sparkling with happiness and relief too. I'm unable to resist, so I lean in and kiss him, just a quick press of my lips to his. Like I need his kisses to give me life.

"Fuck yeah, I do," I say with a grin.

Alex's bright smile as he gives me a thumbs up squeezes my heart.

"Awesome, I'll meet up with you tomorrow to sign the new contract, and Blaine?"

"Yeah?"

"I wanna meet Alex. Make a reservation for lunch because it's time I meet the man who has turned you into a sap."

We both laugh.

Alex leans in and says into the phone, "I'd love to meet you, Hayden."

"You might regret that!" Hayden sings through the phone.

I laugh. "Don't be a dick."

"I won't, scouts' honor. Anyway, I gotta go, but keep your lips sealed about Petford until the team announces it."

"Wait, how do you know?"

"It'll all make sense when you find out, but for now, keep it a secret, and I'll see you in the morning."

We say our goodbyes, and when I place the phone back on the nightstand, a huge sigh of relief escapes me. Dropping my head into my hands, I take a moment to come to terms with everything.

"Fuck," I say into my hands, "I've never been so fucking scared in my life."

"I know, baby," he whispers, crawling into my lap and wrapping his arms around my shoulders. His palm rubs soothing circles across my back, and I hide my face in his neck, breathing in his scent, and wrap my arms tight around his waist. I'm afraid to let go in case I wake up and this has all been a dream.

"I meant what I said," he mumbles into my hair.

"Are you trying to say the trade deadline didn't really matter?" I ask.

"It never did. I would follow you to the ends of the earth if it meant I got to be with you."

I lift my head, meeting those gorgeous eyes that captivated me that first night. "I love you."

And I fucking love the pink flush of his cheeks, and how his ears turn a deep crimson every time I say those three words.

"I love you, too."

I press my lips against his, and what starts as a gentle kiss ends up in a heated assault of tongues and muffled moans. My hands graze over the soft expanse of his back before cupping his neck as our mouths fuse together, exchanging kisses like oxygen.

We're gasping for breath when we part, and I lean my forehead against his.

"I love everything about you, every inch of your body. I love the way you smile, the way you laugh. I love the way you blush all the way to your ears. I love how curly your hair goes when it's wet and how you press your freezing toes against my leg in bed," I begin.

He lets out a small, choked laugh as a single tear falls down his face.

"I realize now that it was you I needed in my life to complete me. You're the reason my relationships and dates didn't work out, because the universe knew it was *you*. I was meant to be with you. I was scared I wasn't worthy of love, then you walked into my life."

"Blaine." Fat tears roll down his cheeks, and his smile

makes me feel like the luckiest man on the planet. "You are everything to me."

"I adore every little thing about you, and I am so in love with you it hurts to be five feet away. You are the sun to my moon, the light to my darkness, and the love of my life."

Thirty-Eight

Alex

"I'm really nervous," I admit, twisting my hands in my lap.

Blaine casts a quick glance at me before focusing back on the road, his brows furrowing. "Why?"

"To meet Hayden. What if he doesn't like me?" I internally roll my eyes at myself.

How old am I? I'm acting like I'm five, not weeks away from twenty-five.

But it does worry me.

This is the guy who tries to keep Blaine's image all sunshine and roses, and while past Blaine made that a difficult task, future Blaine's image includes me, and I'd hate to cause any problems.

Blaine chuckles, reaching over and placing his hand on my thigh, giving it a gentle squeeze.

"Of course he's gonna like you, and if he doesn't, I'll fight him."

I scoff. "No, you won't. He's your agent, who's just got you an eight-year extension with a no-trade clause. If you fight him, he might take it back."

He gives a hum of contemplation. "Okay, maybe you have a point, but I could glare at him really evilly until he likes you."

I shake my head and laugh.

After Blaine got off the phone with Hayden last night, he slept better than he has in weeks. The pressure from the trade deadline was finally lifted, allowing him to completely relax.

Me, on the other hand?

I'm still a bag of nerves because I'm about to meet an important person in Blaine's life.

Blaine flashes his badge at security, then parks his car outside the players' entrance at the Thunder arena. He's signing his contract first and doing some press before we take Hayden for lunch.

We were supposed to meet him here, but his flight from California is delayed.

"Is anyone else going to be here?" I ask, hoping I'll know someone while I wait for Blaine to do his professional hockey player duties.

"Yeah, El and Zach should be here, maybe Ethan," he replies, taking my hand in his and lacing our fingers together.

He leads me through the security doors with another flash of his badge, and then we walk down the hallway, which is lined with photos of players from across the decades. Images of players lifting the Stanley Cup, team photos, and framed jerseys cover the walls. I stop when I spot one of a young, fresh-faced Blaine grinning from ear to ear with the Stanley Cup in front of him.

"Look at you!" I grin, tracing his smile with my finger. "You look so young."

"I was twenty-one then." He stands behind me, wrapping an arm around my waist and resting his chin on my shoulder. "Fresh out of college and living my ultimate dream. I never in my wildest dreams thought I'd win the Cup in my rookie year, let alone win it twice."

I look up at him. "I never doubted you for a second, neither did my grandpa. He knew you were something special."

Blaine dips his head, trying to hide the proud smile on his face. Whenever I mention my grandpa and how much he adored him, he goes all bashful and shy.

I lean up, pressing a gentle kiss to his lips, then squeeze his hand. "Come on, we don't want you to be late to sign your contract."

When we arrive outside the conference room, the Thunder's GM and Coach Harris are waiting, and Blaine gives me a quick kiss.

"Have a look around, you won't get lost, and I'll find you when I'm done."

The fan in me is screaming over being able to snoop behind the scenes, so I start walking down the rest of the hallway, taking in all the photos and engraved plaques on the wall.

"Impressive, eh?" A deep voice startles me.

I spin on my heels and see Ethan leaning against the entrance to the gym, his thick arms folded over his broad chest.

"It is." I nod.

It's on the tip of my tongue to pull the protective brother card and tell him if he does something to upset Jacob then he'll have me to deal with, but my inner voice just laughs at me.

Like I could take Ethan Parkes on.

He's bigger than Blaine at six three and must weigh at least two hundred pounds. The guy could probably bench me single-handedly.

"You don't need to worry," he says, almost reading my mind. His steps fall in line with mine as I continue my way down the hall. "About Jacob," he clarifies. "I want to help you both out."

Blaine speaks very highly of Ethan, but apart from the night at his house on New Year's Day and when he came to the bakery, I don't really know him. I'm unable to read him because he's so guarded. A closed book with high walls built around him.

I trust him only because Blaine does, and Jacob said he understands our situation, but I'm still curious as to *why*.

"I don't want to sound ungrateful, but why? It's a lot of money to give to someone you don't really know."

He rubs the back of his neck, and for the first time, I see a hint of vulnerability.

"Growing up, my mom struggled with money. She worked three jobs so I could keep playing hockey, and she did everything she could to keep a roof over our heads, food on the table, and buy me hockey gear. Whatever she needed to do so I could keep playing."

There's a pang in my heart for young Ethan and his mom. I've never heard of this before, as he always shuts down any talks about his personal life in interviews, and there isn't much on the internet apart from his youth hockey stats.

"I had no idea…"

He leads me around a corner to the players' lounge, where large couches fill the space and several fridges are filled with any drink you could think of. Televisions mounted on the wall play different sports channels, and in the far corner, Elliot and Zach are playing a video game, but they've not heard us come in.

"It's not something I talk about, but now, I have more money than I know what to do with. I'm set for life, and I give my mom whatever she needs because I want to show her how thankful I am for everything she's done for me. So when Blaine mentioned your struggles, I wanted to help. I know how hard it is to be drowning in a never-ending spiral, and I'm separate enough that you wouldn't feel trapped. Not that I think anything bad will happen between you and Blaine, but with me loaning the money, there wouldn't be that element of pressure there that borrowing money from a loved one can bring."

He sits down on one of the couches and pats the cushion next to him. I sit down, curling my legs underneath me.

"Thank you." I smile. "For helping us out. It really means a lot."

Ethan's hard features turn soft as he smiles. "You're welcome." He bumps my shoulder with his and grins. "Just keep Blaine in check, eh? You really do bring the best out of him."

X

"Blaine, you motherfucker! You didn't tell me you were punching above your weight!"

I freeze on the spot when my eyes land on the blond-haired man who just called out to my boyfriend.

A familiar blond-haired man.

"You're Hayden Cassidy," I say in disbelief, finally picking my jaw off the floor.

I was never really a Boston fan growing up, but there was something so spectacular about Hayden Cassidy. He was one of hockey's diamonds in the rough who didn't get picked in the draft but ended up making the history books.

I turn to Blaine, slapping his chest with the back of my hand. "And you never told me that Hayden was *the* Hayden Cassidy."

Blaine rubs his chest with his fingers. "H-how... What... What is going on right now?"

Hayden gives Blaine a wide, cocky grin that could rival his own.

Blue eyes glisten behind thick, black-rimmed glasses as he points his finger at me. "I like him."

Blaine flips his middle finger up at Hayden.

"I used to have a poster of you on my bedroom wall," I confess, then cringe. "Sorry, that was really weird."

Hayden bursts into laughter, and Blaine's eyes are so wide, his eyebrows nearly touch his hairline.

"What?" His voice is high-pitched. "Please tell me that's not true and you're pranking me right now."

I shrug one shoulder, rolling my lips together to suppress my laughter. I'm finding it far too amusing how flustered Blaine's getting. "What can I say? He's always been hot."

Hayden holds his hands out to the side. "Can't argue that. The guy speaks the truth."

"Fuck off." Blaine glares at his agent, then slumps onto the bench at our table opposite Hayden, putting his head in his hands. "Can't believe my boyfriend has a crush on my agent."

"I don't have a crush on him *now*," I chuckle, kissing the top of his head before taking a seat next to him.

"I'm starting to regret inviting you," Blaine grumbles.

"No need to feel threatened, Olsen; I'm not gonna steal your man," Hayden teases and winks at me.

Teenage me would be dying right now because Hayden Cassidy was one of my first crushes. He has that typical Californian boy-next-door look about him—a face made for billboards.

I place my hand on my man's thigh in a sign of reassurance, because as much as I'm startled by meeting Hayden, I'm still very much in love with Blaine and *no one* is hotter than him.

A few moments later, a waitress walks over to take our orders, and I'm stunned speechless at the amount of food the two of them order.

"Did the contract get signed?" Hayden asks.

Blaine nods. "Yeah, thank you for sorting it out. It's a big weight off my shoulders."

Hayden waves him off. "Don't sweat it, it's what you pay me for." He takes a sip of water, then leans forward to rest his forearms on the table and lowers his voice. "Did you hear about what went down?"

Blaine shakes his head.

"It turns out Petford's been sleeping with Peyton's wife. I

don't know how long it's been going on, but shit hit the fan yesterday, and Peyton threw down the gauntlet. He told Harris that it was either him or Petford."

My jaw drops open in shock. "His own teammate's wife?"

Hayden nods as Blaine says, "Yeah, it's pretty common. Hockey players can be pigs."

Wow.

Now that's something you don't hear about in the press.

"I also found out who was behind the bullshit tweet about you the other night," Hayden announces.

Blaine lifts his head, "Who was it?"

"Remember the red-haired bunny from that blog post? Caitlin?"

My spine straightens at the name. It can't be the same person, right?

Blaine grunts. "Why am I not surprised?"

"She must've been feeling bitter that you moved on to someone better," Hayden says, "because she went straight into the arms of Petford."

While Blaine and Hayden discuss the drama surrounding Petford and Peyton, I take my phone out of my pocket and go onto Instagram to find the original profile that started sending me the vile messages.

I blocked her, and several other accounts, but her profile is still visible.

"Is this her?" I hold my phone out to Hayden.

He takes my phone, then nods. "Yeah, that's her."

"What's her?" Blaine asks, concerned.

"She was one of the people sending the awful messages."

"No fucking way." Blaine's features harden as the anger rises. "Fuckin' bitch." He turns to Hayden. "Can I get someone banned from games? I don't want her anywhere near me or Alex."

"Possibly? It's been done before but I wouldn't know where to start…"

Blaine turns to face me, his hand cupping the side of my face. "I'm so fucking sorry, baby. I'm sorry it didn't click in my head when you showed me the messages, but I promise you that she won't be bothering you anymore."

I lean into his touch, smiling at his protective ways.

Because I know this man would fight to the end for me.

Thirty-Nine

Alex

May

"Are you sure about this?" Nate asks as he parks his car outside Paw-loved Adoption Center.

"Yeah, he's going to love it."

I'm pretty certain Blaine's going to love the surprise I'm planning. He hasn't stopped talking about how much he loves Boomer since they got him five months ago, and I know it bums him out that he can't bring him home. But as I moved in with him last month and Blaine signed an eight-year deal to stay with the Thunder, I knew this is the right time for him to finally get the dog he always wanted growing up.

With Ethan's help, we've managed to hire two new assistants to help run the shop, allowing me to do a bit more graphic design work and giving Jacob more time to have a life again.

The door beeps as we push it open, alerting the assistants to our arrival. I've already gone through the thorough background checks a week ago and notified Brent—who was handling it all—that it's a surprise for Blaine and about his occupation.

It turns out Brent is the one who helped the Thunder choose Boomer, so he fully understood our situation.

"Hey, Alex!" Brent greets me with a warm smile. "How are you? Excited to take him home?"

"I'm so excited; it's been really hard keeping it a secret from Blaine. I'm pretty sure he suspects something is going on."

I've already chosen the dog for Blaine and me.

I just hope Blaine loves him, too.

Brent laughs. "Let's hope he isn't too mad. He gets home tonight, right?"

I nod.

The Thunder made it to the playoffs, and their flight lands tonight. Luckily, it's only from Calgary, so he'll be home before midnight.

Brent swipes his key card over the door and leads Nate and me through the corridor to the kennels. The sound of dogs barking fills my ears, and my heart crumples at the sound of sad howls.

I wish I could take them all; maybe I can convince Blaine to get a house in the country with loads of land so we can rescue all of the dogs.

Maybe one day when he's retired.

The dog—nicknamed Puppy Dog as he's currently

nameless—I've chosen is a golden retriever-german shepherd mix, and when I heard the story of how he ended up in the shelter, I cried. My heart broke for the poor, sweet puppy, and I knew he was meant to be ours.

"How has he been?" I ask.

"Good, really good. He's gained a few pounds since you saw him last," he replies with another bright smile as he approaches his kennel. He's tossing the toy I bought him last week up in the air, pouncing on it when it lands before throwing it up again.

My eyes fill with happy tears.

"Hey, puppy dog, it's time for you to go to your forever home!" Brent says cheerfully.

The puppy bounds up to the gate; his tail wags in happy swishes and jumps up my legs the second I step into his kennel.

"Oh, Alex. He's fucking adorable," Nate coos, scratching the excited puppy's head.

"I know. I think Blaine's going to love him."

"Hey gorgeous, you better be naked and ready for me because I am *desperate* to get my hands on you!"

Blaine's voice echoes through the hallway as the front door slams shut. The puppy's head jerks up at the sound. I quickly grab hold of his collar, scooping him up in my arms to stop him from running through the house and ruining the surprise.

My heartbeat increases as I hear the thunk of Blaine's

bag being dropped to the floor and his footsteps getting louder as he gets closer.

"Close your eyes!" I say nervously.

His footsteps falter.

"Um, why?"

"I've got a surprise for you!" I grin at the wiggling puppy in my arms. "A special surprise."

"Oh yeah, baby! I'm so excited to be reunited with your fine ass."

Blaine appears with his eyes closed, as instructed. His navy tailored suit pants hug those thick thighs I love so much, and his white dress shirt is creased from his flight, his tie and jacket long discarded.

"Are you ready to meet your other daddy?" I whisper into the puppy's ear as I walk over to Blaine, and once I'm in front of him, I say, "Open your eyes."

Blaine opens his eyes slowly, and I watch his face change from confusion to surprise to absolute awe. "Oh my god, you got me a puppy?" His voice falters, getting higher with each word, his eyes filling with tears.

"Yes, he doesn't have a name at the moment, but I've been calling him Puppy Dog for now." I chuckle as the puppy wriggles, trying to get to Blaine.

He scoops him up in his arms, holding him up above his head, wearing the widest smile I've ever seen.

"I know how much you wanted to keep Boomer, so I thought now was the time for us to have our own." I chew on my bottom lip with worry.

Blaine's busy talking to the puppy like a baby, cradling him in his arms and allowing his face to be licked to an inch of its life. When he looks up at me, his eyes are filled with so much love and joy that my heart squeezes.

"How? What? When… when did you do all this?"

"I've been researching for a while, finding suitable adoption centers and what dog would be right for us, then I reached out to Colleen to find out where you found Boomer, and she pointed me in the direction of Paw-loved. Brent was the one who helped us, and when he introduced me to this little guy, his story broke my heart."

Blaine freezes, worry etched into his brow. "What happened to him?"

"He was abandoned when he was fourteen weeks old because it turns out the owners couldn't afford the vet bills. He had an infection, which has now been treated, but they just left him in a box on the side of the road."

"Assholes," Blaine curses under his breath, then his expression softens as he looks at the puppy going wild in his arms. "But we've got you now; you're going to be so fucking loved. I promise."

"And don't forget spoiled." I wrap my arms around the two of them, leaning in to steal a kiss from Blaine, but the puppy manages to slip his tongue between us.

"Are you going to be a cockblocker?" Blaine raises a brow at the puppy.

We burst into laughter.

"So now you've gotta think of something to name this little guy," I say, scratching the pup's head.

"I think I have the perfect name."

I raise my head. "Oh, yeah?"

Blaine nods.

He then looks down at the puppy, then he melts my

heart, and I fall even deeper in love with him as he says, "This is Ernie."

I open my mouth, but I'm speechless. He wants to name him after my grandfather?

Blaine puts the puppy on the floor, and he instantly starts attacking the laces on his shoes.

His hands cup my face, and it's only when his thumb wipes under my eyes that I realize I'm crying.

"Is that okay? That we name him Ernie?"

"Y-yeah." I give a shaky nod. "He'd be honored to have our first fur baby named after him." And then I crash my lips against his.

I fucking love this man with every atom in my body.

He loves me like there's no tomorrow. He cares for me in ways I didn't know I needed.

He thinks about me and includes me in everything he does, and despite the trouble I'm still receiving on social media, I have never once doubted his love for me.

And that's all I need.

All we need.

Because we have each other.

Epilogue

Blaine

Seven months later

"Ernie, come on! Don't let me down now, dude." I whistle to get Ernie's attention, but he's too busy trying to pull a tree root out of the ground.

The Chicago Thunder groundskeeper is going to be so mad with me.

"Dude!" I tug on his collar, and he finally lets go, only to run a few more laps around the grassed area outside of the arena.

How this dog has so much energy, I will never know.

Usually, Ernie and I go to the dog park near our apartment block to try and exhaust his never-ending energy levels. This allows for Alex to come home from helping

Jacob at the bakery to a nice, peaceful night working on his graphic design business.

I'm so proud of how far Alex has come in the last twelve months.

With the money worries settled, he's really been able to come into his own. The bakery is thriving, and he's been able to develop his graphic design business. He still works a couple of days at the bakery because he doesn't want to give it up completely, but his clientele is growing, and he now has a waitlist of people eager to get on his list. I couldn't be prouder of him.

And as for me?

Well, today we have a different plan.

If you'd asked me a year ago if I would be walking through the doors to the Thunder arena with an engagement ring in my pocket, I'd have laughed in your face and called you insane.

But there is nothing I want more than to be married to the love of my life and my best friend.

Ernie comes running back, this time with a tree branch, and rubs it against my leg. I lean down to stroke the top of his head. "You can't bring that inside, buddy; leave it out here, and we'll ask Ethan if you can take it back to his place."

Ethan Parkes, top man and a brilliant captain, has offered to give me and Alex some uninterrupted alone time and take Ernie home with him tonight.

We walk down the hall to where I'm meeting Ethan, who's helping me execute my plan, and Ernie makes sure to say hello to every person we pass.

When we reach the door to the locker room, I spot him

standing near the start of the tunnel, a trolley full of carpet next to him.

"Hey!" I give Ernie a nod to let him know that he can go see Ethan.

My teammate reaches down and ruffles Ernie's fur, crooning to him in that high-pitched baby voice I'd never have expected Ethan to be capable of.

"Are you all ready?" he asks.

I knew I wanted to propose to Alex at the rink where I first met him, but I was driving myself crazy over how to make it special. I wanted it to be memorable. Like when you see it in the movies and everyone cries when the story is being retold.

I wanted that.

I wanted people to cry because I'm such a fucking romantic.

But I just didn't know how, so as always, I went to Ethan for help, because it turns out Mister Grumpy and Broody is actually a big softie.

"I think so." I rub the back of my neck. "I'm fucking nervous, man."

Ethan chuckles. "That's normal. Did you bring the candles?"

I nod.

"The jersey?"

I nod again, removing my backpack and unzipping it, taking out the mini jersey I had custom made and handing it over to Ethan. He pulls it out of the bag to examine it, then gives a nod of approval.

"It looks good."

"Do you think he'll like it?"

Ethan laughs. "Yes, he's going to love it. Now let's get to work because we have an hour before he shows up."

I follow him through the tunnel and onto the bench. We begin rolling out the red carpet we use for special pre-game events, starting from the bench all the way to the penalty box where I sat that first night. Ernie is busy zooming around the rink, chasing a puck Ethan threw for him.

We line the edge of the red carpet with battery-operated tea light candles.

I debated using real candles but then thought against it—knowing Ernie, he'd kick them over and cause a fire.

There's been a few times we've wondered whether we've adopted Elliot in dog form because Ernie and Elliot are like two peas in a pod.

"Blaine, your flowers are here!"

I lift my head, and Zach's holding the bouquet of twelve long-stem roses that I ordered—one for every month I've known Alex.

"Did you tip them?" I ask when I get to the bench and take them from Zach.

He nods. "Yeah, I did."

I go to grab my wallet from my back pocket, but Zach waves me off. "You can pay me back in donuts." He grins.

Ernie runs over, slipping and sliding on the ice, then jumps up to bite the end of the bouquet.

"Quit it!" I hold them up out of his reach.

Zach looks out at the ice. The arena lights have been dimmed; only the spotlight lights up the penalty box, and the projector light is casting heart shapes onto the ice.

"Okay, I think you're set." Ethan claps a hand on my

shoulder; his head tilts slightly as a wide smile crosses his face. "I'm fucking proud of you, Blaine."

I bring him into a hug. "Thank you for everything."

"Anytime, bud."

When Ethan and Zach leave, I put the jersey I had made on Ernie, and we head into the penalty box and wait for our man to turn up.

Luckily, I don't have to wait long, as ten minutes later, the sound of voices alerts me to Alex's arrival. I spot Ethan walking out of the tunnel first, with Alex shortly behind. He flashes me a wide grin, then squeezes Alex's shoulder, and next thing I know, the soft melody of Elvis Presley's "Can't Help Falling in Love" filters through the sound system.

Alex gazes around the rink before he sees me as I stand up in the box, my heart pounding in my chest. The doors open, and Ernie's sitting on the bench with the warm-up puck from the first night in his mouth, wiggling in excitement. He doesn't move, though.

I've trained our boy well.

Alex takes a tentative step onto the carpet, then heads toward me. I watch as he wipes his palms down the side of his jeans and takes everything in.

"Hey." His voice is like warm caramel on a winter's day, warming my insides.

Ernie's going crazy on the bench, his tail thumping wildly at Alex's arrival.

"Hey, baby," I say softly as I step out of the penalty box.

Alex warily takes another step forward, his brow furrowing in confusion as he accepts the flowers. "What's going on?"

Taking his hand in mine, I rub my thumb over his

knuckles. "Twelve months ago, on this day, I'd woken up to a shitshow. I thought I was about to lose everything, but little did I know it was the other way around. I was about to win it all."

His breath hitches.

"I didn't know that when I knocked into those boards," I say, pointing to the boards next to me, "that I'd just laid eyes on my forever. The guy who'd challenge me in ways neither of us knew. Who would show me that I'm worthy and someone who could experience this type of love. That I could love with everything I am."

With his hand still in mine, I kneel down on one knee and slip the small velvet box out of my pocket.

I click my tongue, causing Ernie to jump off of the bench and come to my side, where he sits down again. He drops the warmup puck to the ground, then turns around.

Alex's watery eyes go from mine to Ernie's, and when he notices the words *"Marry Me?"* on the back of the Thunder jersey Ernie's wearing, with my number, a choked cry escapes his throat.

I open the box to reveal an eighteen-karat white gold band.

"I want to love you for all of my days. I want to dance with you to Elvis every Sunday. I want us to adopt all the dogs together and have a house in the country for them to run around. I would love for you, Alex, to be my husband."

Alex's mouth drops open, then closes and opens again. A small tear rolls down his cheek.

"Will you marry me, Alex? Will you be mine forever and ever?"

I hold my breath in anticipation for his answer, letting it out on a whoosh as he nods.

He drops to his knees in front of me, taking my face into his hands, and presses his lips to mine in a desperate kiss. My cheeks are wet with my own tears, and when Ernie pushes his nose between us to give us both kisses of his own, we break apart and laugh.

"Yes." Alex nods, the smile that captured my heart spreading across his face. "Yes, I would love to be your husband."

"Good, and you should get two minutes for holding…" I grin. "Because you're going to be holding onto my heart forever."

I kiss him again and again and again.

I kiss him because he's mine.

I kiss him because he's my lover.

I kiss him because he's my forever.

He's my everything.

The End.

Want to see what happens when Alex and Blaine's date at the zoo gets gatecrashed? Head to my website for a bonus scene!

https://www.jodioliver.com/bonus-content

About the Author

Jodi Oliver is a British author who writes MM sports romance, happily ever after guaranteed. She loves donuts, dogs and ice hockey, and when she hasn't got her head in a book or hiding in the writing cave, you can find her at an ice hockey game.

She lives in England but dreams of living in the Canadian countryside, with some highland cows and otters.

You can find her on Instagram @JodiOliverAuthor

Sign up to her mailing list: https://www.jodioliver.com/newsletter

Join my FB reader group for the latest updates:
Jodi Oliver's Sin Bin

Acknowledgments

Well holy freakin' shit, I did it! I wrote a damn book!

I have been writing since I was 13, and if I could tell younger me that one day I would be releasing a book, she would have cried (I mean, I am crying right now, too.)

But I couldn't have done it without some of the most incredible people in my life.

Jo, Emily, Lottie, Rachel, Ella, Brooke, April, Colleen, Steve, Ellie, and so many more. I cannot express how much your support means to me, for being there for me during the moments I didn't think I could do it, for helping me with plot holes and being the constant beacon of light throughout. I will be forever grateful for you believing in me.

Emma, I'm sorry you forgot what I looked like while I was writing this! I promise to be better at leaving the cave!

Bethany and Charli, thank you for being wonderful betas!

Jenn for your words of wisdom!

Julia and Leticia for polishing up my words and helping me fix the Britishism's that slipped through.

And to everyone who has believed in me, who has come along on this journey on Bookstagram and have been my cheerleader throughout. I couldn't have done it without all of your support and excitement for these boys.

And thank YOU, awesome reader, who took a chance on me by picking up this book and giving Blaine and Alex a shot, thank you so much!

www.ingramcontent.com/pod-product-compliance
Lightning Source LLC
Chambersburg PA
CBHW061616210726

48287CB00001B/161